Also by Sharon Sala

Blessings, Georgia

SOMEBODY to *Love*

SHARON SALA

sourcebooks
casablanca

Published by Sourcebooks Casablanca, an imprint of Sourcebooks
P.O. Box 4410, Naperville, Illinois 60567-4410
(630) 961-3900
sourcebooks.com

Printed and bound in the United States of America.
BVG 10 9 8 7 6 5 4 3 2 1

CHAPTER 1

HUNTER KNOX HAD NEVER PLANNED ON COMING BACK TO Blessings, so the fact that he was riding up Main Street in the middle of the night was typical of his life. Nothing had ever gone according to plan.

It was just after midnight when he pulled his Harley up beneath a streetlight, letting it idle as he flipped up the visor on his helmet and glanced up at the Christmas wreath hanging from the pole.

From the sounds going off in town, a lot of people were ringing in the New Year. He could hear fireworks, and church bells, and someone off in the distance shouting "Happy New Year."

He wasn't looking forward to this visit, and he'd planned to get some sleep first, but he couldn't. Too much time had passed already, and there was someone he needed to see before it was too late. So his reservation at Blessings Bed and Breakfast, and the bed with his name on it, were going to have to wait. He flipped the visor back down, put the bike into gear, and rode up Main Street, watching for the turn that would take him to the hospital.

═══════════

The Knox family had just ushered in the new year in total silence—eyeing each other from their seats in their mother's hospital room—already wondering about the disposition of the family home before their mother, Marjorie, had yet to take her last breath.

It wasn't as if she had a fortune to fight over. Just a little three-bedroom house at the far end of Peach Street that backed up to the city park. The roof was old. It didn't leak, but it wouldn't sell in that condition. The floor in the kitchen had a dip in the middle of it, and the furniture was over thirty years old, but right now, it appeared to be a bigger issue than watching their mother still struggling to breathe.

Marjorie had given birth to six children. The oldest, a little girl named Shelly, died from asthma before she ever started school.

Four of her children—Junior, Emma, Ray, and Bridgette, who they called Birdie—were sitting with Marjorie in her hospital room. Only Hunter, the second child and eldest son, was missing. No one knew where he was now, and all knew better than to mention his name.

Their father, Parnell Knox, had died six years ago of emphysema. Marjorie always said he smoked himself to death, and while she'd never smoked a day in her life, now she was dying of lung cancer from someone else's addiction. The diagnosis had been a shock, then she got angry. She was dying because of secondhand smoke.

———

Sometimes Marjorie was vaguely aware of a nurse beside the bed, and sometimes she thought she heard her children talking, and then she would drift again. She could see daylight and a doorway just up ahead, and she wanted to go there. She didn't remember why, but she couldn't leave yet. She was waiting for something. She just couldn't remember what.

———

Ava Ridley was the nurse at Marjorie's bedside. Ava had grown up with the Knox kids because Marjorie had been her babysitter from the time that she was a toddler. Her childhood dream had been to grow up and marry Hunt. But at the time he was a senior in high school, she was a freshman in the same class with his brother, Ray.

She'd spent half her life in their house, making Ray play dolls with her when they were little, and learning how to turn somersaults and outrun the boys just to keep up with them. As they grew older, they hung out together like siblings, but she'd lived for the moments when Hunt was there. At that time, he barely acknowledged her existence, but it didn't matter. She loved enough for two.

And then something big—something horrible that no one ever talked about—happened at their house and Hunt was gone.

After that, no one mentioned his name, so she grieved the loss of a childhood dream, grew up into a woman on a mission to take care of people, and went on to become a nurse. After a couple of years working in a hospital in Savannah, she came home to Blessings, and she'd been here ever since. Ava had cared for many people in her years of nursing, but it was bittersweet to be caring for Marjorie Knox, when she had been the one who'd cared for Ava as a child.

Ava glanced at Emma. She was Emma Lee, now. Married to a nice man named Gordon Lee. Her gaze slid to Junior, and Ray, and Birdie.

Junior was a high-school dropout and divorced.

Ray worked for a roofing company and had a girlfriend named Susie.

Bridgette, who'd been called Birdie all of her life, was the baby, but she was smart and driven to succeed in life where her siblings were not. She was the bookkeeper at Truesdale's Feed and Seed Store, and still waiting for her own Prince Charming.

Ava thought the family looked anxious, which was normal, but they also seemed unhappy with each other, which seemed strange. However, she'd seen many different reactions from families when a loved one was passing, and had learned not to judge or assume. And even though it was no business of hers, she knew the Knox family well enough to know something was going on. Her job was to monitor Marjorie's vitals and nothing else.

The door to Marjorie's room was open, and the sounds out in the hall drifted in as Ava was adjusting the drip in Marjorie's IV. So when the staccato sound of metal-tipped boots drifted inside, they all looked toward the doorway.

The stride was heavy, likely male—steady and measured, like someone who knew where he was going. The sound was growing louder, and they kept watching, curious to see who it was who was passing by at this time of night.

Then all of a sudden there was a man in the doorway, dressed in biker leather and carrying a helmet. He glanced at them without acknowledgment, then went straight to the bed where Marjorie was lying.

Ava's heart began to pound. Hunt Knox had just walked in, and the years since she'd seen him last had been more than kind. His face was leaner, his features sharper. He was taller and more muscular, and his dark hair was longer, hanging over the collar of his leather jacket, but his eyes were still piercing—and unbelievably blue.

She forgot what she was doing and stared as he approached. It took her a few seconds to realize he didn't recognize her.

"Ma'am. I'm Hunt Knox, her oldest son. Is she conscious?"

"Not ma'am, Hunt. It's me, Ava Ridley. And to answer your question, she's in and out of consciousness. You can talk to her if you want."

Hunt's eyes widened. He was trying to see the young girl he remembered in this pretty woman's soft voice and dark eyes.

"Sorry. You grew up some. I wouldn't have recognized you," Hunt said. "Is she in pain?"

"Doctor is managing that for her," Ava said.

When his four siblings finally came out of their shock, Junior stood up.

"Where did you come from? How did you know?" he asked.

Hunt turned, staring until they ducked their heads and looked away, then shifted focus back to his mother. She had wasted away to nothing but skin and bones. Disease did that to a body. He put his helmet aside and reached for her hand.

"Mom…it's me, Hunt. I came home, just like you asked." He waited, and just when he thought she was too far gone to hear, he felt her squeeze his fingers. Relief swept through him. He wasn't too late after all. "I'm sorry it took so long for your message to reach me, but I'm here now."

Her eyes opened. He knew she recognized him. Her lips were moving, but she didn't have enough lung capacity to breathe and talk at the same time.

Finally, she got out one word.

"Sorry," and then, "love."

Everything within him was shattering, but it didn't show. He'd just as soon shoot himself as reveal weakness.

"It's okay, Mom. I love you, too. I made you a promise and I'll keep it. I'm sorry it took me so long to get here. I was out of the state for a while and didn't get your last letter until I got back, but I'm here now and I'll take care of everything you wanted."

Marjorie's eyelids fluttered.

Hunt waited.

His siblings stood and moved around the bed, waiting. They hadn't seen her respond to anything in days, and all of a sudden, she was conscious. Then her lips parted.

They leaned closer, not wanting to miss a moment of her last words.

Then she said, "Hunt."

"I'm here, Mom. I'm right here," Hunt said, and gently squeezed her hand. "I'll do what you asked."

Her lips parted again. "Promise?"

He leaned over and spoke softly, near her ear.

"I promise. I'm here now. You're free to go."

Marjorie exhaled. The light was brighter, and there was no longer a weight on her heart. She let go of her son and let God take her home.

Now all four siblings were staring in disbelief, wondering what the hell just happened. Their mother had been hanging on to life like this for almost a week, and the prodigal son walked in and told her it was okay to go. And she died? Just like that?

Ava was trying to find a pulse, but it was gone.

Marjorie's heartbeat had flatlined on the monitor.

Emma's voice rose an octave. "Is she dead?"

Tears were rolling down Junior's face, and Ray was wiping his eyes.

Birdie, the youngest daughter, covered her face and started to weep.

Moments later an RN came hurrying into the room. She felt for a pulse, then looked up at the clock.

"Time of death, 1:15 a.m."

There were tears on Ava's cheeks.

"I'm so sorry. My sympathies to all of you."

Emma hugged her. "Thank you for taking such good care of Mama," she said.

Hunt had yet to speak to any of his siblings, and was still holding on to his mother's hand. He knew they were gathering up their things and walking out of the room, but he had nothing to say to any of them now. That would come later.

He felt a hand on his shoulder. It was Ava.

"I'm so sorry, Hunt, but grateful you made it. At the last, you were all she talked about."

"Thank you for taking care of her," he said, then let go of his mother's hand, picked up his helmet, and walked out.

Ava had heard pain in the pitch of his voice, but he did not need her concern or her care. Losing a patient was the hardest part of being a nurse, but in this instance, Ava was at peace. Marjorie Knox had suffered a long time. She was no longer sick or in pain, and that was a blessing.

Hunt was on his way back up the hall when he saw his siblings getting in the elevator. He pictured them standing in the lobby downstairs, waiting for him to come down next, and took the stairwell instead.

He was already out in the parking lot and on his Harley as they finally walked out of the building. They watched him ride away without acknowledging any of them.

"Well, dammit, there he goes," Ray said.

"Did any of you ever know where Hunt went when he left town?" Birdie asked.

"I didn't," Emma said.

"Me either," Junior said, while Ray shook his head.

"Mama must have known," Birdie said.

The others looked at each other in silence, finding it hard to believe that the mother they'd taken for granted had kept a secret like that for so long, but the three of them knew why.

"I wonder what Mama asked him to do?" Junior said.

"What do you mean?" Ray asked.

Junior frowned. "You heard him. He told Mama he'd keep his promise and do what she asked him to do."

"Oh yeah," Ray said.

"I wonder where he's going?" Junior asked. "Do you think he's going to stay at Mama's house?"

Emma shrugged. "I don't know. Why don't you drive by the house on your way home and see if he's there. If he thinks he's gonna just move in, he has another think coming. I want to—"

"What you want and what's going to happen are two different things," Junior said. "There are four of us standing here."

"But there are five heirs," Birdie said. "Whatever money comes from selling Mama's house will be divided five ways, not four. The house is old. It's not going to bring anything worth fighting over."

"Nothing is worth fighting over," Ray said.

Emma glared at all of them. "We've already talked about Mama's funeral and stuff, and there's just enough money in Mama's bank account to bury her and nothing more. Let's go home and get some rest."

"Did Mama leave a will?" Birdie asked.

They all stopped.

"I don't know," Emma said.

Junior shrugged. "I don't either."

"How do we find out?" Ray asked.

"Maybe Hunt knows. He already knows something about Mama that we don't know," Birdie said.

"I'm going home. If you want to know where Hunt is at, go look for him yourself," Junior muttered.

Ray got in his car and left, and Junior did the same.

Emma ignored him. "I'm sad Mama is gone, but I'm glad she's not suffering." Then she glanced at Birdie. "I wonder where Hunt's been all these years."

"I don't know, but he sure turned into a good-looking man," Birdie said.

———————

Hunt rolled up to the bed-and-breakfast as quietly as he could manage on a Harley, cognizant of the other guests who were likely asleep. He locked up his bike, grabbed his bag and helmet, then headed to the door and rang the bell.

Bud Goodhope was still up and waiting for their last guest to arrive, and when he heard the doorbell, he hurried through the hall to answer the door.

"Welcome to Blessings Bed and Breakfast," Bud said.

Hunt nodded. "I'm Hunt Knox. I have a reservation."

"Yes, come in, Mr. Knox. I'll get you registered and show you to your room. You must be exhausted."

A short while later, Hunt was taken upstairs and given a room at the end of the hall.

"It's quieter back here," Bud said. "Breakfast will be served from 6:00 to 10:00 a.m. If you need anything, just press seven on the house phone and either my wife, Rachel, or I will answer."

"Thanks," Hunt said. "Right now, all I want is a shower and a bed."

"Then rest well," Bud said as he put Hunt's bag on the bed. "We'll see you in the morning for breakfast."

Hunt locked the door, put his jacket and helmet on a chair, then sat down and took off his boots. The room was well-appointed and had a warm, homey feel. It had been a long time since he'd been in a place like this.

He poked around and found a basket of individually bagged, homemade chocolate chip cookies, as well as a mini-fridge of cold drinks. He hadn't eaten since noon, and it was already tomorrow, so he chose a cookie and a cold Coke and ate to dull the empty feeling in his belly.

When he was finished, he stripped and walked into the bathroom. The full-length mirror reflected the milestones life had left on his body. The scars of war weren't just within him. Some, like the thin silver ropes left from wounds that had healed, were visible, too.

He turned the water as hot as he could stand it to loosen tired muscles, and then washed his hair before he washed himself. By the time he got out, all he could think about was crawling between clean sheets and sleeping for a week. But there'd be no sleeping in. He'd come a long way to keep a promise, and it wasn't going to be accomplished by staying in bed.

———————

Ava's shift ended at 7:00 a.m.

Normally, she would be looking forward to a little breakfast and then sleep, but Hunt Knox was on her mind as she headed home. She wondered if he was married—if he had children—where he lived— what he did. But it appeared she wasn't the only one in the dark. From the little she'd overheard, his brothers and sisters didn't know, either. Again she wondered what had happened to drive such a rift within their family, and what promise he'd made to his mother before she died.

Ava was still thinking about him as she pulled up beneath the carport. The morning was cold and the sky appeared overcast. But weather wasn't going to affect her day. She let herself in and then went through the house, leaving her coat in the front closet and her purse on the hall table.

Getting out of her uniform was always paramount. It went straight to the laundry, then she went to the bathroom to shower. The ritual of washing all over was both a physical and an emotional cleansing— leaving behind all of the sadness and sickness of the patients she'd cared for last night to the capable hands of the day shift.

She was off for the next two days, and then she would be going back on days. She hadn't minded filling in while one of the nurses had been out of town for a family funeral, but she was ready to go back on her regular shift in the ER.

As soon as she was out and dry, she put on her pj's, switched her laundry to the dryer, ate a bowl of cereal while standing at the sink, then crawled into bed. She was still thinking of Hunt Knox when she fell asleep.

———————————

Rachel Goodhope met their latest guest when he came down for breakfast. She hadn't seen him in biker gear, but he cut a fine figure in the black Levi's and the gray chambray shirt he was wearing. He hung a black leather coat over the back of a chair, set a biker helmet in the seat of the chair beside him, and then went to the buffet.

"Welcome to Blessings," Rachel said, and added a fresh batch of crisp bacon to a near-empty chafing dish.

"Thank you," Hunt said. "Everything looks good."

"Enjoy," she said. "If you want something to drink other than hot tea or coffee, just let me know."

"This is fine," Hunt said. "Oh…can you tell me where Butterman Law Office is located?"

"Sure. He has an office in a building directly across from the court-house. There's a sign out front. You can't miss it."

"Thank you," Hunt said, and began filling his plate.

Rachel went back to the kitchen to take a batch of hot biscuits out of the oven. She put them on a counter beneath a heat lamp to keep them warm and was going to bake up some more waffles when her cell phone rang. She wiped her hands and then answered.

"Hello, this is Rachel."

"Good morning, Rachel. This is Ruby. I'm on the church calling committee, so I'm giving you a heads-up about an upcoming funeral."

"Oh no! Who died?" Rachel asked.

"Marjorie Knox finally passed, bless her heart," Ruby said.

"Oh, of course! I heard they'd called in the family," Rachel said, and then gasped. "Oh! Oh my! I didn't put two and two together until now. We had a guest sign in really, really early this morning. His name is Hunter Knox. I'll bet he's family."

Ruby gasped. "Oh my word! That's the oldest son! He disappeared right after high school and never came back."

"Well, he's here now," Rachel said. "And a fine-looking man he is, too."

"I hope he made it in time to see Marjorie," Ruby said.

"He just asked me where Peanut's office is," Rachel said.

"I don't know if Peanut will be in the office or not, since it's a holiday. I guess time will tell how this all plays out," Ruby said. "In the meantime, just giving you a heads-up about a family dinner at church in the near future."

"Noted," Rachel said. "I've got to make some more waffles. I'll talk to you later."

"And I have more people to call," Ruby said. "I'll be in touch."

―――――――

Hunt ate his fill of eggs, biscuits, and gravy, then went back for waffles. He was making up for having gone so long without real food and had no idea what the day would bring, so eating what was in front of him seemed like a good idea.

He'd reserved the room here for at least a couple of nights, until he had a chance to check out his mother's house. If it was habitable enough to stay in while he repaired it, he'd stay there. Once it was fixed, it would be up to him to see to the auction and pay outstanding bills.

When he'd received her letter, Hunt had been shocked to find out his mother had named him the executor of her estate. Even though they'd stayed in touch, she never mentioned his brothers and sisters, and with good reason. She knew he wouldn't care. By the time the letter caught up with him, the postmark was almost two weeks old, and the date on the letter she'd written was a month before that. When she confessed her days were numbered, he panicked and called her, but never got an answer. The thought that she would die without knowing he would do what she'd asked had sent him on a wild sixteen-hour ride from Houston to Blessings. He knew now she'd been waiting for him to come. She'd trusted him enough to wait. Now it was up to him to do the job.

CHAPTER 2

HUNT WENT BACK UP TO HIS ROOM AFTER BREAKFAST. HE HAD the lawyer's number in his mother's letter. He didn't think anyone would be at work today, but he sent a text anyway, just in case.

It wasn't long before he got a response.

I'll be in the office until noon. You're welcome to drop in at any time.

Hunt returned the text.

I'll be there soon. Thank you.

At that point, he put on his jacket, grabbed his helmet, and left the B and B. He knew his brothers and sisters were going to be pissed that she'd given the control of her estate to him, but he didn't care. They'd betrayed him years ago. He owed them nothing, and certainly not respect.

He felt the curious stares as he rode down Main Street, and couldn't help but remember the day he left Blessings. Back then, no one even noticed he was leaving, because they would have assumed he would be back. The memory was as vivid now as it was the day it happened.

———————

It was the day he was supposed to leave for college when all hell broke loose. By the time the fight was over, his world and his future had been destroyed—betrayed by his own family.

His mother didn't know he was gone or what had happened until she came back from dropping Birdie off at school and found her family in an uproar. She began begging them all to tell the truth about what happened, but Emma, Junior, and Ray clammed up, and his father, Parnell, told his wife the same thing he'd told Hunt.

"What was done was done, so get over it."

What none of them knew was that Hunt left the house and went straight to Savannah to an army recruitment office and signed up. After testing revealed an aptitude for flying, he went from high school to flight school, and was still in flight school when the United States invaded Iraq.

His first deployment was to Fallujah, flying Apache helicopters, and for the next seven years, he went wherever he was deployed. He was shot at nearly every time he flew out—but somehow always managed to get back. He was fighting a war he didn't fully understand, running from a betrayal he couldn't forget.

And then the inevitable happened. After all those years of taking fire and limping back to base, they were shot down.

His gunner died, and the wounds Hunter suffered sent him stateside. It took eight months to fully heal, and then he mustered out.

It took another six months before he found a job doing the only thing he knew how to do—fly choppers. But now, instead of carrying Hellfire missiles, he ferried oil-field workers back and forth to offshore rigs, and had been doing it ever since. It was what he was doing before he got home to find his mother's letter. And now he was here, carrying out his mother's last wishes.

He found the lawyer's office with ease, parked at the curb in front, then dismounted and went inside.

———

Betty Purejoy was at her desk when the stranger walked in. When she saw the bike helmet he was carrying, she guessed he must have been the rider on the motorcycle she heard outside.

"Good morning. How can I help you?" Betty asked.

"Morning, ma'am. My name is Hunt Knox. Marjorie Knox was my mother."

Betty thought she remembered him as a teenager, but he'd certainly changed.

"Mr. Butterman is expecting you, and I'm so sorry about your mother. I'll let him know you're here."

"Yes, ma'am. Thank you," Hunt said, and sat down as the secretary picked up the phone.

Within moments, a tall fortysomething man with sandy-brown hair emerged, his hand outstretched.

"Mr. Knox, I'm Peanut Butterman. My sympathies on your loss. Please come into my office."

"Just call me Hunt," he said, and took a seat in front of Peanut's desk.

Peanut waved a hand to his secretary.

"Betty, would you please bring me the file on Marjorie Knox?"

Betty stepped into an adjacent room where hard copies of clients' files were kept and pulled the one for Marjorie Knox, then laid it on his desk before leaving them alone.

Peanut quickly scanned the paperwork, which included a cover letter and the will he'd written for her a few years back.

"Okay… You do know she named you the executor?" Peanut asked.

Hunt nodded. "I didn't until I received her letter. It took a few weeks for it to catch up to me," he said, and took the letter out of his pocket and handed it to Peanut to read.

Peanut read it, then handed it back.

"Of course, I'm not going to pry, but she alludes to hard feelings between you and your siblings. However, the will is straightforward. The property is to be sold and proceeds divided five ways, so that shouldn't be an issue."

"I guess you could call it hard feelings," Hunt said. "One of them, or maybe all three of them—they never would admit any of it—stole money I'd saved to go to college. Over $8,000. It took me over four years of mowing yards, raking leaves, and sacking groceries to save it up. And the morning I'm leaving for school, it was gone. We had one hell of a fight about it. But all of my siblings backed each other, and no one would say who'd done it. My dad told me to forget it and figure something else out. Mom wasn't there. She'd taken my little sister to school, so she came home to me gone and everyone clammed up as to what had happened. Mom and I stayed in touch, but I never came back. Until today."

"Good lord," Peanut said. "That must have been devastating. What did you do?"

"Joined the army. Flew Apache helicopters in Iraq until I was shot down. Now, for the most part, I fly oil-field workers back and forth to offshore drilling rigs."

Peanut leaned back in his chair, eyeing the man before him with new respect.

"I know she wanted the house fixed up before it was sold. Do you intend to do what your mother asked?"

Hunt nodded. "I arrived in time to see her before she passed. I told her I'd keep my promise."

"Well, that explains a part of what's in her will. If your siblings have copies, then they already know it. Do you have a copy?"

"Yes, she sent me one," Hunt said.

"Good. In it, she states that once her property is sold, you are to receive eight thousand dollars off the top, and then what's left is to be divided five ways. So keep the receipts of what you spend as you remodel it, and you will receive that back after the sale, as well as the eight thousand, and then what's left will be divided among the five of you."

"They might not like that she did that," Hunt said. "But they won't fight me about it. Now that they're all grown, I doubt they would want that coming out as public knowledge."

Peanut nodded. "Yes, I understand. And as executor, you are to have access to her checking account, although there's not much in it… probably just enough to bury her. I'll get all of the paperwork started for that. Do you plan to live at the house while you're working on it?"

"Yes," Hunt said.

"Do you have a key?"

"There was one in the letter," Hunt said.

"I would advise changing the locks first thing," Peanut said. "If any of them have keys, and they stole before, they may be tempted to do it again before a sale can be held."

"Already thought of that," Hunt said, and then pulled a business card from his pocket. "This has all of my contact info on it. Just let me know when you hold a reading of the will, and anything else I need to do. I've never been an executor of an estate before, so I'm kind of flying blind on procedure."

"I'll be in touch, don't worry," Peanut said.

"Are we through here?" Hunt asked.

"Yes," Peanut said.

"Pleased to meet you," Hunt said. "Thank you for seeing me on a holiday." He was up and out of the room in seconds.

Peanut followed him out and handed Hunt's card to Betty.

"Hang on to this info. We'll need to contact him again later," he said.

"Yes, sir," Betty said. "He's a nice-looking man, but he seems very stern."

"War and betrayal will do that to a man. As soon as you finish what you're doing, go on home, and thank you for coming in this morning," Peanut said, then went back into his office.

———————

Hunt rode across town, past the park, and then west down Peach Street to the little house at the end of the block. He'd seen this house a million times in his dreams, but it hadn't looked sad and run-down like this.

A black pickup was parked beneath the carport, so he rolled up and parked beside it. He got the house key out of his pocket, but as he headed toward the back door, the hair stood up on the back of his neck. He didn't believe in ghosts, but this house didn't feel like it wanted him there. That was fair.

He didn't want to be here, either, but a promise was a promise.

He unlocked the door and walked into the utility room just off the kitchen, turning on lights as he went. All of the furnishings were here. If it hadn't been for the faint layer of dust all over everything, he could imagine his mom had just stepped out to run an errand and would be back soon.

There was a low spot in the middle of the kitchen floor—probably floor joist issues. The old hardwood flooring was scarred and worn, and the furniture was threadbare. The sight of this neglect made Hunt angry. How could his brothers and sisters let this happen? They were all right here in the same town together.

The year Hunt began high school, they'd remodeled the attic enough to call it a bedroom, and for the first time in his life, he'd had a room of his own. Curious to see what it looked like now, he went straight up the narrow stairwell at the end of the hall and opened the attic door. The single window was bare of curtains or shades, and the dust motes in the air stirred as he moved through the space now filled with boxes of old memories that should have been laid to rest years ago.

The bed he'd slept in was gone. The closet door was missing, the closet empty. Even the rod where his clothes used to hang was gone. It was as if they'd wiped away all memories of him. If only he'd been able to do the same.

He went back downstairs, glancing in his mother's room and accepting it was the only one decent enough to sleep in, then began eyeing all of the things that needed repair.

He went back to the kitchen to check out the appliances. The burners on the gas stove lit, the oven came on. The dishwasher was clean, and the single glass in the top rack told him it had recently been in use and was likely in working condition—something he'd find out later.

The water pressure was good, and the washer and dryer appeared to be in working condition. The refrigerator was the newest appliance in the house, but nearly everything inside it needed to be thrown away. He didn't know for sure how long his mother had been in the hospital, but the carton of milk was over a month out of date, and the single container of peach yogurt had long since expired.

The ice in the bin beneath the icemaker had all frozen together, which meant the electricity must have been off at one time long enough to melt it. Then when the power returned, it froze back. So he took the bin out and dumped the ice in the sink, then put it back beneath the icemaker to start making fresh ice, then dumped everything that was in the freezer and refrigerator into the garbage.

The central heat and air were still working, and they looked newer than he remembered, which was good. There was a big job ahead of him to do this right, but in the long run, it would make a huge difference in the sale of the house. However, this task was going to take tools as well as supplies, so he went out back to the toolshed to see what, if anything, was left.

The light bulb was burned out in the shed, so he left the door open as he went in to look around, and it was just as he feared. There was nothing left in it but a couple of old hammers, a hand saw, and an old sack of roofing nails. Seeing the nails reminded him he needed to check on the condition of the roof as well. He could rent tools and hire help. It wasn't the end of the world, but it was going to be a pain in the ass coping with his family while it happened.

He found a set of car keys hanging on a hook in the kitchen and guessed it was to the truck. If it ran, it would be handy to use while he was hauling stuff to the house to make repairs, so he went out to check. The insurance verification in the glove box was in Marjorie's name. He turned the key to see if it would start, and the engine turned over immediately. So he locked the house and drove to the bed-and-breakfast to pack up his things and check out.

Bud was scanning Hunt's card to pay for his room when Hunt thought about the locks he needed to change.

"Hey, Bud, is there still a locksmith here in town?"

"Yes, there sure is. Mills Locks, next door to Bloomer's Hardware on Main Street. The owner's name is Cecil, but everything is probably closed today."

"Okay…I remember him," Hunt said. "Thanks, and thank you for your hospitality," he said, then carried his bag out to the truck. Out of curiosity, he drove straight to the locksmith, saw the Open sign on the door, and went inside.

The man at the counter looked up.

"Welcome to Mills Locks. I'm Cecil Mills. How can I help you?"

"I need a couple of new locks put on a house I'll be remodeling. Would you be available to do that today?"

"Yeah, sure. Here in town?" Cecil asked.

"Yes, where Marjorie Knox lived. I'm her oldest son, Hunt. I'm going to fix it up some before it's put up for sale."

"Lived?"

Hunt nodded. "She passed away early this morning."

Cecil frowned. "I hadn't heard. I'm real sorry about that. I'm waiting on a customer who's on the way in from his farm, but I can get away around noon, if you don't mind me coming at your lunch hour."

"I'm not on any schedule. You sure you're okay working on New Year's Day? It could wait until tomorrow," Hunt said.

Cecil shrugged. "I've already been called out twice today for emergencies, and my wife is home and sick with the flu. I'd just as soon be here."

"Then noon is fine. Do you know the address?" Hunt asked.

"It's the last house on the right at the end of Peach Street, right?"

Hunt nodded. "Yeah. My Harley and her black pickup will be under the carport."

"Then I'll see you at noon."

"Right," Hunt said, and left the shop, then stopped by the grocery store. He was surprised to see that it was no longer a Piggly Wiggly, and had a new facade and a new name to go with it. The Crown.

Nobody recognized him, which made shopping easy, until he got up front to pay. The cashier who was checking him out kept looking at him, and when he put his credit card in the reader, she finally spoke.

"You sure do look familiar. Are you from around here?" she asked.

Hunt nodded as he put his card back in his wallet. "I'm Hunt Knox. I used to sack groceries here back when it was still the Piggly Wiggly. You're Millie, aren't you?"

"Yes! I'm Millie Garner! I knew you looked familiar. I just heard about your mother's passing. My sympathies to the family," she said.

"Thanks," he said, and began putting his bags back in the shopping cart.

"Do you plan on staying here?" she asked.

"Only long enough to fix up the family house so it can be sold at auction. I promised her I'd do that," Hunt said, then walked out pushing the shopping cart.

By the time he got back to the house and unloaded the groceries, it was getting close to noon. He took off his jacket, then began emptying the sacks and putting up the things he'd just bought.

By the time he was through, Cecil Mills was knocking on his door. He let Cecil in, and then pointed out the locations where new locks were needed.

"There's just the front door, and then a back door in the kitchen."

Cecil nodded. "I'll get those switched out for you and get both locks synced to open with one key. How many keys are you going to want? It comes two keys to a set, so you'll have four."

"That's plenty. I'll be the only one using one here, but when it sells, then that will be handy for the new owners."

"Then I'll get right to work," Cecil said.

"Call out if you need me," Hunt said, then took a notepad and a pen and started in the kitchen, making a list of the things that needed to be fixed.

━━━━━━━━━━━

Emma slept in, but when she finally woke up, she was startled to see her husband, Gordon, sitting on the end of the bed staring at her.

"What on earth are you doing?" she muttered, combing her fingers through her hair.

"You were talking in your sleep," he said.

Her heart skipped a beat.

"I had nightmares all night," she said. "My mama died. I'm sad."

"You were crying in your sleep. You were muttering something about a secret, and don't tell Mama."

She stifled a moan. "Well, it doesn't matter now, does it? Mama's dead, and I have to go to the house and get clothes to bury her in."

Gordon stood up. "I thought you and Birdie already did that a week ago. You said Birdie took them to her house."

Emma wiped her hands across her face. "Oh. Yes. You're right. I'm so confused. This is a horrible time for all of us…what with Hunt coming back and all."

He frowned. "Why does it matter if your oldest brother came back for his mother's funeral? It would be weirder if he had not."

Emma was beginning to feel trapped. "Well, because he left us all so long ago, and now—"

Gordon shoved his hands in his pockets, eyeing the flush on his wife's face. He knew she was lying, but wondered why.

"Why did he leave, anyway? Every time I ask, someone always changes the subject."

"I'm not talking about it," Emma said, and got up and went into the bathroom, slamming the door behind her.

"Right! Just like you're changing the subject now," he yelled. "Just for the record, I'll be glad to meet your brother. Maybe he'll be nicer to me than Ray and Junior are."

Emma heard him and groaned, then turned on the shower and stepped in beneath the spray, wishing she could wash away the demons from her past as easily as she washed the sleep from her eyes.

———————

Birdie Knox worked as a bookkeeper at Truesdale's Feed and Seed just off Main in Blessings. She'd gone to work there straight out of high school, and considering the lack of jobs there were in a place this small, she considered herself lucky she was so good with numbers.

Because it was New Year's Day, the feed store was closed, but tomorrow was payday, and since she'd taken the last two days off to be with her mother, she was behind in her work. With only four hours of sleep, she'd gotten up to a cold, quiet apartment, eaten toast and jelly, then taken her coffee with her as she headed to the store.

The building was dark, except for the night-lights, and she left it that way as she went down the hall to her office. Once inside, she turned on the overhead lights, turned up the thermostat, and got to work.

At first it was difficult to focus, because she kept thinking of her mother. There was no longer anyone to call for advice—no shoulder to cry on.

Her mother had been failing and they'd all been so wrapped up in their own lives that they hadn't noticed something was wrong until she began to lose weight, and the bottles of pills on the kitchen counter grew from two to seven, and then more. And then she'd told them she was dying, and to let her be. She'd wanted to stay in her home until she dropped.

They were all in denial and let her call the shots when there were days she was too weak even to feed herself. The house was let go. The laundry piled up. And they'd ignored the dust and pretended the situation would resolve itself.

They were stupid…and selfish, and Birdie felt horrible.

They'd taken their mother's presence for granted. They'd taken her for granted. And so her mama had sent for Hunt. It made Birdie feel sad that they'd failed their mother and their brother, and she still didn't fully understand why it had happened.

Then she glanced at the clock and got down to business. Emma would call when she was ready to go to the funeral home, but until then, Birdie had work to do.

———————

Junior Knox was still asleep when his phone rang. He woke abruptly, thinking it was the hospital calling about their mom, and then remembered she was already gone. He rolled over and grabbed the phone.

"Hello?"

"Junior, it's me. Did I wake you?"

"Hi, Emma. Yeah, but that's okay. So what's up? Did you go by Mom's last night? Was Hunt there?"

"I went by but he wasn't there. His motorcycle was at the bed-and-breakfast," Emma said.

"Oh, well then," Junior said. "So, what do we need to do?"

"I'm not sure. But I just got a text about the reading of Mama's will. Mr. Butterman is holding it at his office tomorrow morning at nine. We're all supposed to be there."

"Yeah, okay. I guess that means Hunt, too."

"I guess."

"Are we supposed to tell him?" Junior asked.

"Butterman just asked me to let the three of you know, and that's all I'm doing. Hunt is not my responsibility."

Junior was silent a little too long. Emma knew immediately what he was thinking, and it made her mad.

"Don't go getting a conscience at this late date," she said. "You were fine with it fifteen years ago, and you will still, by God, be fine with it now. Tell Ray about the reading. I'll tell Birdie."

"Yeah, yeah, I will. Calm down," Junior muttered.

"Calm down? Really?" Emma snapped, then hung up in his ear.

She was in a mood now and didn't want to go to the funeral home in this state, so she went to the kitchen, popped a coffee pod into her coffee maker and pressed Start. She needed food in her stomach before she faced this day, so she put a couple of frozen waffles in the toaster.

Gordon had gone to Granny's Country Kitchen to hang out with the other guys who were home from work today. They had time to kill before all the football games began, and for a while, Emma had the house to herself. If she was lucky, Gordon would go to his buddy's house and watch the games on the new 65-inch HDTV they had given themselves for Christmas. It's all Gordon had talked about since he found out, and she knew he wouldn't be happy until they had one, too. Men were such babies. It didn't occur to her that women were no different. They just had a different set of wants.

Her waffles popped up. Her coffee was done. So she took them to the table and ate in silence, thinking about the upcoming funeral. Thinking about Hunt being back in their lives. She didn't know where he'd been, but it had changed him. He looked hard—even grim. All she knew was that she didn't want to stir anything up again, because this Hunt Knox wouldn't run.

Birdie had just finished payroll and hit Send, routing the money into the employees' respective bank accounts via direct deposits. It felt good to know she would not be the cause of anyone suffering a financial hardship—even if only for a day. But now she wasn't thinking of numbers anymore. She was thinking of Mama again.

She'd been the baby and was still living at home when Ray finally moved out, leaving her and Mama home alone, and she stayed until she turned twenty-one. On the morning of her twenty-first birthday, her mama had come in to wake her up with her special birthday breakfast—a jelly doughnut.

Birdie closed her eyes, still remembering that morning as if it had been yesterday, and her mama's sweet voice as she woke her up.

"Happy birthday, sugar. This morning you are an adult, and I want you to know that if you ever want to be out on your own, I do not expect you to stay here with me. I'm proud of the woman you've become, and I want you to spread your wings and fly. This home is not your forever nest. It's mine. You do what pleases you now. Find a man who will love you forever, but don't ever let him control you."

Birdie sighed. She could almost hear what Mama would be saying to her now.

It's okay to grieve, but do not bury yourself in my grave. That belongs to me.

Birdie wiped away tears. God, but she was going to miss her. Then she turned off her computer, grabbed her coat and her purse, and left, turning off the lights in her office as she went. She was just getting into her car when her cell phone rang. It was Emma.

"Hello."

"Hi, Sis, where are you?"

"Just leaving the office. I had to do payroll," Birdie said.

"I think it's time we head to the funeral home. I'll meet you at your apartment to get Mama's clothes. We can go together from there."

"Okay, I'll be on the way there now. See you soon," Birdie said.

CHAPTER 3

It was habit that made Birdie turn down the block that would take her past their old house. But when she saw Hunt's motorcycle there, and the van from Mills Locks, she slowed down, then on impulse braked and pulled up in the drive behind the old pickup to see what was going on.

Cecil Mills was on his knees at the front door, replacing the doorknob, when she walked up the steps.

"Hi, Cecil," she said.

"Oh, hi, Birdie. Hunt's inside."

"Thanks," she said, and slipped by him as she went inside, then paused in the living room and called out. "Hello?"

"In the kitchen," Hunt said.

She was hesitant to face the angry stranger he'd been at the hospital. She was barely ten years old when he left, so her memories of him were vague. She paused in the doorway, uncertain of what he'd say.

Hunt wouldn't have recognized this Birdie as his little sister. She'd grown up to be a pretty young woman, but she was still one of *them*, and he didn't know where he stood with any of them anymore.

"What's going on?" Birdie said.

"Getting ready to fix the place up to sell," Hunt said.

"Changing out the locks, too?" she asked.

"On advice of Mom's lawyer," Hunt said.

She blinked.

"Why?"

"I guess so people can't come and go and carry stuff off that doesn't belong to them."

"Are you talking about us?"

He shrugged.

"But it was Mama's stuff. Who else would it belong to but us?" Birdie asked.

"And now it belongs to five people. Not just one. And while we're asking questions, didn't anyone ever come in here and clean for her after she got sick? And what happened to the middle of the kitchen floor? It sags. A lot."

Birdie's cheeks reddened with anger. "We checked on her. And why do you think you have the right to criticize? You went off and left everyone fifteen years ago and never came back. What's that all about?"

Hunt's eyes narrowed. "You don't remember? Any of it?"

"Remember what? You were here when Mama left to take me to school, and when I came home that evening you were gone and everyone was acting like something bad had happened."

"Oh, something bad happened all right. Someone in this house stole my college money. Eight thousand dollars I'd worked and saved for four years, and the morning I'm leaving for college, it was gone. Someone in this house took it. They all knew who did it, but they covered up for the guilty one, and Dad told me what was done was done… to get over it and figure something else out, so I did. Mom didn't know what happened, either, but she knew where I went. She always knew. The fact that she never shared that with any of you is telling."

Birdie was stunned.

"Oh, Hunt. Oh my God. I didn't know. Where did you go?"

"To war. Now, I've got a lot to do to keep the promise I made. I'll be staying here until I've finished, and then the house will go up for sale, as stated in Mom's will."

"You've seen the will?"

"She sent me a copy, along with a key to the house and a request to get it fixed up to sell."

Birdie's eyes welled. "I'm so sorry."

Hunt shrugged. "You didn't take it. One of them did. So you don't have anything to apologize for. And just for the record, I didn't come here expecting a warm welcome. I am a bad reminder of someone else's sin."

Then he turned his back on her and went back to work measuring the kitchen floor.

Birdie's heart ached for him in a way she couldn't put into words. But she offered what she knew.

"About the floor. Blessings flooded a while back during a hurricane. Water never came into the house, but it was beneath it. That might be why it's sagging. I guess I never noticed."

Hunt sighed. Her voice was trembling. Dammit.

"It's okay, kid. I'll fix it," he said.

Birdie turned on her heel and left.

Hunt closed his eyes briefly, gathering himself and his emotions, and then went back to work. At least now they'd all know he was in the house, and why.

He got a text from his boss, expressing his sympathies, and after he answered it, noticed he also had one from Butterman, the lawyer. So the reading of the will was at nine tomorrow morning. That should be interesting.

Birdie cried all the way to her apartment, then went in to gather up the things they needed to take to the funeral home. She was still in tears when Emma knocked on the door and let herself in.

"It's me!" she said, and tossed her purse on the sofa.

Birdie came out of her bedroom, red-eyed and glaring.

"Oh my God, honey! What's wrong?"

"Hunt was at Mama's house, and so was Cecil Mills. He's changing the locks on the house. Hunt's going to stay there to fix up the house before it's put up for sale."

Emma frowned. "Why does he think he has the right to change out locks and keep us out of our own mama's house?"

Birdie turned on her with a vengeance. "Maybe because Mama sent for him? Maybe because Mama sent him a copy of her will and asked him to do it? Maybe because he doesn't trust anyone not to steal things that don't belong to them? Maybe because someone in our family already stole his college money from him, and he has no reason to believe we have morals or a conscience?"

Emma froze. "He told you that?"

"Not intentionally…I challenged him about it, and he just reminded me of what had already come to pass, thinking I already knew."

"Jesus," Emma muttered.

Birdie swiped at the tears on her face. "Who did it? And why, for the love of all that's holy, would the rest of you protect a thief? I am so shocked and so hurt for him right now that I don't really even want to look at you. Mama's clothes are in a bag on the sofa. Take them and go."

Emma picked up the sack. "Just so you know, there's a reading of the will at Peanut Butterman's office tomorrow morning. Nine a.m. We're all supposed to be there," she mumbled, and started out the door.

Birdie followed her, then slammed it shut behind her.

Emma flinched, and when she heard Birdie turn the lock, she swallowed past the lump in her throat. This wasn't going to get better. Mama wasn't here anymore to be the wall between them and Hunt. He didn't have to play nice anymore.

She got back in her car and headed to the funeral home to give them the clothes. They still had to get through a funeral in some semblance of family unity—or not.

Ava woke up just after 3:00 p.m., trying to remember why today felt different, and then she remembered.

Hunt Knox came home, and Marjorie died.

She rolled over onto her back, snug beneath her covers, thinking about the next two days. She didn't often have two days off in a row, and she was looking forward to a little time to herself. She wondered if Hunt was staying at his old home, and then decided if he was, she was going to bake him a pecan pie. It would be a simple gesture of kindness to the family during this time, and she remembered it used to be his favorite.

She also had laundry to do, groceries to shop for, and bills to pay, so she got up and headed for the shower. As soon as she was dressed, she stripped her bed, tossed the bedding in the washer, and started her day by making a grocery list.

Later, she made herself a sandwich and a glass of sweet tea and read the local newspaper while she ate, only vaguely aware of the washer chugging away in the little alcove off the kitchen. As soon as she was finished, she grabbed her jacket and purse, stuffed the list in her pocket, and headed out the door. It wouldn't hurt to drive by Marjorie's place. She'd seen Hunt walk in with a biker helmet, so she guessed he was riding a motorcycle. If it was parked at his old home-place, then she would know he was staying there.

A few minutes later, she turned down Peach Street and saw the black truck. But when she got closer and saw a big black and silver Harley parked between the truck and the house, she knew he was there. So now she knew where to find him, and drove past without stopping, heading for the Crown to get groceries. If she hurried, she could get that pie made and over to Hunt before suppertime.

―――――――――――

Junior called Ray, but Ray's girlfriend, Susie, answered.

"Hi, Junior. Ray forgot and left his phone here at the house, but he's not here. He went to get some snacks for the game. It starts soon. Are you coming over?" she asked.

"I guess, if it's okay," Junior said.

Susie laughed. "Of course it's okay. Two of the neighbors and their wives are coming over, too."

"Do I need to bring something?" Junior asked.

"A bag of chips and a six-pack of your desired beverage would not go to waste. Oh...I'm real sorry about Marjorie," she added.

"Yeah, thanks. I'll see y'all later," Junior said.

The fact that they were all getting together wasn't unusual, because their mother just passed. But they were getting together to watch a football game, not reminisce about her. However, there was nothing more they could do for her today, and it was New Year's Day. Football was a religion in the South. They figured their mama would understand.

Junior sat in the silence of his empty house, contemplating how everything in his life started going wrong after Hunt left. He'd dropped out of high school, then couldn't get a decent job. Even after he got married, he bounced from one job to another until his wife got fed up and walked out. He was drawing unemployment money now, but that wouldn't last much longer. He needed to do something, but he couldn't think past the guilt. His mama had made her feelings toward them all too plain when she'd sent for Hunt instead of depending on them to see to her last wishes. He'd never felt more like a loser than he did right now.

Ava got home with her groceries and started making pie crust, then mixed up the filling and put it in the oven to bake while she switched out a load of laundry. Her parents were in Las Vegas ringing in the New Year, so she was free to putter without her mother organizing some party at their house that Ava would have to attend and put up with all of the single men her mother continued to invite, hoping one of them would tempt her daughter into marriage. In the South, and at the late age of twenty-eight going on twenty-nine, Ava Ridley was considered past her prime.

When the timer finally went off on the pie, she took it out of the oven. Pleased with how it looked, she set it aside to cool. Once she finished her household chores, she went to clean up and change. She was looking forward to seeing Hunt again, but wearing something nicer than pink scrubs.

———

After the locksmith was gone, Hunt spent the afternoon cleaning up the house. He was going to mess it up again when he started fixing things, but for his own comfort he wanted the dust off the furniture, the floors clean and mopped, and the bathroom scrubbed.

He'd washed the sheets on his mother's bed and made it back up, and then left his bag in the closet. After all his years in the military, he needed things to be neat, clean, and in their places to feel comfortable in the space.

He was hot and sweaty and tired when he finally finished, and took a quick shower, dressing only in a pair of jeans and his stocking feet as he went back to the kitchen to make himself a sandwich. It was almost five and tomorrow would be a big day. First the reading of his mother's will, and then off to the lumberyard for supplies. There were so many little things that needed doing that it could be a whole week before he tore into the kitchen floor to see exactly what all was wrong.

He was just finishing up a ham sandwich and chips when he heard a car pulling up at the house, and braced himself for another sibling at the door. Only when he went to answer the knock, he was surprised to see Ava. And in the blue jeans and white sweatshirt, she looked markedly different from the nurse in pink scrubs. Her dark hair was down, and longer than it had appeared clipped on top of her head, and her smile was an invitation to return it.

Ava didn't know whether to be impressed by the rock-hard abs and Hunt's bare chest, or horrified by the thin silver scars laid across it like a roadmap. But instead of commenting on either, she offered the pie she was holding.

"Hello, Hunt. I hope I'm not intruding. I brought you something."

"Not at all," he said, and then saw what she was holding. "Oh wow...pecan... It's my favorite."

"I know. It's why I made it."

"Come in," he said.

"I think I know the way," she said, and smiled as she sailed past him and carried it into the kitchen. She set it down on the counter, then turned around. "I spent half my life in this house. Some of the best times I ever had were here with your family." Then she grinned. "I had the biggest crush on you when I was a kid."

Hunt blinked. "Uh...I don't guess I knew that. I hope I wasn't a jerk around you."

When Ava threw her head back and laughed, Hunt felt it all the way to his bones.

Ava shook her head. "Thank God. You weren't supposed to know it. It was one of those little-girl crushes on someone's older brother, and no, you weren't a jerk. You were my hero."

Hunt grinned. "Okay then. So, while we're talking about how obtuse I was as a teen, how about we cut this pie? Would you eat a piece with me?"

"Sure!" Ava said.

"Give me a second and I'll go put on a shirt," he said.

"Don't bother on my account," Ava said. "I like the view."

He shook his head and went to get the shirt anyway. When he came back, he got out plates and forks while Ava cut two pieces of pie, plated them, then carried them to the table.

She waited, watching as he took the first bite, and when his eyes went shut, she smiled.

"Mmmm, oh my lord, this is good," Hunt said, and then chewed it slowly, savoring every taste and texture.

"Thanks," Ava said, hoping the little-girl crush he'd just resurrected in her wasn't as obvious as it felt.

Hunt ate the whole piece without saying another word, and then after he was finished, he pushed the plate aside.

Ava felt every nuance of the steel-blue gaze upon her, but had to make herself look up and face it.

"You're a nurse. And you bake like a pro. What else cool do you do?" he asked.

She leaned forward, her elbows on the table, instantly at ease with him.

"Not much. Just work, take care of myself, and work some more."

He frowned. "No significant other?"

"One while I was in nursing school. But that was such a bust I kind of lost faith in the opposite sex…present company excluded," she added.

"Sorry that happened," Hunt said.

She shrugged. "Life lesson. What about you? Are you married… or taken, as my mother would say?"

"Not now. Not ever. I don't have a job that lends itself to relationships."

"What do you do? Where do you live?" Ava asked.

"I live in a house in a suburb of Houston. I'm a chopper pilot."

Ava's eyes widened. "You're kidding! Whatever led you to do that?"

"The army. It's where I went when I left Blessings," he said.

The scars. Ava was stunned. All he'd ever talked about was going to college. "You were in the army?"

He nodded. "Want something to drink? I have water and Coke."

"Water is fine," she said, and watched as he got up. She didn't say anything else until he sat back down. "Did you serve active duty… like in Iraq?"

He nodded again. "I flew Apaches for Uncle Sam."

She took a small sip of water, but her mind was racing.

"Aren't those the ones that were…that, uh…that carried missiles?"

"Hellfire missiles, among other weaponry, and aptly named. Those choppers have one gunner and one pilot, which was me."

Ava waited until he finally looked up at her.

"I'm not going to pry," she said. "But I will say I'm glad you made it home."

He was surprised by her sensitivity to his reluctance to talk about it.

"Thanks. I'm glad I did, too," he said.

"And on that note, I think I need to go home and let you get some rest. Will you all sell the house, or are you planning to stay?"

"I promised Mom I'd fix it up to sell," he said.

"Then you have a big job ahead of you."

When she stood up, he stood with her, then walked her to the door.

"Thank you for the pie…and the visit," he said. "It was really nice to see you again."

"Even if you didn't recognize me," she teased.

He grinned. "You were a kid when I left, and I come back to find a very pretty nurse standing beside my mom's bed. I should get a pass on that."

"Pretty, huh? Okay then. Pass granted," she said. "Don't worry about the pie plate. I'll pick it up in a few days, and I hope you don't mind if I pop in now and then to see the changes you're making."

"Sure. No problem," Hunt said. "And thanks again for the pie."

"My pleasure," Ava said. "Rest well, and if there's anything I can do to help, just let me know."

Hunt turned on the porch light, walked out with her onto the porch, then waited until she got in her car and drove away. After he went back inside, he ate one more piece of pie, then cleaned up the kitchen and called it a night.

Gordon was still at his buddy's house watching football when Emma sat down at the kitchen table to eat her supper alone. She was upset that Birdie was angry with her—and knew before tomorrow was over, they would all be on Birdie's hit list. But there wasn't anything she could say that would ever make it better.

A couple of neighbors had brought food to the house earlier in the day, so she was picking at that without really tasting it. They had to go view Mama's body tomorrow after the reading of the will, and if they were satisfied with her appearance, then the funeral home would open her casket for public viewing.

She'd known this day was coming, but the reality of it, coupled with Hunt's unexpected appearance, was more than she'd bargained for.

She pretended she was asleep when Gordon finally came home. She could smell beer on his breath and knew from the way he was stumbling around trying to be quiet that he'd had too much to drink. But she didn't want to talk. She didn't even react when he literally fell into bed, and within minutes he was sound asleep and snoring. She rolled over so that her back was to him and cried herself to sleep.

Ava thought about Hunt all evening, and then couldn't sleep after she went to bed, remembering all the times when she was growing up that he'd been her hero and he'd never even known it.

Like the day she fell on her way to Marjorie's after school and walked in the house sobbing, her elbow and a knee dripping blood. Marjorie ran to get a washcloth and water to clean up the scrapes, and when Hunt walked in behind her and saw the blood, he dropped his books and sat Ava in his lap while his mother cleaned her up. She was eight years old and he was twelve. In her mind, he was nearly grown.

As she plumped the pillow beneath her neck, she thought about the time he caught Junior and Ray teasing her and pulling her hair.

He walked up behind them, grabbed both of them by the hair, and yanked so hard they fell backwards, yelling and begging him to stop.

"Did that hurt?" he asked.

"Yeah! What's the matter with you?" Junior yelled.

"Now you know how Ava felt. Do it again and I'll shave you bald," he said.

He was fourteen, and in her eyes, practically perfect.

Ava sighed, then rolled over onto her side, remembering how he'd helped her with math she couldn't get, and given her the last cookie on the plate for a treat when she finally understood.

Hunt was always my hero.

Then she closed her eyes and finally fell asleep.

———————

Hunt woke early and lay there for a few moments, wishing for his NordicTrack or access to some weights. He was used to running at least two miles every morning before work, and the change in routine was just another aspect of what was happening.

But he could still exercise, and so he rolled out of bed, put on a pair of shorts, dropped to the floor, and started doing push-ups. He quit after a hundred and went to shower. At least he'd worked off a little of the nervous energy he was feeling at having to appear at the reading of the will. He did not look forward to another cold reception, but considering the circumstances, it was to be expected.

———————

The New Year's Day marathon of football games, and the ensuing party at Ray's house, had lasted up into the wee hours of the morning. Junior set his alarm after he got home so he wouldn't miss the reading, then after he'd had breakfast and dressed, he left to go get Ray.

Ray came out of his house carrying a cup of coffee.

"You look like hell," Junior said, eyeing his little brother's blood-shot eyes.

Ray winced. "I feel like it, too. I had a little too much to drink last night…but it was a good game, right?"

Junior nodded. "Yeah. Anytime the Atlanta Falcons win a game is good for me."

They rode in silence for a couple of blocks, and then Ray glanced out the window into the side-view mirror.

"Hunt's behind us," Ray said.

Junior glanced up in the rearview mirror and saw his mama's old black pickup and frowned. He wasn't looking forward to facing Hunt. Still, he felt the need to be defiant.

"So?"

Ray sighed. "You know, he was gone so long, and no one ever mentioned his name… I almost forgot we had another brother."

"Mama obviously didn't forget," Junior said.

Ray took another sip from his cup and let the conversation slide.

They drove up to the law office of P. Nutt Butterman, Esq., parked, and got out.

Hunt parked off to the side and headed into the building without acknowledging they were even there.

"Shit," Junior muttered. "Let's get this over with."

And then Birdie arrived as her brothers were getting out, and sailed past them without speaking.

"What the hell?" Ray said.

Emma arrived and hurried to catch up.

"What's up with Birdie?" Junior asked.

"She found out about the missing money yesterday," Emma said.

Junior frowned. "Who told her? I'll bet it was Hunt."

Emma sighed. "It came out by chance when they were talking. He assumed she knew. She is pissed at all of us. But she's going to have to get glad in the same pants she got mad in, because we've still got to bury Mama and do it with dignity. Not some family squabble. Understand?"

They nodded and followed her inside.

Betty Purejoy had already seated Hunt and Birdie in the outer office, and when the other three arrived, she took them all into Peanut's office.

"Good morning," Peanut said. "Please take a seat. This won't take long, and then you'll be on your way."

Birdie stared at the floor.

Emma was verging on tears, and Junior and Ray were red in the face, but silent.

Hunt was the only one who was calm.

Peanut could feel the tension in the room and guessed it had more to do with their past than with their mother's will. He couldn't imagine how Hunt was feeling, but gave him props for coming back to such a cold welcome. And the sooner he got down to business, the sooner they would all be able to leave. He cleared his throat and picked up the papers.

"I'm going to give each of you a copy of the will so you can read it as thoroughly and as many times as you wish later, but it's very straightforward. And I'm not going to dwell on the details of which you already know…like your mother's name…the fact that she owns the house, and the black truck, and whatever money is in her checking account at the present time. I need you to know that if money comes in via direct deposit from Social Security next month, don't assume it's part of the estate and spend it. That legally ends with her death, and they will take it back once it's discovered that she passed. What you may or may not know is that she has named Hunter Knox as the executor, and he has informed me that at her request per the letter he received from her only weeks before she passed, and which I have read, he will be staying in the home long enough to do the necessary repairs to make the house ready for sale."

Both of Hunt's brothers shifted uncomfortably in their seats, but stayed quiet as Peanut continued.

"Once the house repairs are finished, it will be offered at public auction. At that time, the executor will turn over all the receipts for the costs he has incurred in the repair of said house, and they will be held by me until the house sells. No matter what the house brings, Hunt is to receive full compensation for cost of the repairs off the top, plus the sum of eight thousand dollars, and after that, the proceeds will be divided five ways. This is in your mother's will, which she made right after your father's passing. So she was of sound mind and body when all of this was decided. Do you have any questions?"

"What about Mama's personal things? Her jewelry…her clothes?" Birdie asked.

"I think that should be settled between the five of you," Peanut said. "It's the property and truck that are in question."

Birdie was crying now.

"Don't cry, Birdie," Hunt said. "As far as I'm concerned, all that stuff should belong to you and Emma. You have my vote to do what you want with her clothes and jewelry. As for the pictures in the house, all of you take what you want. I'm not in any of them, so it appears I ceased to exist in this family after my college money disappeared. And the way you're all acting, one might think I'm the criminal in the room."

CHAPTER 4

HUNT'S COMMENTS TOOK THEM ABACK. IT WAS THE FIRST THING he'd said since they sat down, and neither Emma nor her brothers could bring themselves to look at Peanut, or each other.

"Thank you, Hunt," Birdie said.

"No problem, kid. I don't need earrings to fly choppers," he said.

Emma gasped, her eyes widening as she and her brothers exchanged glances. *He can fly helicopters?*

"Where did you learn to do that?" Junior asked.

"In the army," Hunt said.

"Were you ever in a war zone?" Emma asked.

"Seven years of it," Hunt said. "But we're not talking about me."

Peanut felt the need to speak for him. They needed to know what Hunt had gone through.

"He flew Apaches...the attack choppers," Peanut said. "And he forever has my appreciation for having served, and he is truly blessed for surviving being shot down."

Birdie's eyes widened.

"Oh my God," Emma whispered, and then covered her face. Junior was speechless.

Ray couldn't look at Hunt.

But they were all thinking the same thing. If it hadn't been for what happened and the lie they all hid, he would have gone to college, not to war, and they would have still been family.

"Is there anything else?" Emma finally said.

"Betty will have a copy of the will for each of you as you leave. I'm suggesting, in honor of your mother's last wishes, that you maintain a sense of decorum, at least in public," Peanut said.

"Yes, yes, we wouldn't have it any other way," Emma said.

"And if that's all for us here, the funeral home is expecting us. We need to give them the okay before they put Mama in a viewing room."

"You don't need my opinion about that, and I need to get to work," Hunt said. "If anybody needs to talk to me, you know where I am."

He stood up, shook hands with Peanut, patted Birdie on the shoulder, and walked past the others as if they weren't there.

Hunt was already gone by the time they got outside, and then Ray brought up the money.

"By the time they get through paying Hunt, there likely won't be much for any of us divided up five ways," he said.

"They're not giving Hunt anything. He's being paid back money already owed. There's a great big difference," Birdie snapped. "I don't know who stole it, and I don't know why the whole lot of you decided to protect a thief at the expense of your own brother, but whatever's happening now is karma for what you already did to him. Now let's get the funeral home business over with. I seem to be the only one of us who has a job to go to."

She got in her car and drove away, leaving them in shock.

"I got a job," Ray muttered.

"Whenever your boss says come to work, you do," Junior said.

"Junior! You have no room to criticize anyone," Emma said.

"I don't believe we're practicing decorum here," Junior said. "Ray, get in the car."

They headed for the funeral home, with Emma driving behind them. The trip across town was brief. They walked in together and were soon escorted into the back parlor.

They approached the pale-blue casket with trepidation, as if Marjorie was going to suddenly sit up and chastise them for the mess their lives were in.

"I was dreading this, but she looks peaceful," Junior said.

Ray was crying. "It don't seem right that she's gone."

Birdie's voice was trembling. As the baby, it hadn't been all that long ago when she was still living with their mother.

"Everybody dies," she said. "Mama was worn out with her sickness. I'm gonna miss her like crazy, but I wouldn't have her back still sick and suffering."

Emma slid her arm around her sister's waist.

"She looks pretty, doesn't she, Birdie?"

Birdie sighed. "That pale-blue dress was her favorite. I'm glad we chose it." Then she looked up at the funeral director. "She looks beautiful. Thank you."

"It's my small part in helping families deal with the transition of their loved one's passing," the director said. "So, as of now, she will be available for public viewing?"

They nodded.

"And the service is set for day after tomorrow, right?"

"Yes. Two p.m. at the First Baptist Church," Emma said. "The family viewing will be tomorrow evening. And the day of the funeral there will be a dinner for friends and family at the church after the burial in White Dove Cemetery. I'll be dropping off a notice at the newspaper office, but I'd appreciate it if you'd spread the word, too," Emma said.

The director nodded. "Of course, and again, I am so sorry for your loss."

They walked out in silence, then Emma paused on the steps. "People have been bringing food to my house. Y'all want to come over for dinner tonight?"

Both brothers nodded.

"I'll come," Birdie said. "But not one hateful word about Hunt, or I'm leaving."

"Think we should invite him, too?" Emma asked.

Birdie rolled her eyes.

"I believe he's already sent his regrets on how he feels about all of you. Don't insult him further. I have to get to work. What time tonight?" she asked.

"Six o'clock okay for you?" Emma asked.

Birdie nodded. "Yes. I get off at five," she said, and then she got in her car and left.

"Okay then. See you this evening," Junior said. Then he and Ray drove away, leaving Emma standing.

Her steps were dragging as she got in the car, but she didn't want to be alone. Gordon was at work. She had a few errands to run, and then maybe she'd go for a walk in the park before going home.

As the oldest girl, she had an inborn urge to become the hub of their family like Mama had been for them. But the crime and the secret was there instead. If she could take back the decision she'd made to stay silent, she would, but it was too late to change that. As their daddy had said, what was done was done.

Ava was having a video chat with her parents, Larry and Karen Ridley, when she mentioned Marjorie's passing.

"Oh, bless her heart," Karen said. "She suffered something awful."

"Yes, she did, but you won't guess who showed up at the hospital."

"Who?" Karen asked.

"Hunt."

"You're kidding! Where has he been? How did he know?"

"I don't know much, but evidently he stayed in contact with Marjorie because from what he said to her at the hospital, it appears she sent for him. I think that's why she was hanging on."

"You used to have such a crush on him. How does he look? Is he married? Did you talk to him?" Karen asked.

Ava sighed. "That was years ago, Mom. He looks good. He's not married, and yes, of course I talked to him. We all grew up together. He's staying at the family home long enough to fix it up and then they're putting it up for sale."

"Well, we have four more days here in Vegas and then we'll be home. I'm sure we'll get a chance to say hello before he leaves, but we're going to miss the funeral. Please give the family our condolences, okay?"

"Yes, I will," Ava said. "Are you having fun? Did you win any money?"

"Oh, we're winning a little and losing a little. It's all in fun. But we're going to some more shows before we leave. Your dad says hello. Gotta go. Love you."

"Love you, too," Ava said and disconnected, then went to get her purse.

She had a ten o'clock hair appointment at the Curl Up and Dye, and then she was picking up some food from Granny's to take to Emma.

The day was clear but chilly, so she added a heavy jacket to the red sweater and blue jeans she was wearing as she headed out the door. She thought of Hunt again as she was driving away, and swung past the house just to see if he was there. The Harley was there, but the pickup was not. It occurred to her as she headed toward the hair salon that it had been years since she'd been interested in a man's whereabouts, but she wasn't going to let fantasy go to her head. Hunt was obviously not interested in anything but getting out of Blessings as soon as possible. This saddened her, and she wished she knew what had happened that had broken a loving family apart.

Hunt was at the lumberyard picking up what he needed to replace the caulking in the house. The bathroom, the kitchen, and all of the windows were in serious need. Some of the windowpanes were so loose that they rattled when the wind blew. When he got what he needed, he headed back to the house.

He was coming to realize that his grudge against the others had not served his mother's obvious needs. Even though he'd been too far away to help her when he was on active duty, after he was stateside and no longer in the military he still had made no attempt to come home.

He'd let their phone calls and texts suffice for "staying in touch," without realizing she was losing her hold on both her health and the upkeep of the house. Yes, his siblings should have stepped up, but looking back, he wondered why he trusted they would care for her when he no longer trusted them.

He was on his way home when he saw Ava getting out of her car and going into the Curl Up and Dye. He was still trying to wrap his head around the fact that the little girl his mother used to babysit had turned into such an amazing woman—and a beautiful one, at that.

Her smile was genuine. It went all the way to her eyes, but it was her laugh that pulled at his heart. It had been a long, long time since he'd been around a woman who made him curious to know more, who made him want more.

Then he reminded himself he'd come here to fulfill a promise, not get attached to someone he was going to leave behind. As soon as he got home and unloaded supplies, he got to work scraping out the old caulk and got lost in the memories as he worked.

———

Ava came out of the Curl Up and Dye with a bounce in her step. Getting split ends trimmed and a shampoo and style did wonders for a woman's attitude.

She'd called in an order to Granny's while Ruby was doing her hair, so she headed up Main Street to pick it up. She'd already sent Emma a text letting her know she was bringing food. The feeding of family during their loss of a loved one was a time-honored ritual in the South, and since she'd known all of them on a personal level, she felt like she was straddling the line between friend and family.

The parking lot was nearly full at Granny's. Ava had to park toward the back and then dodge cars coming and going as she made her way to the door.

Hope Talbot honked, and then stopped and rolled down the window.

"Hey, Ava! Happy New Year, honey!"

Ava grinned. She hadn't seen Hope since she quit working at the hospital.

"And to you, too, little mama. How's the baby business going?"

Hope laughed. "Well, I'm getting bigger and the little critter kicks like a mule. I miss seeing everyone, but I'm really glad I decided to quit working for now."

"I would agree. Those times are precious. I'm twenty-eight and moving into a never-going-to-get-married-let-alone-become-a-mother mode," Ava said.

"It'll happen when it's meant to happen," Hope said. "I better get home. Jack worries if I'm out of his sight for too long." And then she drove away.

Ava waved and then sighed. She didn't have anyone to come home to, or anyone worrying about her, either. But that was mostly her fault for being picky. Still, it didn't stop her from wanting somebody to love.

She turned around and hurried inside the café.

Lovey's son, Sully, was at the front desk and smiled at her as she walked in. "Hi, Ava."

"Hi, Sully. I need to pick up a to-go order."

He nodded. "Give me a sec. I'll go get it for you."

She leaned against the counter, listening to the murmur of voices and the undertones of laughter with them. Her stomach growled, a hunger complaint she had yet to address, but that would come later. She had a yen for a chili dog and fries from Broyles Dairy Freeze, and as soon as she delivered the food to Emma, she was heading that way.

Then Sully reappeared carrying a large sack. "A rack of ribs, baked beans, and coleslaw…is that right?"

"That's it," Ava said, then paid and left without lingering.

She drove across town to where Emma and Gordon lived, and pulled up in the drive. Gordon's car was gone, which she expected because he worked in Savannah, but Emma's car was there. Ava grabbed the sack and hurried to the house, then knocked.

When Emma opened the door, she stepped aside to let Ava in.

"Come in, honey! It's so good of you to do this," Emma said.

"Good doesn't have anything to do with it," Ava said as she gave Emma a quick hug. "You're all like family to me." Then she handed over the sack. "It's ribs, baked beans, and coleslaw from Granny's. It will taste way better than if I'd made it myself."

Emma chuckled. "You're a good cook, but thank you so much. The brothers and Birdie are coming over to eat supper with me tonight. They'll enjoy all this, and so will I."

"Is Hunt coming, too?" she asked.

"No," Emma said, and made no further explanation.

Ava frowned. "I'm sorry for whatever happened. You all used to be so close. I was so jealous of you. I wanted to have brothers and sisters, too, but Mom and Dad quit with me."

Emma's eyes welled, but she didn't comment. "Thank you again," she mumbled.

Ava nodded. "You're welcome. If you need anything, I'm off today and tomorrow. After that, I'll be back on days at the hospital."

"Okay," Emma said, and then stood in the door as Ava hurried back to her car.

She drove away, still thinking about the divide between Hunt and his siblings. It just made no sense to her, and she felt sad for him—for all of them.

She passed the Knox house again on her way to the Dairy Freeze. Impulsively, she turned up the driveway and parked, then ran up the steps and knocked.

When she heard footsteps inside, her heart skipped a beat. Then Hunt opened the door.

"Hey! I'm on my way to Broyles Dairy Freeze to get a chili dog and fries. I knew you were here working. Thought you might be hungry. Want me to pick up a couple for you?"

Hunt was speechless. "Uh…yeah, that sounds great. Hang on and I'll get my wallet."

"No need. It's on me," Ava said. "Two chili dogs enough?"

"Sure. Thanks," he said.

"No problem. I'll be back in a few… Just leave your door unlocked. I'll call out when I'm back."

And just like that she was gone.

Hunt shook his head and grinned when she leaped off the porch and made a run for her car. He had a vague memory of her doing the same thing when she was a kid…always jumping off the porch instead of taking the steps down.

He closed the door and then went back to the bathroom where he was removing old grout from around the tub. He cleaned up what he'd done, then washed up and headed for the kitchen. All of a sudden he was hungry, and happy to be seeing Ava again.

Ava smiled all the way to the Dairy Freeze and then all the way back, thinking of actually sitting down and eating with Hunt. It would be just like old times—except that Marjorie wouldn't be there riding herd on them while they ate.

She pulled up and parked, then grabbed the sack and ran inside.

"I'm back!" she yelled.

"In the kitchen," Hunt answered, and when she came in and set the sack on the table, he groaned. "That smells so good. Best chili dogs in Georgia, right?"

Ava nodded. "That's what we always said," she replied. She put two chili dogs on Hunt's plate and one on hers, then took out the fries and gave him more than half of the double order.

"I have Cokes. Want one?" Hunt asked.

"Yes, please," she said, and sat down.

Hunt took the chair across the table from her and took a big bite.

"Oh wow," he mumbled, chewing, then swallowing his first bite. "That's better than I remember. Thanks, Ava."

Her mouth was full, so she just nodded and gave him a thumbs-up.

He grinned, delighted in her unabashed enjoyment of food, and how easily they'd fallen back into an old friendship. Only difference was she wasn't the kid anymore. She was a peer, and a pretty one at that.

They dunked fries in ketchup while trading war stories—his from overseas, hers from inside a hospital ER. It was a strange twist of fate that as adults, their jobs had taken them into the sadder and harder sides of life.

"How did you wind up working for an oil company?" Ava asked.

Hunt licked ketchup off his thumb and shrugged.

"I don't have a lot of marketable skills, but I can fly the hell out of a helicopter. I knew a guy who knew a guy and the rest is history. I ferry oil-field workers back and forth to offshore oil platforms, and the bigshots who come and go from there, as well."

Ava could tell by the changing expressions on his face that he liked what he did.

"Life took you a long, long way from Blessings, didn't it, Hunt?"

He nodded. "Not what I planned, but you know what they say about best-laid plans."

Ava wanted to ask. But she also didn't want to ruin this ease between them.

"I sure was sad that I didn't get to tell you goodbye before you left, but I was even sadder when I realized something had happened. You all felt like family to me, and all of a sudden I'd lost a friend and didn't know why."

Hunt was silent for a long while. Almost to the point that Ava feared she'd made him mad.

"I'm sorry. I shouldn't have brought it up," she said. "Don't be angry with me."

"No, no, it's nothing like that," Hunt said. "I guess by not talking about it, I'm still protecting a family who betrayed me, which makes no sense, does it?"

Ava's heart skipped. Betrayed? *Oh my God!*

"I'm sorry. Please. Say no more. It's none of my business."

Hunt glanced at her, judging her obvious reaction of shock.

"I don't want to do or say anything that will ruin the friendship you still have with them, that's all."

Now Ava was struggling not to cry. The hurt in his voice was evident.

"You're my friend, too, Hunt. I love all of you."

"Warts and all?" he said.

She nodded. "Warts and all."

He reached across the table and took her hand.

"Thank you, Ava. I dreaded coming home. In my mind, I'd already lost the others, and now I was losing Mom. She was all the family I had left and now she's gone. What happened happened. They won't deny it, but it's not my story to tell. One of them took something from me that changed the course of my life, and the others lied for the thief. Dad told me what was done was done, and to figure something else out. Mom and Birdie weren't part of it. Birdie didn't even know it happened until the other day, but she was just a kid and I guess they didn't tell her."

Ava's eyes welled. "Did Marjorie know?"

"I told her later what happened to me. I don't know if they ever told her the truth, and now it doesn't matter. As soon as I get the place fixed up, I'm out of here."

"I'm sorry that happened, but I'm even sorrier that I'm going to lose you all over again," she said, then stood and began gathering up the trash from their meal. "I need to let you get back to work."

Hunt stood. "No, ma'am. You cooked. I'll clean up."

Ava managed a smile.

"Oh wait... I need to return your pie plate," Hunt said, and picked it up from the sideboard. "It was delicious...and so was lunch. Next time, the meal is on me."

Ava sighed. *Next time.* It was something to look forward to. She saw a pad and pen on the counter and picked it up.

"This is my cell number. I'm still off tomorrow, but I'll be going back on the day shift so I'll be at the hospital from seven to three after that."

She started to pick up the pie plate, but Hunt wrapped his arms around her instead and gave her a hug.

"Thank you. You're the welcome home I never expected."

She looked up, searching his expression for something more than gratitude, but it wasn't there.

"Well, we're even then, because I never thought I'd see you again. I'm sorry Marjorie had to die for it to happen, but I'm really glad to see you again." Then she picked up her pie plate.

"I'll see myself out," she said, and left him in the kitchen with the remnants of their meal.

Hunt stood until he heard her driving away, then gathered up the trash and carried it out to the garbage can. The house felt empty after he returned, and he wished they'd parted on a happier note. But he didn't lie…not for anyone.

CHAPTER 5

AVA WAS IN SHOCK. THE URGE TO DRIVE STRAIGHT BACK TO Emma's house and demand the truth was huge, but again…she wasn't real family. Just the friend they grew up with, so she went home instead, sad for Hunt and sad for herself. No use daydreaming about him all over again. He didn't want anything from Blessings but a ticket out of town, and that would come when he'd fulfilled his promise to his mom.

Hunt was thinking about tomorrow, and the southern rituals regarding a funeral, but he was staying out of it. There would be the traditional family viewing…where everyone came and stared into the casket, remarking upon how nice Marjorie looked and what a sweet woman she'd been, and then they'd shake hands with Emma, Junior, Ray, and Birdie and leave their condolences.

Later, they would remark upon who seemed to be taking her death the hardest, and then if there was any scandal attached to the family in generations past, it would be mentioned in whispers behind closed doors.

Hunt would attend the funeral, but he wasn't in the mood to put himself on display and field all of the usual questions about where he'd been and why he never came home. His siblings obviously had their own story in place about his fifteen-year absence, and there was no need to bust it wide open by saying something that didn't fit.

He worked all day at the house, in between making appointments with a roofer. When he found out the man also happened to be Ray's boss, he wasn't surprised. Blessings was a small town. There was always a connection to someone else here by blood, friendship, or employment.

Later, he contacted a plumber, who turned out to be Billy Younger, a guy he'd gone to school with, and set up a timeline for him to come fix some leaks.

When evening came, he swept up the mess he'd made that day, then cleaned up before going to the kitchen to figure out something for supper. He ate without tasting it, showered, and settled in with a bottle of beer to watch TV. He was unaware the family was gathering at Emma's house for a meal and wouldn't have cared even if he'd known it.

Gordon had rushed home from work to help Emma get the leaf in the table, and then began helping her by heating up food that neighbors had been bringing.

Junior arrived first with a liter of Coke and handed it over as if it were a bottle of fine wine.

Gordon grinned. "Thanks, Junior. Come in. Emma's in the kitchen."

"Thanks for having us," Junior said, and walked past his brother-in-law.

Gordon started to close the door, then saw Ray and Susie driving up and waited in the doorway for them, as well.

"Come in, come in," he said as they hurried in out of the night chill.

"Hey, Gordon," Ray said, and then helped Susie off with her coat.

"I'll take those," Gordon said and hung their jackets up in the hall closet. "Emma is in the kitchen."

Susie gave him a quick smile, and Ray took her hand and walked her through the house.

Birdie was the last to arrive, and when the doorbell rang, once again Gordon went to the door.

"Welcome, Birdie. Hope you brought your appetite. There's a lot of food here."

Birdie smiled as she took off her coat, then followed Gordon into the kitchen.

Emma was taking plates down from the cabinet when they walked in.

"Hey, honey, I'll get those," Gordon said, and took them out of her hands and set them at the end of the counter.

Emma had the food laid out buffet-style so they could fill their plates and then sit at the table.

"I think we're short a plate," Gordon said.

Emma turned and looked. "No...that's it."

"Hunt's not coming?" Gordon asked.

Emma frowned. "Hunt wasn't invited because he isn't talking to us," she said.

"Well, with that attitude, the issue will never be resolved, that's for sure," he muttered, and set the plates down without further comment.

There was a long moment of silence, and then Ray shifted focus by grabbing a plate.

"I'm starving. Can we eat now?" he asked.

"Sure," Emma said. "Help yourselves. All of you." She gave Gordon a hard look, which he ignored, and the moment passed.

Birdie filled her plate, then sat and ate, letting the conversation roll over her. She was tired and sad, and whatever she swallowed felt like a knot in her stomach.

But when they began telling their favorite stories about their mother, she got up to get herself a piece of pie. Something sweet would surely settle this ache in her heart. The family she'd thought she had wasn't real, and her mother was gone. She'd never felt so abandoned in her life.

Ava hadn't been hungry at suppertime, but now that she was getting ready to watch a little television before going to bed, she decided to make some popcorn.

She put the bag into the microwave to start popping, and then on impulse called Hunt. Now that she knew a little more about what had driven him from Blessings, she hurt for the boy he'd been. The phone rang a couple of times, and then when he answered, she shivered. Even his voice made her ache, wishing he had loved her like she'd loved him.

"Hello?"

"Hey, Hunt. It's me, Ava. I just wanted to make sure you were doing okay."

Hunt smiled. "I'm fine, but I'm glad you called. I was thinking about you and those chili dogs. You were a sweetheart to feed me today."

She grinned. "It was my pleasure. If I'd known all it would take to get you to notice me was chili dogs, I would have done that years ago."

Hunt laughed out loud, and Ava's smile widened.

"You're good for what ails a man," Hunt said. "No wonder you're such a good nurse. Your instinct for comfort is on point."

Ava sighed. There was so much she could say to that remark, but she was afraid it would come across as fishing for compliments, so she settled for the safe response.

"Thank you," she said. "So what's on your agenda for tomorrow?"

"Just work at the house. I don't suppose you'd want to go to Granny's with me tomorrow," Hunt said.

Ava rolled her eyes, then was glad he couldn't see her. "Is that a question or an invitation?"

Hunt sighed. "My bad. Whatever it was, it was half-assed, and I can do better. Ava, I would love to take you out to eat tomorrow if you're free."

"That was an invitation, and yes, I'm free then. How about Granny's around eleven thirty? I'll meet you there."

"I'll be looking forward to it," Hunt said and realized how much he meant it.

Then Ava's microwave dinged. "Oops, that's my signal that my supper is ready," she said.

"I heard the microwave. What are you having?" Hunt asked.

"Popcorn. I wasn't hungry earlier, so this is supper and snack. Wish you were here. I'd share."

"Wish I was, too," Hunt said. "Sounds like a good time. Maybe another time we'll do popcorn at your place."

She laughed. "It's a date. In the meantime, I'll see you tomorrow at Granny's. Take care and sleep tight."

"You too," Hunt said. "And thanks for calling." He was still smiling when he disconnected.

Ava pocketed her phone and then dumped the popcorn in a bowl, grabbed a bottle of pop, and headed for the living room. All of a sudden she was starving and happy and couldn't wait for tomorrow to come.

Morning dawned with Ava thinking about seeing Hunt today and knowing it was time to get up and get busy. This was her last day off for a bit, and there were always things waiting to be done.

Hunt was up and making coffee, knowing there was still more caulking to do and walls to scrape to get ready for painting. By the time he had coffee and cereal in his belly, he was back at work and thinking about Ava.

He knew tonight was the family viewing, but his mother would not judge him for staying away from the ritual, any more than she'd judged him for not coming home again.

She not only understood why, she had never blamed him for how he felt. Only once after he left did he ever mention it, saying how hard it was to grasp that the children she'd raised and the man she'd married had turned into people she didn't know. She told Hunt she still loved them, but except for Birdie, who was her rock, she didn't much like them anymore, and apologized to him for not being there for him when he needed her most.

So, Hunt didn't care what they thought because he was honoring his mother in a different way by making good on his promise.

———

Emma had an early appointment at the Curl Up and Dye. Tonight was Mama's viewing, and she wanted to look better than she felt.

Junior woke up, remembered what was happening this evening, and went back to sleep.

Ray took a more practical approach to the day and went outside early to begin cleaning out his car, while Susie left to run errands.

Birdie was getting ready for work with a heavy heart. She didn't want to see her mother in a casket. But she reminded herself that being an adult meant doing the hard things, too, and this was hard. So far, the hardest thing she'd ever had to do.

———

Ava had errands to run, and after picking up some cleaning and a quick stop at the grocery store, she was pushing her shopping cart out to the car when a man in a red Porsche drove right in front of her and then slammed on the brakes.

Ava gasped. He was so close she'd almost hit him with her cart, and now he was blocking her. The fact that she didn't recognize the car and the windows were tinted sent a dozen scenarios racing through her mind, ranging from an angry patient to human trafficking. Her fingers tightened around the handle on the shopping cart, even as she reminded herself there were dozens of people coming and going and she was fine.

Then the window came down. At first, all she could see was a silhouette, and then she heard a laugh, and the hair crawled on the back of her neck. It couldn't be! But it was.

When she leaned down, she got a clearer look at his face and shivered. Vince Lewis! Her first thought was where the hell did he come from? And then, why was he here? She hadn't seen him since nursing school.

"Hey, baby! Long time no see!" he said.

Ava backed up her cart and tried to go in front of him, but he drove forward, blocking her again. She shifted her direction, trying to push the cart behind him, and he backed up, laughing.

"Come on, baby. Get in! Let's talk."

She'd had enough. "I'm not your baby and you're still a jerk, Vince Lewis. Move it now, or I'll ram this cart right into the side of your fancy little car."

He frowned. "Damn! You're still the cold bitch you always were," he said, and peeled out.

Ava was in shock and trembling by the time she got to her car. She unloaded her groceries and headed home, keeping an eye in the rearview mirror to make sure he wasn't following her as she went.

Once she got her things inside, she immediately locked the door behind her and then started putting them up, while keeping an eye on the time to go meet Hunt.

But the whole time she was working, she was worrying about Vince's sudden appearance in Blessings. Why was he here...and why now? He'd only been to Blessings once with her when they were dating, and she was still in nursing school when they broke up. She'd seen him from a distance a couple of times when she was still in Savannah, but the breakup was so volatile and ugly that they'd never spoken again.

Showing up at his apartment early for their date had been the downfall. Finding him in bed with another woman had been shattering, but having him laugh in her face and invite her for a threesome had ended her feelings for him in a rush of disgust.

She'd thrown the key to his apartment into the bed where they were sprawled and walked out. The weird part was that she was so shocked by who he'd revealed himself to be that she wasn't even hurt by the betrayal. She just considered herself fortunate to have found out the truth about him early in their relationship.

But his behavior today bothered her. She knew Vince well enough to know he hadn't come to Blessings on an impulse. She'd find out soon enough what he was up to.

———————

It was eleven fifteen when Ava left the house to meet Hunt, and again she kept a look out for the red sports car as she drove through Blessings, although it was nowhere in sight.

She saw Hunt's black pickup the moment she pulled into the parking lot and tried not to make a big deal out of this. But to her, it was a big deal. She assumed Hunt was buying her lunch in return for the pie and the chili dogs she'd brought him, but she was secretly calling it a date. She'd always wanted to be Hunt Knox's girl, and for a little while today, she could pretend it was true.

She parked and then hurried into Granny's. Hunt was waiting, and stood up when she entered.

"Hi, Ava. That color of yellow is sure pretty on you," Hunt said as he gave her a quick hug.

"Thanks," she said. "Come say more nice things to me while we eat."

Hunt laughed. He hadn't felt this lighthearted since he was a kid. Ava Ridley all grown up was good for his bitter self.

"Where's Lovey?" Ava asked, as Sully grabbed a couple of menus and seated them in a booth.

"Oh, Mom had a flat on the way to work. She'll be here shortly," he said, and then ran back to the register and the people waiting to pay.

Ava glanced around the dining area and then breathed a little easier knowing Vince wasn't here. Hopefully, he'd already left Blessings.

But Hunt caught the look on her face and noticed she had just scanned the entire dining room.

"Is everything okay?" he asked.

Ava jumped and then shifted focus back to Hunt. "Yes! Why?"

"You seemed to be looking for someone."

Ava sighed. "I guess I was, but not like you think. I was confronted in the parking lot at the Crown this morning. Scared the heck out of me, and then it made me mad. I guess I was just making sure the creep wasn't here."

Hunt frowned. He didn't like thinking someone had scared her.

"What happened, and what creep? Do I know him?"

"No, you don't know him. Remember you asking me if I'd ever been married or engaged, and I told you I'd only had the one serious relationship when I was in nursing school and none since because it was a less-than-positive experience?"

Hunt nodded.

"So, that same person nearly ran me over in the Crown parking lot this morning, and then kept blocking me from going around his car, going forward or backward, and laughing. He kept calling me 'baby' and wanted me to get in his car. I told him I wasn't his baby, and if he didn't get out of my way, I was ramming my shopping cart into the side of his fancy red car. He called me a bitch and sped off."

The hair was standing up on the back of Hunt's neck. He knew men like that. Bullies who got a kick out of intimidating other people.

"What's his name?" Hunt asked.

"Vince Lewis."

"What's he driving?"

"A red Porsche."

Hunt's face was suddenly expressionless. "Does he live in Blessings?"

"No. That's the weird part. And he only came here with me once for Sunday dinner with my folks when we were dating."

Before Hunt could ask more, their waitress appeared with a basket of Mercy's famous biscuits.

"Sorry about the wait. We're slammed today. Do y'all know what you want to drink?"

They ordered drinks and their food at the same time, and as soon as she was gone, Ava reached for a biscuit.

"Want one?" she asked, and scooted the basket toward Hunt.

"I want to know if you're afraid of this man," Hunt said.

Ava sighed. "I honestly don't know how I felt. But unsettled, for sure."

"Did he ever hurt you before? Or threaten to?"

Ava rolled her eyes. "No, just cheated on me, and when I walked in and caught him in bed with another woman, he laughed and tried to get me to join them. I walked out and never looked back."

Hunt took a deep breath. "You're serious?"

"Unfortunately, yes," she said, and then leaned across the table and smiled. "But that's enough about the jerk. When I was a kid, I used to dream about you asking me out on a date, so right now I'm living out that fantasy and I'm not letting anything spoil that dream."

Hunt was falling deeper under Ava's spell, and she wasn't even trying. She was genuine in every way, and so matter-of-fact about her childhood crush that it was actually charming.

He wanted to pursue this, but at the same time, she was entrenched in Blessings, and he wouldn't live here again if it were the last place on earth. So he sat listening to her chatter and laughing in all the right places.

A short while later, their food came, and as they were beginning to eat, Lovey finally showed up and began going through the dining room greeting her customers.

When she got to their booth, she saw Hunt and smiled.

"Hunt Knox! It's good to see you again. I heard you'd come back for your mama. Bless your heart. I am so sorry for your loss. Marjorie was dearly loved here in Blessings."

"Thank you, Lovey. It's good to see you."

"I see you and Ava are catching up," Lovey said. "Enjoy your food…and it looks like you two need some more biscuits."

"Hunt's really enjoying them," Ava said.

Lovey beamed. "They're good, aren't they?"

"Yes, ma'am. Best I've ever had," Hunt said.

"We have acquired a new baker since you were here. Her name is Mercy Pittman. She's married to Lon Pittman, the police chief," Lovey said.

"Lucky man to have such a wonderful cook," he said.

"She's an amazing lady in more ways than one. Are you staying in Blessings long?" Lovey asked.

"Just long enough to get the old house fixed up to sell. Then I'll be going back to Houston," Hunt said.

"Then I'm guessing we'll be seeing you again before you leave," she said.

"Since I'm tearing up the house some, there's not much cooking going on. I'd say that would be highly likely," Hunt said.

Lovey moved on, and the waitress came by later with more biscuits. The food was as good as Hunt remembered, and Ava was way more interesting and prettier than he would have ever imagined. As time went on, he began to relax. Good food in an empty belly was never a bad thing.

After their meal, Hunt walked Ava out to her car.

"Thanks for taking time out of your day to eat with me," he said.

Ava shook her head. "This was my dream date, remember? I didn't 'take' time to do anything. I would have fought a bear before missing this."

Hunt grinned. "Fought a bear, huh?" Then he leaned over and kissed the side of her cheek. "If it's okay with you, I'd like to call you later."

Ava resisted the urge to touch the place where he'd kissed her.

"Of course it's okay. Tonight is the family viewing, so—"

"I'm not going," Hunt said. "If I show up, then it will be all about me and where did I go? Where have I been? Why didn't I come back. Tonight is for Mom. And my brothers and sisters will be much happier without me, too, so there's that."

Ava frowned. "I'm so sorry. Whatever happened, it's not fair to you, and that's all I'm going to say, other than feel free to call me anytime. Thank you again for dinner."

"You're welcome," Hunt said. "Maybe we can do it again sometime...like in the evening, after you get off work?"

Ava beamed. "I'd love that. Take care."

Then she jumped in her car and drove away.

Hunt was getting in the truck and missed seeing the red Porsche that pulled out of a side street and followed Ava home, but once he left the parking lot, he decided to drive by Ava's house on the way home, just to make sure the old boyfriend wasn't in the area.

CHAPTER 6

AVA WAS STILL DAYDREAMING ABOUT HER LUNCH WITH HUNT and didn't think to check the rearview mirror before heading home. It wasn't until she was pulling up into her drive that she caught a glimpse of red and then a car pulling in behind her. When she realized it was Vince, her heart stopped.

She had a moment of sheer panic, and then anger washed through her. The fact that he was an utter jerk was no longer in question. He was stalking her and it made her mad. She reached beneath the seat, grabbed the old baton her dad had given her years ago when she began working nights at the hospital in Savannah, and got out with it in her hand.

Vince got out, holding up his hands in a joking I-give-up gesture when he saw what she was holding.

"There are laws against stalking," Ava said.

Vince took a step toward her, grinning. "Aw, come on, Ava. I'm not stalking you. I just wanted to clear the air. I didn't mean anything back at the grocery store. I was just surprised to see you and—"

"You weren't surprised. You were looking for me or you wouldn't be here. Why are you in Blessings?" she asked.

He didn't care that she'd caught him out, and just shrugged.

"We were in Tallahassee for the holidays. I had to leave to get back to Atlanta and—"

"Who's we?" Ava said.

"Uh…my wife and I, and—"

"Oh, for the love of God! You're married, and you went out of your way to look up an old girlfriend?" Ava yelled, and then whacked the hood of his car with the baton.

The dent she put in it was immediate, and Vince reacted first in shock and then in anger. He doubled up his fists and started toward her.

"Dammit, Ava, I'll make—"

They both heard tires screeching and turned to look just in time to see a black truck sliding to a stop in front of her house.

Ava sighed. It was Hunt. She'd never been so glad to see anyone in her life.

Hunt started toward Vince Lewis like a wolf stalking prey—his gaze fixed and unwavering, without saying a word.

"Who the hell is that?" Vince asked.

"Ava, is this him?" Hunt asked.

"Yes."

"Is he still bothering you?" Hunt asked.

"Yes."

"Whoever the hell you are, you need to mind your own business," Vince said, but he was backing toward his car.

"Ava is my business," Hunt said softly. "You need to apologize for scaring her, apologize for showing your sorry-ass face back in this town again, and apologize for being on her property. Then you need to get the hell out of Blessings and don't come back."

Vince shuddered. "Look, I didn't mean anything. She's an old friend and—"

"I know who you are. I know what you did. I am not impressed," Hunt said. "Get the hell out of Blessings, and I won't repeat myself again."

Vince glanced at Ava, and then shrugged. "Sorry. Sorry. Sorry."

Ava whacked the hood of his car again.

Vince shrieked. "What the hell? I apologized!"

"You did not sound sincere," Ava said, and raised the baton again.

Vince held up his hands again, and this time the attitude was gone.

"Don't! I'm sorry, Ava. I didn't mean to scare you. I'm sorry I bothered you here in Blessings. I'm sorry I intruded onto your property. As soon as I check out of the B and B, I'm leaving town."

"Then get," Hunt said.

Vince jumped into his car, backed out of her drive, then left rubber on the street as he sped away.

Hunt stood in the street until the man was out of sight. When he turned around, Ava was walking into her house. He followed her inside, and the sight of tears on her face hurt his heart.

"Dammit, honey, I'm sorry," he said and opened his arms.

She walked into them, hiding her face against his chest as he pulled her close.

"I have to say, you're hell on wheels with that baton. I was debating with myself whether I should let you whack him with it, too, and was relieved when you put another dent in his car instead."

Ava snorted softly, then pulled away from him, wiping her face with her hands.

"Thank you for following me home. I put the first dent in the hood when he admitted he was married and still had the gall to look up an old girlfriend for the hell of it. I thought he was going to hit me when I did it, but then you arrived, so I didn't have to test the theory."

Hunt cupped her face, then swiped at the tears on her cheeks.

"You are something of a warrior, aren't you? You stood up to a bully, not knowing what he would do, and you didn't let him back you down. I think I am in serious awe of you right now. Are you going to be okay?"

Ava nodded. "Sure. I've been challenged by worse in the ER and came out bleeding from it. Vince Lewis is just a jerk."

Hunt frowned. "You got hurt in the ER?"

She shrugged. "Big-city ERs can be a little rougher than our little hospital here in Blessings. I've had a few stitches. It's part of why I came home to work. Thank you again for coming to my rescue. Now you have fulfilled two of my childhood fantasies."

Hunt grinned. "What are you talking about?"

"Remember I said I was pretending that eating with you at Granny's was our first date? Well, I've always considered you my knight in shining armor, too. All of the bloody knees you helped patch up, and making Ray and Junior stop pulling my hair, and teaching me how to do long division, and giving me the last cookie for getting it right?"

He shook his head. "You remember all that?"

Ava swallowed past the lump in her throat. "I remember everything about you. And like the knight you always were in my heart...you came to my rescue today. Thank you."

Hunt sighed. "Honey...you're welcome, but I think I'm the one who's hit the jackpot here. I haven't felt worthy of much of anything for a long, long time. You just put a light back in my heart, and for that, I thank you."

He wanted to kiss her. But she'd already endured crap she hadn't asked for, and he wasn't going to add insult to injury. Being old friends didn't give him leeway for anything more.

"I really enjoyed our date today. I'd love to do it again sometime. Maybe an evening after you get off work...and if you're not too tired."

"I'd love that," she said, and then stood in the doorway and watched him drive away.

Later that evening, Ava got dressed and drove to the funeral home for Marjorie's viewing, but she was thinking of Hunt at home alone and feeling bad for the rift between him and his siblings.

═══════════════

Marjorie's children were at the funeral home, dressed in their best, presenting a united front to the people who were coming to pay their last respects.

They mingled about the visitation room, thanking people for coming and listening to them relating their best memories of Marjorie.

Many times they were hearing the stories about their mama for the first time. Some had to do with how Marjorie had helped them, or how they always looked forward to the solos she sang in the church choir. What they had taken for granted, others saw as the loving, generous-hearted woman she was.

So far, none of the people had mentioned Hunt, likely because they were still unaware he'd come back, which was a relief to Emma, Junior, and Ray. They didn't want to talk about him at all, or try to make excuses for why he wasn't there with them tonight.

Birdie didn't have much to say to her siblings and gave all of her attention to the visitors. She was still in shock at what she'd learned and confused about why her mother had never told her. Since she'd found about the theft, she had been thinking long and hard about what she remembered going on inside the house immediately after Hunt was gone.

She remembered Emma going to Florida for the summer to work at Disney World, and being so jealous that she couldn't go, too. And when summer was over, Emma came back all tan and smiling, with a Cinderella T-shirt for Birdie and Pluto and Goofy T-shirts for Junior and Ray.

That fall, when it was time to go back to school, Junior dropped out, and nothing Marjorie could say would change his mind. And Birdie remembered her mama and daddy fighting almost every night after they went to bed. She had never connected the dots of Hunt's absence with it being the trigger of all that upheaval, but she did now.

Birdie looked across the viewing room at Emma. She was a nice-looking woman who took pride in her appearance, and her husband, Gordon Lee, was a good man. Birdie liked him. Sometimes she thought Emma was mean to him, but it was none of her business.

She saw Ava come in, and then a half-dozen people followed her inside, and Birdie lost sight of her in the crowd as she began looking for Junior until she saw him. He looked decent for the first time in ages, but he wasn't going anywhere in life because he had no aspirations for anything better than getting by.

Ray was off in a corner talking to a couple of his pool buddies. His girlfriend, Susie, was at his elbow. Birdie liked her, too, but wondered what she saw in Ray. None of her siblings had pride in themselves. And now she knew why.

Now that Birdie had found out about the secret, she finally understood something even Emma might not know. Emma didn't dislike Gordon. She disliked herself. And Junior and Ray failed their brother, so they didn't allow themselves to succeed at anything in life. She wanted to shake them all until they confessed the secret they were keeping, but after all these years, whatever it was, they'd buried it so deep inside themselves that it was impossible to speak the truth.

Then someone tapped her on the shoulder. She turned around and saw Elliot Graham, the town recluse, standing before her. His hands were clasped against his chest, almost as if in prayer, and he was staring intently into her eyes. To say she was surprised to see him here was an understatement.

"Mr. Graham! How kind of you to come," Birdie said.

"Your mother asked me to deliver a message to you," he said.

"I didn't realize you knew Mama," she said.

"I didn't, not in the sense you mean," Elliot said. "Will you step outside with me a moment? She insisted it be delivered to you in private."

Birdie was confused by what he was saying, but a message from Mama was something she wouldn't refuse.

"Yes, of course," she said, and when he offered his elbow, she slipped her hand beneath it, and they walked out together.

The night was cold, and Birdie was wishing she'd grabbed her coat when Elliot immediately removed his and slipped it over her shoulders.

"Thank you, sir, but I'm puzzled. If you didn't know Mama well, then why did she leave the message with you?"

"Because I'm the only one who can see and hear her now."

For a second Birdie's heart just stopped, and when it kicked up again it was pounding.

"You mean you—?"

Elliot held up a hand. "What I do is of no matter. It's the message I am to deliver. Rest assured I don't know what any of this means, but she said you would understand, and since it's a bit chilly out here I won't waste time. She said she's sorry for not telling you. She said Hunt deserves to know the truth. She said the others won't be free until it's told. She said it starts with Emma, and your father took it because of her. She said Junior and Ray knew and said nothing because your father demanded silence from all of them. She said she didn't know any of this until she passed, and then it was revealed to her."

"Oh my God," Birdie said, and then covered her face.

Elliot sighed. "I can see this is upsetting to you. I am sorry, but when Spirit asks, I can't say no."

"No, no, it's not that," Birdie said. "The upset was already a reality. It's the answer that was shocking. Tell Mama thank you for the message. And I thank you for delivering it."

Elliot smiled. "You can tell her yourself. She'll always hear you, even if you don't know she's there."

Birdie threw her arms around Elliot's neck and hugged him.

"Thank you, sir. Thank you from the bottom of my heart." Then she gave him back his coat. "And God bless you."

"He already has, countless times in my life," Elliot said. "My sympathies for your loss," he said, and walked away.

Birdie went back inside and walked straight to the casket and looked down at her mother. She almost looked like she was sleeping.

Oh, Mama…thank you. I'm going to figure out a way to get them all together, Hunt included, and give him the answers he deserves.

She blinked away tears and slipped into the crowd, glad her absence had not been noted.

———

Hunt had gone back to Granny's for supper, but only because he didn't want to spend the evening alone. When he was finished, he left a tip on the table and went up front to pay. He felt the stares as he moved through the room, suddenly wishing for the anonymity of Houston. Nobody knew him at Granny's, but after the funeral tomorrow, everyone in town would know he was back.

He drove through the quiet peace of a night in Blessings, thinking about the frantic hustle and bustle of Houston traffic. As soon as he got home he went inside, but he was too antsy to settle. His mother's body was on display, and that was somewhat offensive to him, so he moved through the house, kicking off his boots, hanging up his jacket, and then stripping down to a pair of sweatpants and a T-shirt.

But the old house and the disarray it was in bothered him, and it was too early to go to bed. There were many things he'd learned while in the army that mattered to him now—like order and neatness, and enjoying the burn of muscles and the surge of adrenaline from physical activity.

He needed to run—to get lost in the rhythm of his body and the hammer of footsteps to earth, and thought of the path through the park just beyond the backyard. Without hesitation, he put on some running shoes and headed out the back door, then out the gate and into the park.

There was just enough moonlight and security lights in the park to see the sidewalk that wound through it, and he took off at a lope, taking it easy until he got into the rhythm, and then he amped up his stride. From a distance, he was little more than a dark shadow on the path, and then he disappeared into the trees and was gone.

Two hours later, he'd circled the park more than a dozen times. He was dripping sweat and his legs were burning, but he felt good. He'd worn out the sadness and the anger of this place for the night—at least enough to be able to sleep.

He stripped in the laundry room, tossed his clothes in the washer and started it up, then went to shower. After he was clean again, he crawled into bed and turned on the TV. Just to be on the safe side, he set the alarm so he wouldn't oversleep. After flipping channels without finding anything to catch his attention, he turned the TV off and closed his eyes.

He was halfway between dozing and dreaming when Ava's face suddenly appeared before him. She looked scared and she was crying. Then his dream shifted and he was standing in the doorway watching her leap off the porch, skipping the steps, as she ran away. He fell asleep, dreaming that he needed to see her but couldn't find her, and woke up to an alarm.

It was already tomorrow. The day they buried Mom.

He turned it off, then rolled over onto his back, staring up at the ceiling.

God give me the strength to endure and the wisdom to keep my mouth shut doing it.

Then later as he was leaving for the church, he thought of Ava again and how she'd made him feel yesterday.

Her knight in shining armor.

If only.

He knew she'd gone back to work today, so he wouldn't see her at the service. He also knew he was opening himself up to complications by being around her, but the bottom line was he wanted to see her again.

———

Gordon was exceptionally patient with Emma this morning. He knew the day was going to be grueling for all of them and would do anything he could to make it easier, even making breakfast for them while she was in the shower.

Emma came into the kitchen in her bathrobe, smelled the pancakes and coffee, and burst into tears.

"Oh, Gordon, you are such a sweet man."

Gordon hugged her. "I love you, honey. I'm so sorry for your sadness. Come eat a little before we leave for the church, okay?"

Emma slid into the chair, letting her husband serve her, and then they sat and ate, talking about nothing in particular as married people often do. But it was the comfort of his presence and the kindness that touched her most. By the time they were leaving the house, she felt better able to cope with the day ahead.

———————

Junior ate two Pop-Tarts and drank a cup of coffee before getting ready. The silence of his house was never more obvious than it was this morning. Now that his mother was gone, he didn't have anyone in his life who cared about his welfare. He wanted to find a way to change, but he didn't know how. Every dream he'd had as a kid died when the secret became more important than the people who kept it.

By the time he was leaving for the church, he'd worked himself up into a bundle of nerves. They were going to spend the whole freaking day with Hunt. He didn't think Hunt would make any kind of scene, but the guilt alone was enough to make his brother's presence uncomfortable.

———————

Ray and Susie were walking out the door to go to the funeral at the same time that Ava was on the job in the ER, cleaning an open wound on a teenager's head. The ER doctor was standing by, ready to glue it shut. Life didn't stop for one family just so another family could lay a loved one to rest.

Even though that ceremony was a vital end to the circle of one life, the lives of others still went on.

———————

The siblings arrived at the church one by one and were escorted into a classroom near the sanctuary to wait until it was time for the service to begin.

Emma and Gordon were the first to arrive, but Junior was right behind them. Ray and Susie came in arm in arm, then hugged the others, making small talk without knowing what to say.

Mama had been present when they'd buried their daddy, but now they were the adults in charge and this felt awkward and wrong.

Birdie came in wearing blue in honor of her mother's favorite color, but her eyes were red-rimmed and swollen.

It broke Emma's heart to see her little sister so sad, and she went straight to her.

"I'm sorry, Birdie. This is sad for all of us."

Birdie nodded. There wasn't anything to say.

And then Hunt walked in, and before anyone could stiffen up or turn away, Birdie went straight into his arms and laid her cheek against his chest.

Hunt wrapped his arms around her.

"We can do this, kid. We can do anything for Mom, right?"

Birdie nodded. "Yes. We owe her everything. She kept a roof over our heads and loved us all so much, despite our flaws. We can do this for her, and do it right."

Hunt looked over Birdie's head to the others. They met his gaze briefly, then looked away. He felt a moment of sadness for the shit storm that was their lives, and then let it go. They had created their own reality.

A few minutes later, an employee from the funeral home came to get them and escorted them to the sanctuary. As soon as they reached the doorway, the congregation stood in silence, watching as the Knox family walked single file down the aisle and took their seats in the front row.

Hunt heard a few shocked gasps and hasty whispers as he was passing. Now they knew he was back. Blessings would have something new to gossip about for a while.

Because he was the last to walk in, he wound up being the one to sit at the end of the pew nearest the aisle, and Birdie was beside him. It seemed fitting that the oldest would be sheltering the youngest in their time of grief.

And so the service began.

Hunt looked once at the closed casket in front of him and then never looked at it again. He felt Birdie trembling and put his arm around her shoulders and left it there. From the moment the music ensued through the reading of the eulogy and the pastor's message upon the passing of Marjorie Knox, it all felt surreal.

Hunt had been a world away when they buried his father. But he'd seen far too many people die in the last fifteen years to come undone today. His mother's death was just one more scar to add to his life.

———

Birdie began shaking when she saw her mother's casket, and if it hadn't been for the solid presence of Hunt walking behind her down the aisle, she might have collapsed. They made it to the pew and sat down, but it wasn't until Hunt put his arm around her that she regained her composure.

She glanced down the pew to where Emma and Gordon were sitting, and saw Emma clenching Gordon's hand so tightly that her knuckles were white. Junior had tears on his cheeks, and Ray was staring at the floor. Birdie took a deep breath, and then looked away.

The service began at ten, and by eleven, they were in the family car on their way to White Dove Cemetery.

Marjorie and Parnell had buried their first child, Shelly, in White Dove only four years after she was born. When Parnell died, Marjorie buried him on one side of Shelly, and Marjorie's final wishes had been to be buried on the other side of her baby's grave.

Hunt sat beside Birdie all the way there, holding her hand without talking, and because Hunt was in the car with them, the others stayed silent. The day was chilly but clear. A perfect day to say goodbye.

Hunt sat beside Birdie again while the preacher prayed, but was of the personal opinion that there was too much ritual to burying. It just drew out the sadness.

A hawk circled the sky above them, floating on the air current like a kite, dipping and soaring with outstretched wings. The preacher was talking again, but Hunt had tuned him out. He didn't want to hear one more word about the glory of God. It wasn't like he'd given up believing in Him, but he'd seen too much ugliness to believe God was ever going to interfere and fix it.

That which man has wrought, man will suffer, he thought. And today was not the day he wanted to be hammered with biblical promises, so he was grateful when the graveside service was over. All he knew was that three members of his family were now buried beneath the black dirt of Georgia, and it was a sobering sight.

They were driven back to the church for the meal. It was understood that family, friends, and anyone else who wanted to attend were welcome. It was the Blessings way, the southern way, to welcome a new life or to say goodbye to one ending with food and fellowship.

Birdie paused beside Hunt as they walked into the dining hall.

"Sit with me," she said.

He smiled. "You don't have to babysit me, kid. I'm not afraid of these people."

Birdie frowned. "I'm not babysitting you. I'm being selfish. I want to sit by my big brother."

"You're something of a firecracker, aren't you?" he said.

She shook her head. "Ava is the only firecracker I know."

He thought of her whacking the hood of Vince Lewis's car and wondered what else she'd done.

"Really? How so?" he asked.

"Well, for starters, there's a reason she doesn't have a significant other. She doesn't suffer fools. When she first moved back to

Blessings, she was inundated with wannabe boyfriends. She culled them out of her life so fast it made their heads spin, and word got around she couldn't be played. I'm sure guys still ask her out now and then, but I don't think she messes with them."

Hunt already knew why she had trust issues, but was secretly pleased to hear Birdie confirm Ava wasn't interested in anyone else.

Their conversation ended momentarily when the preacher called everyone to attention to say a blessing, and then the meal began.

The food was laid out buffet-style on long dining tables, leaving the guests to serve themselves, then choose their own seats at the tables scattered about the dining hall. The siblings sat at one table together, but Birdie waited for Hunt and then led him to a different one.

"This okay?" she asked.

"Any place is fine with me," Hunt said, and seated her before taking the chair beside her. They hadn't taken more than a couple of bites before a couple came up to their table.

"Hi, Hunt…Birdie. Mind if we sit here with you?"

"Of course not," Birdie said. "Hi, Bella. Sit here by me."

Hunt looked up and grinned. It was Rob Denton. He hadn't seen him since their high school graduation.

"Hey, Rob… Sit yourself down, man. It's been too long."

"Truth, Hunt. It's good to see you again. This is my wife, Bella. We're real sorry about your mom."

"Thanks. It's nice to meet you, Bella," Hunt said.

Before they'd had time to settle, another couple approached.

"May we join you?" the woman asked.

And once again, Hunt was facing another classmate, this time an old girlfriend from his sophomore year.

"Hello, Linda. Thank you for coming," Birdie said.

Linda nodded. "Hunt, good to see you again. This is my husband, Andy Ames. Our condolences on your loss."

Hunt nodded. "You, too, Linda. Nice to meet you, Andy," Hunt said, and gestured toward the last two seats.

Birdie was having a hard time swallowing food. She couldn't get past the fact that they'd just buried their mother, and now everyone was being all chatty and eating like it was any church dinner. She didn't think anyone noticed until Hunt leaned over and whispered in her ear.

"One bite, kid. That's all it takes. The others are easier after that."

She blinked back tears and forked a bite of potato salad into her mouth, then chewed and swallowed. The faint hint of mustard within the mayonnaise dressing reminded her of her mother's recipe.

Love you, Mama, she thought, and took another bite.

After that it was easier, just like Hunt said, and within minutes the conversation turned to Hunt and where he'd been.

"Man, you were missed around here," Rob said. "I thought you went off to college in Savannah, but then you never showed up. Where did you go?"

"The army," Hunt said.

There was a moment of shock, followed by a mental tabulation of what was happening in the army fifteen years ago, and it was Linda who asked.

"Did you see active duty?"

"A little," Hunt said. "I wonder who made this potato casserole. It's good."

"My older brother, Doyle, was in Iraq," Rob said. "Were you ever there?"

"Hunt flew Apache helicopters all over," Birdie said. "Fallujah, Mosul, and Afghanistan. Did I get that right, Hunt?"

He nodded.

"Are you still active duty?" Andy asked.

Hunt shook his head. "No. I mustered out after being shot down. Took a while to heal, but I still fly choppers. I work for an oil company down in Houston, ferrying oil-field workers to offshore rigs all up and down the southern coast, from Texas as far up as Louisiana. Keeps me busy." Then he glanced at Birdie's glass. "I'm going to get a refill. You want more tea?"

"Yes, please," she said, and as soon as Hunt got up and left the table, they peppered her with questions.

"Is he married?" Rob asked.

"No, never has been," Birdie said.

"Was he hurt bad?" Linda asked.

Birdie shrugged. "He doesn't talk about it, but I'd say yes. His gunner was killed. He survived. And when he comes back to the table, no more questions about war, okay?"

They nodded, embarrassed that they'd been thoughtless enough to do it in the first place.

Hunt came back with their drinks and knew by the awkward silence around the table that Birdie must have called them out about their curiosity. He owed her one for that.

It was almost an hour later before he and Birdie were alone again. Before he knew it, the man who'd been sitting with Emma was coming toward their table.

"Who's that?" he asked.

Birdie smiled. "Oh, that's Gordon Lee, Emma's husband. He's really nice."

Hunt stood as Gordon arrived.

"Hunt, I just wanted to come introduce myself. I'm Gordon Lee, Emma's husband."

Hunt shook the hand Gordon offered. "Nice to meet you," he said.

"I work in a sporting goods store in Savannah six days a week, but I'm home every evening around six. If you need help at Marjorie's house, don't hesitate to give me a call. I'd be happy to lend a hand." He handed Hunt his card and then winked at Birdie.

She smiled.

"Thanks," Hunt said. "I appreciate that."

Gordon nodded. "Sure thing," he said, and then went back to where the others were sitting.

Hunt could tell Emma was uncomfortable that he'd done that, but obviously Gordon Lee was a man with his own mind, and that was never a bad thing. Then he glanced down at Birdie.

"I think I'm going to slip out of here," Hunt said. "Are you going to be okay?"

Birdie stood up and hugged him. "Yes. I'll be talking to you again in a day or two."

"I think I can handle that," he said. "Thanks for the moral support," he added.

"That goes both ways," Birdie said. "Love you, Hunt. I'm sorry Mama had to die to get you home, but I'm so glad to see you again."

"Love you too, kid. It's good to see what an amazing woman you grew up to be," Hunt said, and then slipped out of a side door and left.

Birdie saw the others still talking to friends and decided to go home, too. She put on her coat and left through the same door, grateful that this was finally behind them.

CHAPTER 7

HUNT DROVE HOME AND CHANGED INTO WORK CLOTHES. HE still had several hours of daylight and a lot of work to get done. Yesterday, he'd finished caulking. The roofer was delayed in coming out, and Hunt wanted to look at it on his own, but was minus a ladder. So he reverted to his teenage years and went up into the attic that had once been his room and climbed out onto the roof through the dormer window.

He'd been up there a good ten minutes when he saw Ava coming up the street. When she pulled into the drive and got out, his heart skipped. The sun shining on her dark hair made it look like silk, and her ready smile when she saw him was the best thing that had happened to him all day.

"The front door is unlocked. Give me a couple of minutes and I'll be right down," he called out.

"Be careful," she said.

He headed back to the window, crawled inside, and began dusting himself off as he hurried down the stairs.

Ava was standing in the hallway, and when she saw him, she walked straight into his arms and gave him a hug.

The urge to kiss her senseless was so strong within Hunt that he was struggling to focus when she saved him and turned him loose.

"That's the best greeting I've had all day, but what was it for?" he asked.

"I couldn't be at the service today. It's a hug for my regret. I worried for you. Were people nice, or did they grill you mercilessly?"

"They were nice, and Birdie decided to attach herself to me to make sure I wasn't grilled. It was actually pretty sweet of her."

Ava sighed. "Thank God. Curiosity can often take a hateful turn.

I know how nosy and sarcastic some people can be. So how's the roof?"

He was watching the way her mouth shaped words, wondering how they would feel against his lips, when it dawned on him that she'd just asked a question.

"I'm sorry... What did you say?"

"I asked, how's the roof? Are you going to have to replace it?"

"It looks okay, but it's old. I think to get top dollar on the house, it needs a new roof. That kitchen floor is probably going to be the biggest repair. I think I'll replace the cookstove in the kitchen and put in a new sink and countertops after we paint."

Ava nodded. "I love the location of this house. I was always jealous of the fact that your backyard was basically the whole park."

Hunt thought of his run the other night and realized what he'd taken for granted.

"I never thought of it like that, but I guess you're right. We went straight out the back gate and into the park every day when we were kids. I seem to remember pushing you and Ray in the swings a time or two."

Ava shook her head. "Not a time or two. Almost every day... especially if your mom sent you out to babysit us."

"You remember all that?" Hunt asked.

Ava grinned. "Oh, I remember everything about you...I was in love with you forever, remember?"

Hunt took a slow breath. "Want something to drink?"

"I do if you do, and whatever you're having," Ava said, then followed him to the kitchen.

They sat down to iced Coke in glasses and a package of cookies between them.

"If your mom was at the sink, she'd be telling us not to eat more than two or we'd ruin our supper," Ava said.

Hunt smiled. "Even though nothing ever ruined my supper."

"Or mine," Ava said, and took a bite of the cookie.

"Can I ask you something?" Hunt asked.

"Sure," Ava said.

"Birdie said you didn't date, but she doesn't know everything. Is there anyone here you date? Someone special, I mean?"

Ava chewed, swallowed, and smiled. "You mean besides you?"

Hunt didn't smile back. "I'm serious," he said.

Ava's heart skipped a beat as the smile slid off her face. "Maybe I am, too. How would that fit into your here-today, gone-tomorrow life?"

Hunt felt the world starting to spin around him. It had been a long, long time since he'd felt this alive.

"I don't know. What's old with you is new to me. You were a kid to me when I left," he said.

Ava was afraid to hope…afraid to wish.

"I accept that, but what am I now? Curiosity?"

"No. But knowing you haven't been married, or are engaged, and you don't have a special someone in your life…and after running into the jerk who hurt you before, it makes me think you might not want one. I guess I'm just being careful."

She took a deep breath. Saying this now was baring her own secret. It was scary. The rejection would be devastating, but he was worth the risk.

"Maybe I don't have anyone else because I didn't want a second best. Maybe I knew my heart long before I was old enough to speak it. Maybe I'm one of those women who only loves once."

Hunt felt like he was flying. There was no wall, no boundary around him, only the truth on Ava's face, and all he had to do was say yes.

"Fifteen years and a war can change a person. What if you don't like the man I became?" he asked.

"Try me," she said.

He grinned. "Will you go to dinner with me tonight?"

"Early dinner, because I have to be at work at 7:00 a.m., yes, and thank you."

His smile widened. "Then we'll keep it in town, too. Granny's okay? Unless you'd rather do barbecue or—"

"Granny's is perfect. Pick me up at six. That will give me time to get all gorgeous and stuff."

He sighed. "You're already gorgeous…and stuff."

She picked up her Coke and took a last sip before putting it back on the table.

"Now that I have totally disrupted your life, I guess I'll be going."

Hunt got up and circled the table, then pulled her into his arms.

"You haven't disrupted anything…yet. But I have a feeling you're going to."

Then he kissed her.

Lightly.

On the lips.

He heard her sigh.

Felt her yield to the pressure.

And knew he would never be the same again.

She was the first to pull away, but she was not unmoved. There was a film of tears in her eyes. Her voice was shaking.

"I have been waiting for that my whole freaking life, Hunter Knox. Don't you dare break my heart."

And then she was gone.

"Holy shit," he mumbled, then shoved his fingers through his hair, trying to remember what he'd been doing.

Oh yeah, he'd been on the roof, but he wasn't going back up there again. He was so high on life right now, he might try to fly—without wings.

Since he was waiting on a plumber and a roofer before anything else could be done, he grabbed a scraper and headed for the back bedroom, the one that had been Emma and Birdie's room.

There was only one bed in it now, and it was going to be sold in a yard sale because he needed the furnishings to be gone when he got ready to paint the walls and ceilings and refinish the old hardwood floors.

The paint looked gray, but as he began to scrape and saw an undertone of blue, he remembered the walls had been robin's-egg blue. He kept working, but with one eye on the time. He needed a little time to get all gorgeous and stuff, too.

———————————

Birdie had taken the whole day off, and needed it. Even though the services were over and she was home, she was still shaken by the finality.

She put on her oldest sweats, a long-sleeved T-shirt, and a thick pair of socks, then went to the kitchen to make herself a cup of coffee.

She was still thinking about her mama's message from the grave and what she was going to do about it. The whole thing hinged on getting all of them together without revealing why. Maybe they'd gather at the old house to go through Mama's things. That would be a logical reason to gather, and Hunt had already told them to feel free to get what they wanted in the way of keepsakes.

Satisfied that she'd figured that out, she went to the living room with her coffee, curled up in her recliner beneath a quilt, and aimed the remote at the television. She didn't care what she watched. She just wanted to hear something besides the sound of her own heartbeat.

———————————

Hunt walked out of the house at ten minutes to six wearing Wrangler jeans, his brown Justin boots, and a gray sweater under his black leather bomber jacket.

His dark hair brushed the collar of the jacket as he walked to the truck and then made sure the seat was dusted off before he got inside.

He'd backed out of this drive in his mother's car many a time during his high school days to go get his date, but he'd never felt this level of anticipation. He drove the short distance between them in haste and parked behind her car before going to the door.

She answered on the second knock and swung the door inward.

Her long hair was down and in long, soft curls, and the pink sweater and gray slacks she was wearing flattered her curves and long legs. But her dark eyes were flashing in frustration.

"Come in. I'm trying to find my phone."

He took his phone out of his pocket and pulled up the keypad, then handed it to her.

"Call yourself."

She grabbed his phone. "Yes! Thanks," she muttered, and quickly keyed in the numbers.

Almost immediately they both heard her phone ringing.

Hunt grinned. It was a Bon Jovi song. "Your ringtone is 'Living on a Prayer'?"

"Shut up and help me find it," Ava said.

"It's that way," Hunt said.

"That's the laundry. Please Jesus I didn't wash the sucker," Ava muttered.

Hunt laughed out loud. "Well, it's ringing, so I doubt it's been through the wash."

"Oh, right," she said, and made a run for the utility room before her phone quit ringing.

Within seconds, she was digging through the basket of laundry she'd been going to wash.

"Ta-da!" she cried, and pulled it out. "I guess it fell out of my pocket when I was gathering up laundry. Thank you, Hunt."

"So, did I just get a glimpse of you in action?"

Her eyes narrowed. "If you think that was me being upset, it's not even close."

He nodded. "Right. I remember. Good enough. I always say if you're gonna raise hell about something, make it memorable."

She grinned. "Nurses have to keep their cool on the job. I maintain quite well. But on my own time, I lose patience with myself."

"I empathize. Now, are we good to go? Got your jacket? It's chilly out."

"It's in the living room," she said, and then appreciated the view as she followed him back through the house. He had a sexy butt.

He helped her into her jacket and then flipped on the porch light as they were leaving.

Ava couldn't remember a man ever being that thoughtful, and gave him a big check mark in the good manners department. When he helped her into the truck and then made sure she was seated and buckled in before he closed the door, he scored again.

The tension was there between them as they drove to Granny's, but their friendship was older than this new stuff, and they were laughing and talking freely by the time they arrived.

"Remember the time you got sick from eating too many cinnamon candies?" Hunt said.

Ava rolled her eyes. "Are you really going there? Referring to the time I threw up on your shoe at the swings?"

"I guess I am," Hunt said.

"So much for me getting all gorgeous if you're going to bring up my sordid past," she muttered.

He grinned. "Sorry."

"No, you're not, but that's okay. I remember you getting caught making out with that Linda girl when you guys were sophomores. Her daddy brought you home."

Hunt chuckled. "How come you know that?"

"Emma told me. I pined for a good week that you'd forsaken me, and then the next time I saw you, you bought Ray and me ice cream and I forgave you."

"Lord. I had no idea," Hunt said.

Ava shrugged. "I got over it. My mother always said boys are slow on the uptake. Now, we're here. Let's go in. I'm starving."

Hunt already knew he was in over his head, but if this was what drowning felt like, he wasn't going to mind going under.

Hunt smelled barbecue the moment they walked in the door. It must be the special. At any rate, it struck a hungry chord.

"Mmmm, barbecue!" Ava said. "I know what I'm having."

Hunt grinned. "Come on, Ava. Don't be shy."

She turned around and poked him on the arm. "We've known each other too long to be prissy about being hungry."

"That we have, lady. Point made."

Ava grinned, and then turned and waved at Sully.

"Hey, Sully, how's your pretty wife?"

"You know Melissa…still being pretty," Sully said, then picked up two menus. "Booth or table?"

"Lady's choice," Hunt said.

"Table," Ava said.

"Follow me," Sully said, and led them through the busy dining room to a table on the far side of the room.

After the funeral today, Hunt's presence in Blessings was no longer unknown.

The fact that Ava Ridley was walking in with a man was newsworthy, but Hunt Knox being that man made it even better.

Ava waved and talked her way all the way across the room, then smiled when Hunt seated her before sitting in the chair to her right.

"Baby back ribs are the special tonight," Sully said as he gave them the menus. "Enjoy."

Ava shoved the menu aside and then looked at Hunt.

"What?" he said.

"Just checking to make sure I'm not dreaming," she said. "And in my panic to find my phone, I neglected to mention how hunky you look."

Hunt shook his head and then grinned. "You are going to be seriously good for my ego."

She leaned forward and lowered her voice.

"If I brag on how blue your eyes are, do I get dessert?"

He laughed out loud, and everyone in the room turned and looked, then whispered among themselves about what, if anything, was going on between Ava and Hunt.

Someone remembered Marjorie Knox used to babysit Ava, and someone else assumed they were likely catching up on the old friendship, and their presence together was duly assessed and ignored.

They ordered and ate biscuits while waiting for their ribs. Ava was trying not to think about later, but later was all Hunt could think about. He wanted her in his arms—standing body to body—kissing her until she begged for more.

And then their food came, and they got down to business.

"These are so good," Ava said as she finished one rib and then took a drink. "Tell me what you're working on at the house."

"I finished the grout and caulking, and started scraping down walls to get ready to paint," Hunt said.

"Is Emma's room still blue?" she asked.

"It's faded to more gray than blue, but yes, it's the same," he said.

"What about your room…in the attic?"

The smile slid off his face so fast Ava wished she hadn't asked.

"It's just the attic again," he said.

She reached for his hand. "I'm sorry, Hunt. No more talking about the past. Did you see old friends today?"

"It's okay, and yes, I did. I saw Rob Denton and met his wife. It was good to see him again."

The awkward moment passed, and they finished their meal.

"Do you still want dessert?" Hunt asked.

Ava put a hand on her belly. "Lord, no, but thank you. As your mama would have said, my eye was bigger than my stomach."

"You can get some to go," he offered.

"You want pie, don't you?" Ava said.

"Guilty," Hunt said.

She sighed. "Well, good lord, Hunt. Don't stand on ceremony with me. Order it. And you can get one to go for me. Coconut cream, if they have it."

"If you insist," Hunt said.

And this time, it was Ava who laughed.

Once again, the diners turned to look. Some were beginning to think their first assessment of the couple might have been hasty. When Hunt suddenly leaned over and wiped a faint smear of barbecue sauce from Ava's chin, they decided the look he gave her was more wolf than puppy friendly, and knew they were right.

"Y'all save any room for dessert?" their waitress asked as she refilled their drinks.

Hunt nodded. "We need one piece of coconut cream pie to go, and a piece of chocolate for now."

"You got it," she said, and hustled off to fill their orders. When she brought back the chocolate, she brought two forks. "Just in case," she said, and winked. "I'll be right back with your to-go order. Enjoy."

Hunt handed Ava a fork. "You get the first taste. After that, you'll have to fight for a bite."

"Well, maybe just one," Ava said, and forked a little bite of the pie and popped it in her mouth. "Yum…Mercy Pittman is one fine baker. That's so good."

He took a bite and had to agree. "Yes, it's good. But yours is just as good," he added.

She grinned, pleased with the compliment even if it wasn't exactly true.

When they finally started home, Ava was holding her piece of pie, trying to come to terms with the fact that she was sitting in a car with Hunt. This was, to date, the best day of her life. That it had to happen on the day he buried his mother was just enough to temper her emotions.

When they pulled up in her driveway, Ava knew their night was over. She turned in the seat to face him before they got out.

"Thank you for supper. I loved spending time with you."

Hunt smiled. "You're very welcome. I loved spending time with you, too."

Ava sighed. "Lord…that's a little too proper and polite for how I'm feeling. Walk me to the door before I make a fool of myself."

"Well shoot, I was kinda looking forward to you and your fool-ishness," Hunt said, then got out and circled the old truck to help her out.

The porch light he'd turned on before they left shone the way up the steps, and when she unlocked the door and stepped inside, he followed her far enough to make sure all was well.

Ava put down the pie and then put her arms around his neck.

"Thank you," she said, and gave him a quick kiss on the lips. "See you soon?"

He pulled her close. "No question about it," he said, and finally did what he'd been thinking about all night. He kissed her senseless, and didn't quit until she moaned. Reluctantly, he stopped.

"Sleep well, honey. Call me whenever you want. You know where I'll be."

Ava was still reeling from the kiss, and when he turned her loose, she felt off balance...like she was suddenly standing on one leg.

She watched as he drove away and then stepped back inside and locked the door. It was a little after 8:00 p.m. By the time she got her makeup off and her pajamas on, it would be time for her to get in bed. Five a.m. came early, but she needed the two hours before she had to be at work to get mentally ready for another day on the job.

CHAPTER 8

GORDON HAD TAKEN EMMA TO SAVANNAH FOR A MOVIE, MOSTLY to shift her focus from the funeral and all it entailed, and it worked. They drove home later that night, more at ease with each other than they had been in months. He knew there would be other times when the sadness of loss would return, but for one night, he'd made her smile.

Junior was at the Blue Ivy Bar getting shit-faced drunk because everyone was buying him a drink in sympathy for the loss of his mother. It wasn't until he passed out at the bar that May Temple, the owner, called Ray.

Ray had to work tomorrow on a roofing job in Savannah. He and Susie were getting ready for bed when his phone rang. When he saw the caller ID, he groaned.

"What?" Susie asked.

"It's May at the Blue Ivy. How much you wanna bet Junior is passed out drunk again?"

"Oh lord," Susie muttered. "Let me get my shoes and I'll drive you."

"You're the best," Ray said.

"Junior needs a keeper," Susie said.

Ray didn't comment. Susie didn't know anything about what was wrong with them and he hoped she never found out.

"I've got the car keys," Susie said. "Let's go." And out the door they went, straight to the Blue Ivy Bar.

"There's his car. Wait here," Ray said. "I'll get the keys and drag his ass out. When you see us come out, just get out and open the door for me, please. You don't need to be exposed to all the crap in there."

"I will," she said, and when Ray got out and ran inside, she locked the doors. The whole atmosphere of the place gave her the creeps.

Ray was just hoping Junior hadn't pissed himself as he walked into the bar. When he saw Junior passed out on the floor and the wet spot beneath his pants, he groaned. Too late.

"Dammit. I'm sorry, May."

May just shook her head. "This is par for the course here, and it's not your fault. Thanks for coming to get him."

"Thanks for calling. I wouldn't want him trying to drive home like this," Ray said, and then dug in Junior's pockets until he found the car keys.

May pointed at two men at the end of the bar.

"You boys help Ray get Junior to the car."

They got up without argument and hefted Junior up between them and headed out the door. Junior was still out—his chin on his chest—head lolling from one side to the other—feet dragging on the floor as they went, with Ray in the lead.

When Susie saw Ray had help, she stayed in the car, and as soon as Junior was loaded up, Ray waved at her, and then took off. She put the car in gear and followed.

The upside of living in a town the size of Blessings was that it didn't take long to get from one side of town to the other.

Susie turned on the heater as she drove, and then when they got to Junior's place, she parked behind the car and got out to help.

Ray handed her the keys.

"Open the door for me, sugar. It's that red key by the fob. I'll get him in the house."

She ran ahead, unlocked the door and pushed it inward, and then ran back to help. By now, Junior was coming to and staggering enough to walk himself inside with them holding him up.

"Jus' put me on a bed," he mumbled.

Ray sighed and walked Junior to the bedroom, where he promptly collapsed on the bed. Ray pulled off Junior's shoes and covered him with a blanket, pissy pants and all. He walked out without looking back, used the remote to lock Junior's car, and then tossed the keys on the coffee table.

"Let's go home," Ray said, then locked the door behind them as they left.

———————

Ava was in a house she'd never seen before, running through the rooms calling out Hunt's name. She could hear him answering from somewhere far away, but no matter how many rooms she ran through, she couldn't find him. She was out of breath and crying when she began hearing a siren. She turned around.

The alarm was going off. Ava sat straight up in bed, recognized where she was, and groaned as she shut it off.

"Lord have mercy, what a horrible dream," she muttered, and headed for the shower.

A few minutes later she was out, her long hair wound up in a bun at the top of her head. She made a run for the dresser to get underwear and then turned up the thermostat in the hall before getting dressed. Within minutes she was in a fresh set of scrubs and headed for the kitchen.

Coffee was first on the agenda, and after she popped a K-cup in the coffee maker to brew, she got out peanut butter and jelly, popped some bread in the toaster, and went out to get the paper.

It was still dark, but the streetlights were bright enough for her to see the newspaper at the edge of the steps. That paper carrier needed to practice with his pitching arm. He hadn't hit the porch once in the last two months. She glanced up at the sky. It looked cloudy, and it smelled like rain.

She hurried back in to the kitchen. Her coffee and toast were ready, so she sat down to eat as she read. Her cell phone was in her pocket, and she thought about texting Hunt but was afraid it was too early.

After breakfast, she grabbed an all-weather coat and headed out the door. It was fifteen minutes to seven.

She liked early mornings in Blessings. Lights were on in the houses as she passed, and she imagined sleepy-headed children being coaxed out of bed to get ready for school, or people like her who were getting ready for work.

She drove past the Knox house even though it was out of her way, but it made her happy to know Hunt Knox was in the vicinity again—just like he'd been when she was growing up. Even though he'd had no romantic interest in her whatsoever then, the fact that she had been able to see him when she wanted had been enough. And now, fate had brought him back…and with interest to spare.

God was good.

It was beginning to sprinkle when she got to work, and after she clocked in at the ER, her day began.

The loud clap of thunder woke Hunt out of a deep, dreamless sleep. As he rolled over onto his back and glanced toward the window, he could already hear rain blowing against the panes and was glad he'd finished caulking. At least they weren't loose anymore.

When he saw it was after 7:00 a.m., he thought of Ava. She was already at work. He closed his eyes, remembering the way she'd felt in his arms, and the film of tears in her eyes when she'd warned him not to break her heart.

He got the message.

She had waited a long time for the man she wanted, but the warning was clear. If he wasn't on board, he should say so now.

The thing was he was so on board he couldn't think straight. He didn't know how bad he'd wanted somebody to love until the offer came, and now she was all he thought about.

Thunder rumbled again.

Hunt sighed. This was prime sleeping weather, but there was too much to do to sleep in, so he threw back the covers and went to turn up the thermostat, then headed to the bathroom to shower and shave. He'd planned to remove a few boards in the kitchen floor today and see what was up with the sagging middle, but not while it was raining. Today would be a good day to tackle the attic—removing trash, sorting things that his siblings might want to go keep, and setting the rest of it aside to sell.

———————————

It was a little after nine before Ava had a chance to text Hunt.

Thank you for dinner and your company last night. I loved it.

Hunt was going through a box of old Christmas decorations, throwing away everything the mice had chewed on and setting aside the little ornaments they used to put on the tree. When his phone signaled a text and he saw it was from Ava, he dusted off his hands and read it, then texted back.

I loved it, too. How about a repeat tonight...but at your place around 5:00 p.m. I bring the food. You set the table. I promise not to stay too long. I just want to see your face and steal another kiss...or two.

He hit Send, then rocked back on his heels, waiting for the reply. It came quickly.

I would love it. Five o'clock works for me. I'll be all puckered up and waiting.

Hunt grinned. One of the best things about Ava was her lack of self-consciousness. And all the rest of her was pretty damn awesome, too.

When the rain began, traffic in the ER slowed down, giving everyone a little space to catch up on paperwork. But as the rain continued, it began to cause problems.

Wilson Turner, the manager at the Crown, was going too fast coming into town, hydroplaned into a ditch, and rolled upside down. He called in his own accident and was transported to the ER with a broken nose and a cut on his head.

They were wheeling him into X-ray when the ambulance went out again, returning minutes later with Chester Benton, the young man who was the dishwasher at Granny's. He'd gone on an errand for the restaurant and was rear-ended at the stoplight and taken to the ER with whiplash.

Then Sully Raines showed up to check on his employee, and the assistant manager at the Crown arrived to check on Wilson Turner, and the rain kept coming down.

Lunchtime came and went, and it wasn't until Ava was clocking out that she realized she hadn't eaten a single bite of anything since breakfast.

Rhonda Bailey was clocking out as Ava walked up, already wearing her raincoat with her purse over her shoulder.

Rhonda looked at her and grinned. "You look as tired as I feel. Are you okay?"

Ava smiled. "I'm fine. All I need is a soaking bath and a little rest. Hunt's coming over tonight and I don't have time to be tired. Not when my life is just getting interesting."

Rhonda laughed. "Have fun, and drive safe going home."

"For sure," Ava said, then clocked out and left the building, running through the rain to get to her car.

Once inside, she started it up and then turned on the wipers. It was too late to eat a meal, but she was too hungry to wait until Hunt came, so she went through the drive-through at Broyles Dairy Freeze, got a vanilla malt, and drank it on the way home.

She pulled up in the drive, then hit the house running. As always, she threw her scrubs in the laundry, then headed for the shower. Once she had the workday washed off, she tidied the house and set the table before going back to change into something besides sweatpants and a T-shirt.

She'd worn her hair up all day to the point that it had given her a headache, so after brushing it to a dark, silky shine, she left it down for the evening. She didn't want to dress up, but she still wanted to look good, so she opted for jeans and a red sweater, then added a little makeup and called it done. Now all she needed was Hunt.

Hunt worked all day in the attic, lulled by the rain on the roof and the dusty memories of his childhood as he sorted through what had been stored.

He sent Birdie a text, telling her that he had several boxes of things they needed to sort up in the attic, and to let him know when they all wanted to come over and get the clothes still in Marjorie's room.

She replied, mentioning the weekend, and that was all he needed to know.

When four o'clock rolled around, he headed for the shower. He'd been looking forward to seeing Ava again and had no intention of being late. He called in a to-go order at Granny's and then finished getting dressed.

The rainy day had faded into an intermittent drizzle as he was leaving the house, and he was glad he had his mom's old pickup to drive rather than riding on the Harley.

He made a quick stop at Granny's to pick up his order, then headed to Ava's. When he turned the corner and headed down the street to her house, the porch light led him straight to her door.

He knocked and then heard footsteps running toward the door. All of a sudden, the door swung inward.

"Come in! Come in! This is terrible weather," she said.

Hunt crossed the threshold and elbowed the door shut behind him.

"You look beautiful," he said.

"So do you," she said, then laughed. "And you smell delicious."

"It's Granny's fried chicken," he said.

"Yum! Follow me. I have the table set in the kitchen."

He set the sack on the table, then began pulling out boxes and cartons, while Ava went behind him opening them up and putting in serving spoons as Hunt turned around and took off his jacket.

"Everything looks amazing," Ava said.

Hunt looked up, then grinned. She wasn't looking at the food. She was looking at him.

He leaned over and kissed her.

"And 'everything' tastes as good as it looks, too," he added.

"Sit here," she said, patting the chair at the head of the table. "I'm getting butter for the biscuits."

Hunt sat, then waited as she got butter from the counter and honey from the pantry and carried them to the table. Then she sat down in the chair to his right.

"What's your favorite piece of chicken?" Hunt asked.

"Um, anything dark meat, but I like it all," she said.

"There are thighs and drumsticks," he said. "Help yourself. I'm going for white meat."

After adding mashed potatoes and gravy, corn, hot biscuits, and coleslaw to their plates, they began to eat.

"What went on in the ER today?" Hunt asked.

Ava rolled her eyes. "Fender benders, a rollover, all weather related. No serious injuries. I think the worst was Wilson Turner's broken nose."

"Who's Wilson Turner?" Hunt asked.

"He's the manager at the Crown," Ava said. "His eyes were already turning black when they took him home. He'll look like a raccoon before he's healed. With such a rainy day, were you able to work on the house?"

"Not with repairs. I was up in the attic all day going through stuff."

She paused and laid down her fork, suddenly serious. "I'll bet that brought back a lot of memories."

"Yeah, it did, but they weren't all bad. It's weird, though. That was my bedroom for the last four years I was home, and now there's not even a hint that it was ever my room."

Ava frowned. "I don't understand that."

Hunt reached for a biscuit and buttered it. "I do. After I left and didn't come back, they got rid of my stuff so they wouldn't be reminded I still existed."

Ava just nodded and began forking off bits of her chicken, talking as they ate.

"After you mentioned you all had a falling-out before you left, I've been tempted to ask Emma what happened. But I haven't. Even though I felt like part of your family when I was growing up, I wasn't, and it's not my business to cross that line."

"Finish your meal. We'll talk afterward," Hunt said.

Ava nodded, and the tension of the moment passed as they moved into old memories and laughter.

Finally, Hunt wiped his hands on a napkin and pushed his plate back.

"If we're going to give this thing between us a try, then it has to be open and honest all the way because that's how I am. You asked me not to hurt you, and that's the farthest damn thing from my mind. I think about making love to you. I think about life with you. So I have to be honest about all of it. Agreed?"

Ava's heart was pounding. That honesty had just curled her toes inside her shoes.

"Agreed," she said.

"Someone in my family stole all the money I'd saved to go to college—eight thousand dollars—and the others knew who did it and lied to protect them. Mom had left to take Birdie to school. She didn't know it happened until she came home and I was gone. After I called her to tell her I'd just enlisted in the army, she was hysterical, telling me she'd known nothing about it and they weren't telling her anything. Birdie just knew I left. She didn't know anything about any of this and they never told her. She didn't find out until after I came back, and she's pretty pissed at all of them."

Ava was staring at him in disbelief. "Even your father knew?"

Hunt nodded. "He told me what's done is done, and to figure something else out. So I did."

"Oh, Hunt. Oh my God, I am so sorry. No wonder you feel the way you do."

He shrugged. "Old news for me. But I don't keep secrets from people who matter."

An ache began in the back of her throat to the point that she was afraid she would cry if she spoke, but she had to ask. "And I matter?"

He reached across the table and took her hand. "So much it scares me. But there's one other thing you have to know, and then the decision is totally yours. I will never live in Blessings. I like the people here okay. But I don't belong here anymore. My life and my work is in Houston, and there's nothing keeping me here right now but a promise I made to Mom…and you. If you don't want to leave, then you have to know I'll never stay."

There were tears in Ava's eyes, but she was squeezing his hand.

"Do you know my middle name?"

Hunt frowned. "Uh…I don't guess I do."

She turned loose of his hand and stood.

"It's Ruth… And in the Bible, Ruth faced a similar decision, and her answer was…'Whither thou goest, I will go.' That's my answer, Hunt Knox. When you leave, take me with you."

Within seconds, she was in his arms, and then madness ensued.

The kitchen was for kisses.

The shoes came off in the hall.

By the time they got to her bedroom, they were coming out of their clothes.

They fell onto her bed in a tangle of arms and legs, with Hunt's hands fisted in her hair, and her arms locked around his waist. There was no foreplay, no sweet love words whispered in her ear, no promises made that hadn't already been said. One moment she was on her back, and then he was inside her, and after that, nothing mattered. Nothing but a mind-blowing blood rush that was so powerful they couldn't have stopped—even if they'd wanted to. Even if they'd meant to.

Time ceased, and there was nothing but the frantic gasps, the stifled moans, then a change in rhythm as they hit the wall and shattered, falling slowly apart in each other's arms.

The silence that followed was almost reverent. There was nothing to add to what had just happened. Nothing to say beyond the word *love*.

And they did.

Ava's love was old and strong.

Hunt's was new and sharp.

But it was there…and it was theirs.

Hunt rolled over and glanced at the clock.

It was already after seven. He didn't want to leave her, but they both had a duty to others.

He rose up on one elbow to look down at the woman beside him.

"You have to know the last thing I want to do is leave you, but I promised, and this wasn't on the agenda when I walked into your house a couple of hours ago. However, I'm not a damn bit sorry. You're the best thing that's ever happened to me. Thank you for loving me first…but I'm a quick read, and I catch up fast."

Ava reached for him, cupping his face, searching the intensity in his gaze.

"There is no race. I waited this long for my miracle and it happened. I'm not going to second-guess the reasons or the timing. And despite the friendship I've had with the rest of your family, I'm in your corner."

Hunt kissed her one last time, rolled out of bed, then began gathering up his clothes and getting dressed.

"You know where I am. If you need me…just call. Love you, Ava."

She sighed. "Love you more."

She listened to his footsteps as he walked through the house, retrieving his jacket, then leaving the house. If it wasn't for the food still on the table, she would just stay in bed. Instead, she got up wearing nothing but a smile, put on a robe and house shoes, and went to clean up the kitchen.

This was easily the best dessert she'd ever had in her life.

She'd thought she wouldn't sleep at all, but she fell asleep dreaming of Hunt and slept until her alarm went off. It had stopped raining overnight, but there were puddles everywhere when Ava arrived at work.

Traffic was slow downtown except at the grocery store. The parking lot at the Crown was full of people shopping before another rain came through.

It was also the first day back at school after Christmas vacation, and the town had a different rhythm when school was in session. Buses were running, parents in cars dropping off children, and the streets were filled with other children who walked to school.

A new semester was beginning. Whatever had happened last year was now history. Teachers were hoping for the best. Parents were hoping for the best. Kids had their own agendas, none of which involved learning something new.

The last bus to arrive at Blessings Elementary was unloading children. The driver made it a habit to get out first so he could help the little ones who sat at the front of the bus walk down the steps.

Another teacher was standing on the steps of the elementary school, watching the bus riders as they made their way up the walk.

Seven-year-old Davey Randolph was running up the walk when another student bumped into him, making him drop his book bag. When it hit the ground, papers fell out and began scattering, blowing across the schoolyard and then back toward the street.

Davey took off chasing papers without looking where he was going, and when he suddenly abandoned the schoolyard and started running toward the cars, the teacher realized he wasn't going to remember to stop, look, and listen for cars—like the one that just illegally pulled out of line too soon.

She began shouting at the bus driver to stop Davey as she took off running. The bus driver heard her and looked up just as Davey ran past his line of sight.

"Stop, Davey, stop!" he shouted, but it was too late.

Davey had darted between the back of the bus and the line of cars and ran right in front of the moving car.

The sudden screech of brakes, the sickening thud, and then the sounds of dozens of children screaming and crying filled the air. The first day of the new school year was beginning on a tragedy.

———————————

Avery Ames, the day dispatcher at the police station, sent out the call to all patrol cars, dispatched an ambulance, and then all kinds of sirens began sounding across town. They got word at the hospital of the impending emergency and began readying for a trauma patient.

———————————

Hunt was in the kitchen having breakfast when he heard the sirens. He frowned. Ambulance and police were heading somewhere fast. He hoped it wasn't bad, and knew whatever it was, Ava would be in the thick of it.

Last night had been a gift—the beginning of a new way of life. He was in love, really in love, for the first time in his life. It had only taken him thirty-three years of living and less than a week in her presence to make it happen. The thought of belonging to someone again, like he'd once belonged to his family, was an unbelievable gift.

Now, the sound of sirens told him she was likely facing another hectic day. He hoped it was nothing serious, then finished his cereal, put the bowl in the sink, and went back to work. The walls were scraped down and patched, ready for paint. Today, it was all about scraping the woodwork and filling in the cracks with putty.

———————

When the ambulance arrived at the ER, they were ready.

Davey Randolph was unconscious and bloody—and so small and too still as they rolled him in. An IV was already in place, and EMTs were giving valuable info to the waiting trauma team as they wheeled him into the first bay.

Ava was on duty and soon in the middle of it all, helping cut away the child's clothing as Dr. Quick began assessing injuries. There was a large cut on the back of Davey's head that was bleeding profusely. And it appeared he had, at the least, a broken arm, and maybe some broken ribs. But when Dr. Quick raised an eyelid to check for pupil reaction, and then checked the other eye as well, his focus shifted.

"Pupils fixed and dilated," he said. "Get the portable X-ray in here stat. I need film…head, upper body, and pelvis."

Ava recognized the child. She knew the parents. But she couldn't let that matter. In a town the size of Blessings, every patient was someone she knew, and Davey Randolph's life depended upon them doing their job.

When the tests and X-rays came back, it was painfully apparent he needed surgery they weren't equipped to perform.

Dr. Quick began issuing new orders.

"Call Medi-Flight. Get a chopper here, stat. We need to get him to the medical center in Savannah. Ava, you and Rhonda continue to monitor his vitals. Let me know if anything changes. I have to talk to his parents."

Both nurses were focused on the doctor's orders and the job at hand, trying not to think about how close this child was to death. Trying not to think about the internal bleeding in Davey's brain and belly and what would happen if they couldn't stop it…if his brain swelled too much before they got him where he needed to be.

A couple of minutes later, a nurse came running.

"Medi-Flight en route. ETA about sixteen minutes."

CHAPTER 9

BOYD WINSTON HAD BEEN A PILOT FOR MEDI-FLIGHT FOR TWELVE years. Every trip they made was to pick up someone in critical condition, and this trip was no exception. He'd heard the medics on board talking and knew the patient they were picking up this time was a child. But his job was to get there as quickly and safely as possible, and return the same way, making sure the patient had every opportunity to survive.

This was his first trip of the new year, and he didn't want to start the year off losing a patient before he got them where they needed to go.

He was in constant contact with the hospital in Blessing all the way there, and radioed them when he was four minutes out. He'd flown to Blessings before, so when he finally came over the little town and glanced down at the helipad he was approaching, he was shocked when his vision suddenly blurred. And then panic struck as he felt the band of muscles begin tightening across his chest. When he broke out in a cold sweat, he knew what was happening, but he needed to get down before he passed out.

"Help me, God," he muttered, then radioed to the hospital. "Coming in. Be advised. Pilot in distress."

The EMTs behind him heard and leaped to their feet, shouting, "Boyd! Boyd! What's wrong?"

Boyd just shook his head and, with every ounce of focus he had left, set the chopper down on the helipad, shut down the speed of the rotors, then grabbed his chest and passed out.

Dr. Quick was on the site when he heard the call.

"We can't wait for another pilot to get here!" he said. "If I don't act now, this child has no chance at all."

Ava grabbed his arm. "We don't have to wait! There's a licensed chopper pilot right here in Blessings. Marjorie Knox's oldest son flew helicopters for the army, and he's employed by an oil company in Houston, flying oil workers back and forth to offshore rigs. He can do this!"

"Then call him!" Dr. Quick said.

Ava grabbed her phone and ran out into the hall, calling as she went. It rang once, then again, and again, and she was in a panic, afraid it would go to voicemail when she heard Hunt's voice.

"Hey, how's my favorite girl?"

"Hunt, we need you! A little boy was just hit by a car, and we need to get him to Savannah for emergency surgery or he's going to die. The Medi-Flight pilot just landed the chopper and then passed out. We think heart attack. Please! Can you help? There's no time to get another pilot here, and we're not equipped to do this surgery."

"Give me three minutes," Hunt said, and disconnected.

He dropped what he was doing and ran out of the house, jumped on his Harley, and within seconds was on the street—racing to the hospital, taking back streets to avoid traffic to get there quicker.

Ava ran back. "He's on the way!"

Dr. Quick nodded, but Davey's vital signs weren't as strong as they had been, and he was worried.

The pilot was unconscious and ashen as they wheeled him past her down the hall.

Davey's parents were in hysterics, and the EMTs were arguing about the legalities of using some untried pilot when Hunt rolled up on the Harley.

He flashed his ID and his pilot's license.

"Load him up. I'll get coordinates in the air," he said, and just like that, their concern for his ability to do this ended.

Hunt glanced at Ava once and then ran for the helipad and climbed inside the chopper, quickly familiarizing himself with the instrument panel as they loaded up the boy. An EMT tapped him on the shoulder.

"I'm Rolly. We're good to go."

Hunt began increasing the engine speed. The rotors were spinning faster and faster. The hospital personnel ran back toward the hospital as the chopper lifted off.

Ava watched, her heart pounding, and then they were gone.

"Good call, Ava," Dr. Quick said.

Ava's stomach was in knots, but there was another patient in distress to tend, so they hurried to the trauma bay to assess the unconscious pilot.

Meanwhile, Hunt was radioing Medi-Flight and the hospital in Savannah, explaining the emergency that had occurred and requesting coordinates to the destination.

The flight from Blessings to Savannah was brief, but still hair-raising for all involved.

Hunt could hear the medical team behind him in constant contact with the doctor at their destination and knew the child was in crisis, but he couldn't think about that. His job was to get them there. The rest of it was on their shoulders and in God's hands.

They'd been airborne a little over fifteen minutes before he had Savannah in sight. He radioed to the hospital that they were three minutes out and then continued on course.

A couple of minutes later, Rolly came up behind him and pointed.

"That's our destination," Rolly said, pointing to the helipad on the hospital roof.

"In my sight," Hunt said, and within moments, he set the chopper down without a wobble. "What's your protocol?"

"We transfer the patient and the med chart to the waiting team, and return to base," Rolly said.

Hunt gave them a thumbs-up and then watched as the bay door slid open. Two team members jumped out, and two stayed inside to help steady the stretcher.

The hospital team came running, loaded the injured child onto a gurney along with a chart of his info and stats, and then began their own race against time, taking the child into the hospital, then straight to surgery.

Hunt radioed to Medi-Flight that the patient had been delivered, and as soon as the flight crew climbed back inside, they headed to base.

The anxiety of the emergency had passed. The trip from the hospital to their base was less than ten minutes by air, and this time when they landed, Hunt powered down. The medical team had their patient bay cleaned up, ready for their next run. When the door slid back, they began getting out.

"There's the boss," Rolly said, pointing to the man waiting near an office building. "Come with me, Hunt. We'll figure out a way to get you home."

Hunt followed them to the office and was quickly introduced to Niles Morehead, the director.

"Hunt, this is our boss, Niles Morehead. Niles, this is Hunt Knox, the man who helped us out, and he is one fine pilot," Rolly said.

Niles shook Hunt's hand. "I can't thank you enough for stepping in. Dr. Quick called us from Blessings Hospital and gave us the low-down on you. He said one of his nurses knew you and recommended you. So you flew choppers for the army, did you?"

"Yes, sir," Hunt said. "And I still fly for an oil company."

"How is Boyd? Has anyone heard?" Rolly asked.

"He had a heart attack," Niles said. "We're waiting to see if we have to go get him."

"Mind if I wait around?" Hunt said. "If you go back, I'd like to hitch a ride home. Otherwise, I'll have to call someone to pick me up or hitch a ride to a car rental to get back to Blessings."

"No problem," Niles said. "Have a seat inside the office. There's coffee. Help yourself."

Hunt went inside, got a cup of coffee, and settled into an old leather chair to wait it out.

One hour passed, and then another. One Medi-Flight crew went out to pick up injuries from a wreck on a freeway. Hunt was still in the waiting room when the phone rang again. A few minutes later, Niles came out of the office.

"You've got your ride. We're going to get Boyd. They're stabilizing him now. I have another pilot named Conrad getting a chopper flight-ready. I've called Rolly. He's coming to walk you out to the chopper. Conrad knows what's going on. Thanks again for helping us out, and it was nice meeting you."

"Sure thing," Hunt said, and walked out of the office. He saw Rolly running toward the office, and went to meet him.

Rolly arrived, breathless but smiling. "Follow me, Hunt," he said, and led him toward the tarmac where the chopper was warming up.

The rotors were already turning, and the EMT crew was loading up when Rolly walked up behind the pilot and tapped him on the arm, shouting to be heard above the noise level.

"Conrad...this is Hunt Knox, the pilot who brought in Boyd's chopper."

Conrad gave Hunt a thumbs-up and gestured for him to get in.

Hunt nodded and climbed into the belly of the chopper.

The same team he'd flown with was already inside, checking supplies and waiting for takeoff.

Conrad climbed in, and then Rolly shut the door behind them.

Hunt acknowledged their greetings but barely had time to get a seat and buckle in before they were in the air. The ride was strangely silent. He knew the trip would be stressful for all of them because this time the patient they were picking up was also a friend.

Hopefully, Boyd would survive the heart attack and have a lot of years left of his life, although this was going to ground him from working as a pilot again. Then he said a quiet prayer for the little boy he had flown to Savannah and settled in for the flight.

Dr. Quick and the ER staff were getting Boyd ready for transport when they got word that Medi-Flight was only two minutes out. The orderlies were there, ready to move their patient to the helipad.

"Thanks for everything, Doc," Boyd said.

Dr. Quick patted him on the arm. "Of course. That's what we do. Your ride is here, and so are the orderlies to get you to it. Safe travels," he said.

The chopper landed, and when the doors rolled back, Hunt was the first one out. He started walking toward the hospital and saw Ava coming toward him. He opened his arms, caught her in midstride, and held her close.

"Thank you! Thank you!" she kept saying. "We got word that Davey was still stable when they wheeled him into surgery. It's the chance he needed, and you gave it to him!"

"You're selling yourself short," Hunt said. "You're the one who thought of me. I didn't do anything spectacular. I just flew a chopper...like I do all the time. You people are the ones who gave the little guy a chance."

"Can you come inside for a couple of minutes? Dr. Quick wanted to meet you and thank you himself."

"Yeah, sure," Hunt said, and took her by the hand as she walked him back into the ER.

"Everybody! This is Hunt Knox, the pilot who flew Davey to Savannah," Ava said.

Before Hunt could even say 'hello,' he was inundated by staff, all wanting to talk to him.

He recognized an orderly as someone he'd gone to school with, and one of the custodians was a neighbor from his childhood. And then everyone was talking to him, telling him they'd helped care for his mother and thanking him for stepping in for the pilot.

Then Dr. Quick came out of an exam room and went straight to Hunt. Ava made the introduction. "Dr. Quick, this is Hunt Knox. Hunt, this is Dr. Quick, our ER doctor."

"It's a pleasure to meet you, sir. Thank you for stepping up," Quick said.

Hunt shrugged. "I'm glad I was able to help," he said, and shook the doctor's hand. "Nice to meet everyone…but this appears to be a busy place. Looks like I need to evacuate so you all can get back to work."

"I'll be right back. I'm going to walk him out," Ava said, and walked Hunt out of the building and then back to his Harley. "Will I see you later?"

"Count on it," Hunt said, then slid an arm around her waist, pulled her close, and kissed her. "This must be getting old to you. So far, our entire relationship has consisted of eating, or going to eat, or making love. But there are a thousand things I can't wait to show you when we get back to Houston."

Ava slid a hand up the side of his cheek.

"Hunt, you forget. In my eyes, we're old friends who just fell in love. I have memories of all kinds of things I did with your family, you included. I ate half my meals with you then. The fact that we're still doing it just makes everything right. And the plus side of it is you finally fell in love with me. That's all I ever wanted. We both have responsibilities. If our time off revolves around an evening meal, then count me in."

He grabbed her hand, pulled her forward, and kissed her again.

"Consider yourself counted. I'll either bring food to your place, or I'll pick you up and we'll eat somewhere here in town. So do you want me to bring food to you, or do we go eat out? My place is a mess."

"What do you want to do?" she asked.

"Eat and make love to you," he said.

She laughed out loud, then threw her arms around his neck.

"Then we better eat out first," she said.

He grinned. "Pick you up at six?"

She nodded. "I've got to get back to work. See you later."

He started up the Harley and rode away.

Emma was at the Crown getting groceries when Lilah, one of her friends from church, came running up to her.

"Lord, lord, Emma! What a miracle your brother was for the Randolph family. I know you must be proud of him!"

Emma frowned. "Which brother are you talking about, and what happened to the Randolphs?"

Lilah's eyes widened. "Oh my! You haven't heard? Little Davey, their seven-year-old, was hit by a car in front of the elementary school!"

"Oh no! I did hear sirens, but I never knew what was happening," Emma said.

"They said he was hurt real bad. They called Medi-Flight to take him to the med center in Savannah, but the pilot flying the chopper had a heart attack just after landing here. He couldn't fly Davey out, and the child was so critical there wasn't time to wait for another chopper. Then Ava Ridley told them about Hunt, so they called him. He flew the chopper back to Savannah and helped save that little boy's life!"

Emma was speechless. Knowing Hunt could fly choppers was one thing, but hearing him put his skill to a use that saved someone she knew was humbling.

"That's good. Real good. I'm glad he was able to help them out," Emma said.

Lilah nodded. "Well, when you see Hunt, tell him we're all really proud of him."

Emma swallowed past the lump in her throat. "Yes, yes, I'll do that."

She hurried up with the rest of her shopping, then cried all the way home because she couldn't just pop in and see Hunt and hug him…or praise him. She couldn't face him, because the secret and the lie were still between them.

Birdie was at work when her boss, Dub Truesdale, stopped in the doorway of her office.

"Hey, Birdie… Tell your brother Hunt he did good today!"

Birdie looked up from the invoices she was posting and smiled.

"What are you talking about?"

"He stepped in for the Medi-Flight pilot this morning. The pilot landed, then had a heart attack. Ava Ridley told them about Hunt, and he showed up and flew a little kid to the med center in Savannah for emergency surgery," Dub said.

Birdie gasped. "What? When did this happen? What little kid? Why am I the last to know anything around here?"

Dub proceeded to tell her what he'd heard, then ended his story by praising Hunt. "You must be real proud having a brother who can do that," he added.

She nodded, but now she was remembering the chopper coming in and going out, and she'd just heard another one come in and go out, and all that time had no idea Hunt had been involved in any of it. She wondered if he was back, then sent him a text.

I just heard about your morning flight. I'm so proud of you, Hunt.

She hit Send, then got up to get a can of Coke from the mini-fridge before going back to work.

While everyone had been frantically trying to save Davey Randolph's life, Richard Borden, the man who'd been driving the car that hit him, was devastated. All he kept thinking was if he hadn't pulled out of line—if he'd waited like everyone else for his turn to drive away—Davey would have been in class, settling in to the new semester.

Chief Pittman had given Borden several citations, all relating to failure to obey and unsafe driving, with warnings that if Davey Randolph did not survive, further charges, including involuntary manslaughter, could be added.

Richard Borden was so distraught that he refused to get back in his car. Chief Pittman called a tow truck to get the car home, then called Borden's wife to come get her husband.

The turmoil within the Borden family was on a level with the Randolph family. Both of them were desperately praying for Davey to survive. Both of them would be forever changed if he did not.

———————

Junior Knox was still sleeping when Hunt became the hero of the day. When he finally woke up, it was midafternoon. He made himself some coffee and sat staring blindly at the television, thinking about his life. He had no future. He had no plans. He was just here, taking up space.

Later, he checked his bank to see if his unemployment money had come in. It wasn't going to last much longer, which meant he'd need to go find himself another job. But for now, he was getting by. Once he realized he had a positive balance in his account, he left to gas up his car.

He pulled up to the pumps at the gas station and got out with his bankcard. He swiped it at the pump just as one of his drinking buddies from the Blue Ivy pulled up and got out.

"Hey, Junior… Hunt sure did pull off a good one this morning, right?"

Junior frowned. "I don't know. What did he do?"

"He flew a kid to Savannah for surgery and saved his life."

"Why would he be doing that?" Junior asked.

"The Medi-Flight pilot had a heart attack while he was landing, and someone called Hunt. I didn't know he could do stuff like that."

"Yeah… He was in the army. That's really something," Junior said.

His buddy nodded, then shoved his hands in his pockets and leaned against his car while waiting for his tank to fill. He kept trying to talk about Hunt, but Junior wasn't responding. When the pump finally kicked off, Junior got in his car and drove straight to their mother's old house.

Both the Harley and the black pickup were there, and so was a plumber. Junior wished he had the guts to just go in and help, but he couldn't look his brother in the eye.

Hunt worked at the house the rest of the day, but it was hard to focus. He felt the adrenaline rush of the emergency, and then being back in a chopper had made him long to be in the air again. He kept thinking about being with Ava, too, so there was that distraction as well.

He was in the boys' old bedroom, moving the furniture around to check the flooring for loose boards or wood rot. The hardwood was in bad shape, but he thought it could be sanded down and refinished.

He'd taken down the pictures when he was scraping the walls to get ready for painters and had tossed them on the bed out of the way. But as he was moving the furniture back in place, one of them slid off the bed. And when it did, the frame broke, leaving the print and the piece of cardboard backing loose within it.

"Dammit," Hunt muttered, but as he bent down to pick up the pieces, a piece of paper fell out.

It was lined paper, torn out of a school notebook and folded in half. Curious, he unfolded it and read.

I swear on Marjorie and Birdie Knox's lives never to tell why Hunt's money was taken.

> Signed:
> Parnell Knox
> Emma Knox
> Parnell Knox, Jr.
> Raymond Knox

Hunt was in shock. He recognized his daddy's handwriting, as well as his brothers' and sister's handwriting. Whatever the hell had happened, his daddy had written this and made them sign it.

It didn't tell him any more than he already knew, but the fact that his daddy went so far as to make them sign what amounted to a written oath, sworn on the lives of their mother and sister, was shocking.

Hunt folded the paper back up and put it in his wallet, then gathered up the broken pieces and carried them out to the garbage.

But he couldn't get past the fact that his daddy had seen fit to make them do this. His mother was gone now, and Birdie had known nothing about any of this. And the others weren't talking. It was the nightmare that wouldn't end.

He was relieved when it was time to go get Ava. The sun appeared to be as tired of this day as Hunt was as it sank toward the horizon.

He pulled up in her driveway, and before he could get out, she came bouncing out of her house with a smile on her face, her dark hair swinging with every step that she took.

"Hi!" she said as she climbed in the truck.

Hunt grinned. "Hello to you, too, pretty girl. You must have had a good day."

"Not really, but it's over. The good part of my day is you, and it's just now starting."

She leaned over and kissed him square on the mouth.

Hunt groaned, cupped the back of her head, and pulled her closer to kiss her back.

"You don't know how much I needed that…and you," he said, then started the truck and backed out of the drive. "What's your pleasure this evening, honey?"

"It's a little cool, but let's get stuff from the Dairy Freeze and go eat at the park. I just need fresh air and you," Ava said.

Hunt sighed. "Perfect. Not counting the flight, I've had a weird day, too, and you're my touchstone to joy."

Ava's eyes suddenly welled. "Oh, Hunt. That might be the sweetest thing anyone has ever said to me."

"Give me time. I can do better," Hunt said, and then winked to take away the seriousness of the moment.

Ava laughed through tears. "Then feed me. I'm starving."

"Broyles Dairy Freeze, here we come," Hunt said. "Burgers or chili dogs?"

"Chili dog and fries, please," Ava said.

"Anything for my sweetheart," Hunt said.

Twenty minutes later, they were at the park, sitting at one of the picnic tables, and in between sharing ketchup and dipping fries, they were talking about Houston and what he did on the job. After a while, Ava shifted the conversation.

"I don't know if anyone told you, but Davey Randolph's surgery was successful. He's in the ICU, and for the time being he's listed as critical but stable."

"That's really good news," Hunt said.

She nodded. "Every save is a good day. Oh, my parents are coming home sometime tomorrow," she added. "I told them you had come back because of your mom, but I didn't say anything about us yet."

"Are they going to be upset if you leave Blessings?" he asked.

Ava smiled. "Not upset. They'll be delighted for the both of us. Mom's always known I loved you. We both just thought it was for naught, as the old-timers used to say. Knowing Mom, she'll just look at us living in Houston as a plus, giving them another place to visit."

Hunt felt like his future was on a roll. Loving Ava was bringing his years of exile to an end in the most marvelous way.

"What now?" he asked as he dumped their trash.

Ava pointed to the swings.

"For old times' sake, would you push me in the swing like you used to do when I was little?"

Hunt wrapped her up in a bear hug and felt the chill of her cheek against his.

"I would be honored," he said, and then laughed when she tore out of his arms and took off running.

By the time he caught up, she was in the swing, her long legs dangling, waiting.

He got behind her and gave her a quick push, and when she swung back, he pushed harder, and then again, and again, until she was leaned back in the swing, her dark hair flying out behind her, laughing.

Hunt watched with tears in his eyes, his heart so full of love for her that it hurt to draw breath.

CHAPTER 10

RICHARD BORDEN WAS INCONSOLABLE. THERE WAS NOTHING TO be said to make what he'd done okay. He'd worked at the bank for years, but he didn't go in today. He couldn't stop crying and was so sick to his stomach that he couldn't stand without feeling like he was going to pass out. From the moment it happened, he hadn't stopped praying, and he didn't know how he was going to take another breath if that little boy died.

It was nearing 5:00 p.m. when Richard's cell phone rang. When he realized it was Chief Pittman calling, his heart nearly stopped. His voice was shaking as he answered.

"This is Richard."

"Richard. Chief Pittman here. The Randolph family called and asked me to let you know that Davey's surgery is over and it was successful. He's still in the ICU and in critical condition, but his prognosis is good. They know you were at fault, but they also know their child ran into the street. They're being very generous, and I hope you appreciate their intentions to let you know."

Richard dropped his head and started sobbing.

"Oh my God, thank you, thank you for letting me know. I don't think I'll ever be able to get behind the wheel of a car again, but that doesn't matter as long as that child heals and lives a long and happy life."

"Understood," Lon said. "Have a nice night."

"You too, Chief. Thank you again."

Richard put down the phone, then went to tell his family that their prayers had been answered.

At the same time Richard Borden was receiving good news, Dan Amos was about to be on the receiving end of some not-so-good news.

He was in his office posting invoices, entering rental payments, and smelling all of the good stuff Alice was making for supper, when he heard footsteps coming up the hall. He thought it was Alice coming to tell him supper was ready, but it was his son, Charlie, and Booger, the family bloodhound.

Booger ambled over to where Dan was sitting, and Dan stopped what he was doing to give Booger a scratch on the head.

"Hey, Booger... Hey, Charlie."

"Hey, Dad, can I talk to you a minute?"

Dan nodded, thinking how tall Charlie had grown since he and Alice had gotten married, and pointed to the chair at the end of his desk.

"Absolutely. What's on your mind, buddy?"

Charlie closed the door behind him, and when Booger moved to sit between his legs, he reached down and patted the old hound.

Dan frowned. He'd been a lawyer too long not to recognize someone with a problem, and when Charlie looked up, Dan knew he'd been right.

"Charlie...son...what's wrong?"

"If you knew someone was going to do something wrong...something bad...would you tell?"

"Yes," Dan said.

"Even if they are sort of my friends?" Charlie asked.

Dan hesitated a moment. "Uh...now I need to ask you something."

"Okay," Charlie said.

"Are all of your friends the kind of people who do bad things... wrong things?" Dan asked.

Charlie frowned. "Well, no! Of course not!"

"Do you admire these friends of yours who are going to do something wrong? Do you want to be like them?" Dan asked.

Charlie was silent a few moments, and then he sighed.

"No…no, I don't."

"Then what am I missing here? If you know a crime is going to be committed and you say nothing, you're abetting the crime. And if innocent people are hurt or killed in the act of that crime, you're partly responsible. Does that make anything clearer for you?" Dan asked.

Charlie inhaled sharply. "I was in the Crown getting dog food for Booger and overheard two guys talking about robbing Mr. Phillips and stealing his car when he locks up tonight."

Dan frowned. "Their names?"

Charlie sighed. "Teddy and Brian Hollis."

"The Hollis family who rents one of our properties?"

Charlie nodded.

"Damn it," Dan said. "Do they know you overheard them?"

Charlie shook his head. "No."

"You're certain?"

"Yes, sir," Charlie said.

"Don't say anything about this to anyone else. I'm calling Chief Pittman. If they show up, he'll be ready for them, and if they don't, then all the better," Dan said, and stood. When Charlie got up, Dan hugged him. "You did the right thing, Charlie. I'm proud of you."

Charlie hugged him back. "Thanks, Dad. I was scared. I didn't know what to do about it."

"When you become a man, you will carry a man's burdens. But for now, stuff like this is what parents are for. Go help your mom with supper. I'll be along shortly."

Charlie nodded and left the office, but Dan was already on the phone, calling the police station.

———————

Lon Pittman was shutting down his computer and getting ready to go home when his phone rang. He glanced at the clock, then sighed and reached for the phone.

"Blessings PD."

"Chief, this is Dan Amos. I need to tell you something," Dan said and then proceeded to repeat the story Charlie told him.

Lon's thoughts were racing. It was a little bit after five, but the pharmacy didn't close until six thirty.

"Thanks for the heads-up," Lon said. "If the Hollis brothers do show up, we'll be waiting for them."

"For the record, you got an anonymous tip. I don't want Charlie put in danger for being called a snitch," Dan added.

"Understood," Lon said, and disconnected, then headed up the hall.

Larry Bemis, the night dispatcher, was already on duty.

"Hey, Chief, are you heading home for the night?" Larry asked.

"Not yet," Lon said. "We just got a tip on a possible robbery. I don't want anything going out over the radio. Radio the two officers on duty, and tell them to meet me ASAP in the parking lot here at headquarters."

"Yes, sir," Larry said, and began dispatching the call as Lon went out through the back of the building.

As soon as Lon got in his cruiser, he called the pharmacy, and the owner, Phil Phillips, just happened to be the one who answered.

"Phillips Pharmacy."

"Phil, this is Chief Pittman. I need you to listen carefully," he said, and then related the story he'd been told.

Phil was horrified. "What should I do?"

"I'll be there shortly, so proceed as usual. One of my officers will drop me off so there's no visible police car. I'll be inside with you the whole time."

"Okay. I need to put the Closed sign up and get LilyAnn and the last customers out of here. I don't want anyone getting hurt."

"Don't do it early. Keep your normal routine, but say nothing to them. I'm just coming in as a customer."

"Will do," Phil said.

When both patrol cars pulled up behind the station, Lon got out to meet them.

"What's happening, Chief?" Ralph Herman asked as he got out.

"We got a tip on a possible robbery at the pharmacy this evening. Some teenagers plan to rob Phil and steal his car as he is locking up. Do you know the Hollis brothers?"

"Tall, skinny kids with blond hair?" Ralph asked.

"Yes," Lon said. "Those are the ones we'll be looking for."

"We know them on sight," they both said.

"Good," Lon said. "Ralph, I want you to drop me off at the pharmacy now. I'm going inside, and you just drive away. Both of you keep an eye on the alley, because they plan to take him down when he leaves to get in his car. Only it won't be Phil coming out. It's going to be me. So if you see them slip into the alley, let them be. Just back me up."

"Yes, sir," they said.

Lon got into the cruiser, and Ralph drove straight to the pharmacy and dropped him off.

Lon went inside, waving at LilyAnn as he passed. "I'm going back to talk to Phil," he said.

LilyAnn nodded and kept checking customers out.

Phil glanced up and then continued filling a prescription for a customer, but his gray hair was disheveled as if he'd been running his hands through it, and his expression was a little shell-shocked. As soon as the customer moved up front, Phil came out of the pharmacy area.

"I've never had anything like this ever happen before," he muttered.

Lon gave him a quick pat on the back. "Don't worry. We've got this. It's almost six now. You usually close at six thirty, right?"

Phil nodded.

"Then don't change your routine. I need to stay out of sight for a bit and let people forget they saw me come in. Okay if I go into your office?"

"Yes, yes, just down that hall," Phil said.

"When it's closing time, get everyone out as fast as possible. Tell LilyAnn you'll count out the till and send her home. Walk her to the door, lock it behind her, then start turning off lights like you always do. Don't do anything different."

"Yes, yes, okay," Phil said.

Lon went to Phil's office, checked in with his officers, and told them to let him know if they spotted the Hollis boys on the move, then sent Mercy a text and told her he was going to be late getting home.

About twenty minutes after six, Lon's cell signaled a text from Deputy Ralph.

Hollis brothers about a block away from the pharmacy.
Moving up the alley. One has a baseball bat.

Lon responded.

Will be closing up soon. Don't let them see you.

Lon could hear Phil talking to LilyAnn, then heard their footsteps as Phil walked her to the door.

As soon as she was gone, Phil locked the door and then began walking through the store, turning off lights.

Lon was in the hall now, still staying out of sight.

"Now go get your hat and coat and bring them to me," Lon said.

Phil got his things out of the employee break room and came out carrying his brown fedora and a brown leather jacket.

Lon put them on. "I need a bank deposit bag and your car keys. Then you go in your office and stay there. If you hear gunfire, lie flat on the floor behind your desk."

Phil's hands were shaking as he handed Lon the empty bag and his keys.

"Lordy be," he muttered, and slipped into his office. For something to do, he began counting out the night deposit, but his heart was pounding and he was sick to his stomach with fear.

Lon slipped his handgun out of the holster, hid it behind the empty bank bag, and started walking slowly up the aisles toward the front of the store, as if he was making sure everything was locked up. He rattled the front door to make sure it was locked before turning around and heading toward the back of the store.

Teddy and Brian Hollis were twins and seniors at Blessings High School. Technically, they should have graduated last year, but between absences and bad grades, they didn't graduate and were still trying to pass the two classes they'd failed.

They turned nineteen just after Thanksgiving and considered themselves adults, even though they still lived at home with their parents. They needed jobs and diplomas to move on with their lives, but had neither.

It was during Christmas vacation that Teddy came up with the idea of just leaving home anyway. He already knew he was going to fail again, and school wouldn't let them in at this age for a third try. They would have to take GED classes with adults now to ever get a diploma.

It was also Teddy who thought of robbing the pharmacist, because his routine was so well known.

Every evening, Mr. Phillips came out of the back of the pharmacy with a bank deposit bag under his arm, then got in his car and drove away. His unwavering routine was the cherry on their plan.

They planned to disguise themselves so he couldn't identify them, and by the time anyone found Phillips, they'd be long gone. They just needed the car to get out of town and planned to ditch it after they hit Savannah. And the money they got from the night deposit would be their seed money to get them started somewhere else.

They didn't have access to any guns, which was fortunate for all concerned. All they had was Brian's baseball bat from Little League. Their plan was to leave after supper. Their dad would fall asleep watching the evening news, and their mom would be cleaning up the kitchen. As soon as that scenario began playing out, they headed for their room.

They'd already packed, so they tossed their bags and Brian's bat out of their bedroom window, then climbed out. They quickly shouldered their gear, slipped out of the backyard into the alley, and headed for town.

They'd cut up their sock caps to make ski masks, and when the time was right, they would just pull them down over their faces and strike. They talked as they went, their enthusiasm for running away from Blessings overshadowing the deed they had to do to get away. They seemed oblivious to the harm and the crime they were planning to commit.

"It's already after six. We need to hurry," Teddy said, and shifted his bag to his other shoulder.

Brian did the same, and then they lengthened their stride. They arrived in the alley at the back of the pharmacy with less than five minutes to spare, and when they saw the car was still there, breathed a sigh of relief that they weren't too late. They tried the car doors but they were locked, so they dropped their bags behind the dumpster then crouched beside it, pulled their masks down over their faces, and settled in to wait.

It was already dusk, and night was imminent.

One moment they were trying to shoo away a cat prowling around the garbage, and then suddenly the back door opened. They got a glimpse of the familiar hat and coat, and tensed.

"Wait, wait," Teddy whispered, and as soon as Phillips was almost to the car, he leaped out from behind the dumpster with the ball bat raised, ready to swing.

All of a sudden Mr. Phillips spun, and when they saw the gun in his hand, the twins froze. And then they saw his face. It wasn't Phil Phillips. It was Chief Pittman, and he was shouting.

"Get down on the ground! Get down on the ground belly first, and lock your hands behind your heads."

Brian started to run, when all of a sudden there were patrol cars coming up the alley from both directions with lights flashing and sirens screaming. He turned, staring at his brother in disbelief, and then dropped to his knees and locked his hands behind his head.

Teddy Hollis was in shock.

"How did you know? How did you know?" he kept asking.

"Drop that bat, then turn around and get down!" Lon shouted and aimed his gun straight at Teddy's chest.

Teddy stared down the barrel and knew the next few seconds of his life depended on the choice he made. He'd already made one bad decision by trying to rob a man, and dying for it didn't seem worthwhile.

He dropped the bat and went belly-down. He was putting his hands behind his head when he felt the first handcuff around his wrist. He glanced over at Brian, who was belly-down and silent.

When the chief pulled off the masks, Teddy groaned. They were going to jail.

After the officers loaded the boys up and took them to the station to be booked, Lon went back inside.

"Phil! Phil! It's safe to come out now."

Phil walked out, relieved but shaken.

"Were they armed?"

"With a baseball bat," Lon said. He began taking off the hat and coat, then handed the pharmacist the bank bag. "Did you get your money counted for the night deposit?"

Phil nodded.

"Bag it up. I'll ride with you to the bank, and then you can drop me off at the station on your way home, okay?"

"Thanks, Chief. I don't know what would have happened to me tonight if you hadn't been tipped off."

"But we were. And you're safe. Now let's get the place locked up."

A few minutes later, Phil pulled into the drive-through at the bank, dropped his bag into the night deposit, and then took Lon to the police station.

"Thanks again, Chief," Phil said.

"Just doing our job," Lon said. "See you tomorrow. Try and get some rest," he added, then got out of the car and went inside.

The Hollis brothers had been booked and put in cells across from each other.

Brian was lying on his cot with his face turned to the wall and still hadn't said a word.

Teddy was pale and shaken, but silent until the chief walked in.

He stood. "Did you call our parents?"

"Just about to do that," Lon said. "You want to give me their number?"

"No," Teddy said.

Brian turned over. "I will. It's my dad's cell." He gave the number, then asked, "What's going to happen to us?"

"You will be charged with attempted assault with a weapon, attempted robbery, and attempted car theft," the chief said.

"We didn't hit anybody. We didn't steal anything. We didn't take a car," Teddy argued.

"Just because we caught you in the act before you could finish it doesn't give you a pass," Lon said.

"We can't afford a lawyer," Teddy said.

Lon sighed. "Were you paying attention when my officers read you your rights?"

Teddy shrugged. "I guess."

"Then you heard them say that if you can't afford a lawyer, one will be appointed for you. Sit tight, boys. I've got some calls to make."

He left the jail and went straight to his office.

Donna Hollis was a little woman with a big heart. She was in her early forties but looked older. Life had been hard since the day she'd been born. But falling in love with Arnold Hollis had been her blessing. She loved him, and she loved their boys with everything in her.

The boys were tall like Arnold but got their blond hair from her, and even though they seemed to be stumbling their way out of their teenage years, she had faith they would do it. She was cleaning up from supper and could hear her husband snoring as she finished washing the dishes. She wanted him to carry out the trash, but hated to wake him. He loaded and unloaded sacks at the feed store all day long and always came home so tired. If he wasn't loading up a customer's purchases into their vehicle, he was unloading delivery trucks or driving the forklift moving pallets of feed.

She was hanging up the dishtowel when she heard Arnold's phone ring, then heard him grumble before answering. At least he was awake now. He could carry out the garbage after all. She heard him cry out, and then he was running toward the kitchen. When he ran in, the look on his face was one of horror.

"Arnie! What's wrong?"

"The chief called! Our boys are in jail!"

Donna screamed. "No, no! They're in their room! This has to be a mistake!"

Then she ran through the house and into their room. It was empty, the window was open, and the curtains shifting in the slight breeze gave shocking truth to their absence.

"They're gone! Oh my God! What did they do?" Donna wailed.

Arnold could hardly get out the words. "They set out to rob Mr. Phillips. They had a baseball bat for a weapon and intended to steal his car. The police got an anonymous tip that it might happen, so they were waiting for them."

Donna gasped, then staggered toward the bed, but didn't make it. She fell to the floor in a faint.

"Oh my God!" Arnold cried, and then dropped to his knees beside her and began patting her cheek. "Honey...wake up! Wake up!"

A few moments later, Donna began to come around. She opened her eyes, saw the expression on her husband's face, and groaned.

"This is real? It's really happening?" she asked.

"It's real. We need to go to the jail," he said, and helped her up.

Donna staggered to her feet, then stood for a few moments, trying to gather her thoughts.

"Close the window, Arnie. I can't wear my house slippers. I need to change my shoes."

CHAPTER 11

TEDDY AND BRIAN HEARD THEIR PARENTS' VOICES IN THE HALL outside the jail.

"That's Dad!" Teddy said.

Brian stood up. "I hear Mama. We did a bad thing. I don't want her to see me in jail."

"Too late for that," Teddy muttered.

"Aren't you sorry?" Brian asked.

Teddy was sick-to-his-stomach scared, but he wasn't going to admit it. "Yes. But we can't take it back now, can we?"

Then the door opened. Chief Pittman came in, followed by their parents.

Donna Hollis stumbled when she saw them. "Oh my lord!"

Arnold grabbed her elbow to steady her. "Easy, sugar," he said.

"I'll give you a few minutes, but I can't leave you alone with them," Chief Pittman said.

"Mama, I'm sorry," Brian said and started crying.

Teddy wanted to still feel empowered like he'd been when they were hiding out ready to take down Mr. Phillips for his car and money. But he didn't have the guts to be defiant. And the look on his dad's face hurt his heart.

"They said you two attacked Mr. Phillips with a baseball bat. They said you intended to take him down, steal his money, and steal his car. Is that true?" Arnold asked.

"But it wasn't Mr. Phillips. It was the chief," Teddy said. "It was a setup. They were lying in wait for us!"

Donna was horrified by her son's defiance. It made her angry, and her anger was what she needed to get past the shock. She turned loose of her husband's arm and walked into the aisle between their cells.

She was tiny, but she was mighty in her rage. Her hand was shaking as she pointed at both of them.

"Oh…you mean like the setup you two had when you were lying in wait for Mr. Phillips? When you were going to hit him in the head with a baseball bat? When you were going to steal his money and his car? Did you intend to kill him, too?"

Brian wailed. "No, Mama, no!"

"But you could have," Donna cried. "A head injury is a deadly injury. So attempted assault, robbery, and car theft are your solutions to failing school again, while claiming you're both adults?"

Brian stumbled back to his cot and buried his face in his hands.

Arnold walked to his other son, shaking his head in disbelief.

"You have been feeling sorry for yourself because we're poor. But you never offered to get a job. You just complained about what you didn't have. We raised you boys in church. We loved you every day of your lives. We supported you every way we knew how, and you chose to solve your absences at school by smoking weed and drinking with your so-called friends. You didn't even graduate and were screwing off your second chance at that, while wondering why we were upset." Arnold took a deep, shaky breath. "I would have bet my life you two would never do something like this…and I would have died, wouldn't I?"

Teddy shuddered. If his dad had been angry and shouting, he could have maintained the don't-care attitude. But this broken man standing before him hurt his heart.

"I'm sorry, Dad. It was a mistake."

Donna interrupted. "No, sir, Theodore Hollis! You didn't make a mistake. A mistake is something that happens by accident. You planned every bit of this. You two decided it would be okay to attack a man, to rob him, and to steal his car. You both disgust me."

"I'm sorry, Mama. I love you," Teddy said.

"I don't believe you," Donna said.

"I love you, too, Mama," Brian said.

Donna glared at the both of them.

"Love gets your father and me nowhere. While you two are off serving time, your father and I will have to face the judgment and disapproval of people who were our friends. They'll decide we were surely bad parents and that we're the cause of your criminal behavior. That's what your so-called love has done to us...not to mention the fact that you broke my heart. I don't know what I feel right now, other than I don't like either one of you or what you've become."

Then she turned around and walked out on her own, leaving Arnold behind.

Arnold's eyes welled with unshed tears. "Your mother is right. Chances are we'll be leaving Blessings. I don't reckon I want to spend the rest of my days having people remind me that both my sons are in jail. You did a bad, bad thing, and I am ashamed of the both of you."

Brian shrieked. "But Dad...if you move...how will we find you when we get out?"

"Why would you care where we were?" Arnold asked. "You both were already leaving us."

He walked out, knowing no matter what kind of sentence his sons got, they'd be worse by the time they got out. They weren't dead, but they were already lost.

Dan hadn't talked to Alice about what Charlie told him because he didn't know if what he'd reported to the chief had actually happened. But when they had heard sirens during their meal, it made him wonder, and when Charlie looked at Dan, all he could do was shrug.

Alice caught the interaction between them and was starting to ask when Dan looked at her, then at Patty, and shook his head.

She nodded, and the moment passed until they were cleaning up the kitchen and Dan's phone rang.

"It's Chief Pittman," Dan said. "I need to take this."

That's when Alice frowned. "Okay, Dan…I need to know what's going on."

"Just a second, honey. This call will probably have answers for both of us," he said, and then answered. "Hello, this is Dan."

"Hi, Dan. This is Lon. I wanted to let you know your tip paid off."

"Really? Are you serious? They really did it?" Dan asked.

"Well, they tried. Your boy saved Mr. Phillips. They were waiting for him with a baseball bat, but we pulled a switch on them. They got me instead of Phillips."

"Oh my God," Dan said. "I can't imagine. They were going to beat him up?"

"Probably planned on knocking him out, but getting hit in the head with a ball bat can be lethal. At any rate, thank Charlie. And make sure he understands that no one will ever know who tipped us off."

"What's going to happen to them?" Dan asked.

"They'll do some time. I can't say how much or where, but they're both nineteen, so they're too old for juvenile detention."

"That's too bad they turned out that way," Dan said. "The family rents from me. They're a really nice couple."

"Yes, and they were horrified and humiliated and so angry at their boys. Anyway…thought I'd let you know before I head home."

"Thanks, Lon," Dan said and disconnected, then began telling Alice everything that had ensued, from Charlie coming to him to the phone call just now which confirmed the twins had followed through with their plan.

Alice was stunned. "Oh, Dan… What if Charlie hadn't heard them?"

"What if Charlie hadn't told someone is more to the point," Dan said. "He would have felt guilty for the rest of his life, especially if Mr. Phillips had been hurt or killed."

Alice put both hands over her heart, smiling through tears.

"I am so proud of the man he is becoming…but I'm not surprised.

He was trying to take care of Patty and me long before you ever showed up in our lives. He has a good heart and a good head on his shoulders. And you…you are the example he needed of what it means to be a good, decent man. I love you so much and am so grateful you are in our lives."

Dan took her in his arms.

"I'm the one who is grateful for all of you for loving me. I needed what you offered…a family…and your love," Dan said, and held her.

"Let's go tell Charlie," Alice said.

Dan nodded. "As long as Patty doesn't know. It's imperative that no one ever knows Charlie was the anonymous tipster."

"She's in her room watching her hour of television before getting ready for bed, and Charlie is outside with Booger," Alice said.

"Then outside we go," Dan said.

They found Charlie sitting in the dark, waiting for Booger to finish prowling the perimeter. It was the dog's nightly ritual.

Charlie turned around when he heard the back door open.

"Hey, Dad…Mom… Look at Booger. He's on patrol."

"He's a good watchdog," Dan said.

Alice sat down beside Charlie and gave him a hug.

"You did the right thing," she said.

Charlie glanced at Dan.

"Yes, I told her," Dan said. "No secrets ever between husband and wife…and she's your mother. Never any secrets between you and her."

Charlie nodded, then hugged her. "Sorry, Mom. I didn't intend to leave you out."

"No, no, you did the right thing," Alice said. "But you can always tell me anything. Then we'll both go find Dan, right?"

Dan grinned. "Always. Oh…and Chief Pittman says to thank you, Charlie, even though it will be noted in the case as an anonymous tip."

Charlie lowered his voice to a whisper.

"You mean they really did it?"

"They tried. The police caught them in the act. They're in jail."

Charlie was silent for a few moments, and then he looked up.

"What's going to happen to them?"

Dan shrugged. "Chief Pittman said it will be up to the courts, but he believes they'll serve some time. It was attempted robbery, car theft, and assault."

"I can't believe they'd do something so stupid," Charlie said.

"That's all on them," Alice said. "Just remember Mr. Phillips is the real victim and might not even be alive tonight were it not for you."

Booger barked.

Charlie stood.

"I know, Mom. I get it. And thanks, Dad. Now I better go get Booger and bring him in for the night before he stirs up a skunk."

Dan put his arm around Alice as they watched Charlie leap off the patio and run out into the dark.

"That's a really good boy you have, my love."

Alice leaned against him. "We have…and yes, he is."

———————

Night drove Hunt and Ava from the park back to her home, and after the passion of making love had tempered their body heat beneath the covers, Hunt held her in his arms, watching her sleep. Her hair was like silk against his face, and the rhythm of her breathing matched the beat of his heart.

For all these years, he'd considered himself a loner. Sometimes he told himself it was because of the abrupt disruption of his family and the way that he'd been cast out. Other times he blamed it on the war, telling himself it had numbed him beyond repair.

And then he'd come home, and the dark-haired nurse standing beside his mother's bed had both surprised and intrigued him. Now, he couldn't imagine life without her. When she shifted slightly in his arms and sighed, he pulled the covers up over her back and then rested his chin on the crown of her head.

Sweet God in heaven… Hunt had never thought of his father as a loving man, but he couldn't get past that paper he'd found. He didn't know what had happened, but it felt like his father had controlled all of it, including the outcome.

"I love you, Ava. Thank you for loving me," Hunt whispered, and then closed his eyes and slept.

———

Arnie and Donna Hollis couldn't sleep.

Every time Donna closed her eyes, she saw her sons behind bars.

Arnie lay staring up at the ceiling, sick to his stomach and thinking back to when the boys were little, trying to remember if he'd missed the signs that would have alerted him to this future.

He remembered Teddy had always had a tendency to lie about everything. Even things that didn't matter. And Brian was the follower.

A tear rolled from the corner of Arnie's eye and slid down his cheek. Their sons felt like strangers—monsters. It was a thing hard to bear.

He heard Donna crying again and patted her shoulder.

"I'd cry, too, but I'm already sick to my stomach. No need adding to my misery."

"What did we do wrong?" Donna wailed.

"We didn't do anything wrong. They did. And that's the hard truth of it all. They were loved. They were never abused. They just quit trying to do the right thing, and I can't say as how I ever saw this coming."

"It will be the ruin of them," Donna said, and rolled over into his arms and started sobbing. "Why is this happening?"

Arnie kept patting her shoulder. "I wish to God I knew, but I don't."

"I want to go home," Donna said.

Arnie frowned. "You mean back to West Virginia?"

"Yes. My sister, Joy, keeps writing, reminding me that Mama's old house is vacant. We could live there for free."

"But what would I do?" Arnold asked.

"You're nearly old enough to draw social security, and you have your railroad pension for now. I could wait tables somewhere. We wouldn't be paying rent. We'd do fine."

Arnold was silent for a few moments and then he hugged her.

"If that's what you want, then that's what we'll do. I'll give notice at the feed store tomorrow. We can rent a U-Haul truck and tow our car. Do you want to tell the boys where we're going?"

"They'll know where we are. Right now, I'm sorry I ever gave birth to them," Donna said, and then broke into sobs all over again.

———————————

Arnold and Donna weren't the only members of the Hollis family in tears. Teddy was rolled up in a ball beneath his blanket, his face turned to the wall so no one could see his tears, while Brian was flat on his back, sobbing.

Lights were never turned off in jail, the cots weren't their warm, soft mattresses at home, and the blankets they had for cover were scratchy and smelled of disinfectant rather than the lilac-scented fabric softener their mother used in the wash.

The reality of their situation had hit hard. They were criminals. They were in jail and probably going to prison. It was the worst thing that they'd ever done, and there was no coming back from it. Saying "I'm sorry" didn't cut it. Not when they were already nineteen, and not when what they'd done was against the law.

Brian sat up on his cot and looked across the hall to where Teddy was lying.

"Teddy, are you awake? I'm scared," Brian said.

"Shut up, Brian. Just shut up and lie down."

"But what's going to happen to us?" Brian said.

"I don't know. I guess whatever happens to people in jail."

Brian's voice was trembling. "Do you really think Mom and Dad will move away without telling us where they went?"

Teddy sighed. "Why do you care? We were running away from them, remember?"

"But it's Mom and Dad!" Brian said.

"If they leave, they'll go back to Bethlehem," Teddy said.

"You think?" Brian asked.

"I know," Teddy said. "Now shut up. I just want to sleep."

Brian sat there a minute, then wiped his eyes with the blanket and lay back down. Prison. They were likely going to prison. He wondered if he'd die there. He'd heard about people dying in prison. Getting killed there. Getting beat up. The more he thought about it, the more dying seemed like the most equitable way out. But someone else would have to do it to him because it would break his mama's heart if he did it to himself. And he'd already hurt her enough for one lifetime. He couldn't do that, too. The way he looked at it, whatever happened to them was out of their control and they deserved the consequences.

———————

It was morning.

Hunt woke up alone in Ava's bed, and then heard the shower running and glanced at the time. If he joined her, he'd make her late to work. If she didn't show up, sick people suffered. So what he wanted and what he needed to make happen were two different things.

He got up and got dressed and was making the bed when Ava came out. She was barefoot and her hair was still damp, but she was already dressed in her scrubs, and when she saw what he was doing, she smiled.

"Oh wow…you make love like a boss and make beds, too?"

Hunt grinned as he pulled the bedspread up over the pillows and gave them a quick tuck, then took her in his arms.

"It's what's left of my military life. Neat and orderly." Then he nuzzled the spot beneath her ear. "And whatever I do that makes you happy is my joy. Like a boss, huh?"

Ava cupped his face and kissed him.

"The last thing I want to do is leave, but I have to get to work."

Hunt nodded. "I know, sugar. That's why I got dressed...so neither of us would be tempted to linger. Take care. I love you. Call me if you need me."

"You be careful, too," Ava said. "No accidents working on the house."

"Yes, ma'am," he said, and then grabbed his jacket and was gone.

She sat down to put on her shoes, and then got her things, poured herself a to-go cup of coffee, and locked up as she left.

About two hours later, Ava got a text. Her parents were finally home and inviting her to supper. She returned the text, telling them to set an extra place for dinner because she was bringing Hunt. Then she texted Hunt, telling him her parents were home and she'd committed him to dinner at their house tonight.

The plumber, Danny Wilson, was in the bathroom and Hunt was working in the kitchen when he received the text. He sent her a thumbs-up emoji and then called the florist shop and ordered roses for Ava, to be delivered at the hospital before 3:00 p.m.

He was still smiling as he put the phone back in his pocket, when Danny called out, "Hey Hunt. You need to come take a look at this."

Hunt sighed, and headed for the back of the house.

But every day was progress, and the sooner he was finished, the better.

———

Karen and Larry Ridley were glad to be home. Las Vegas had been fun, but they had given up spending the holidays with Ava to do it, even though she had assured them she'd be working more days than not.

The moment they walked into the house, Karen began unpacking and doing laundry, while Larry went through the refrigerator, making a list of what they needed to restock since they'd cleaned it out before they left.

Karen stopped long enough to let Ava know they were home and to come to dinner tonight. When she got the text back from Ava, her heart skipped a beat. Ava was bringing a man to dinner. Even if it was just Hunt, she could always hope.

Karen was a shorter version of her daughter. A little blond Barbie doll of a woman who was not nearly as serious as her girl. Ava was a lot more like her father, Larry, who tended to be the one to get things done. He was still making the grocery list when Karen came into the kitchen.

"Get extra steaks. Ava is bringing Hunt."

Larry looked up. "Hunt Knox?"

"Yes, he came back for Marjorie's funeral, remember?"

"Oh, right. I remember now. But why would—"

Karen rolled her eyes. "Larry, I love you to pieces, but you can be so oblivious. How many times has Ava ever brought anyone here to dinner?"

"Uh…never?"

Karen giggled. "Right! So this could mean our girl is finally on the love track."

Larry frowned. "The love track? Where does this stuff come from that comes out of your mouth?"

"Out of my head, I guess. Stop frowning. Please God this is serious. I want grandbabies while I'm young enough to enjoy them."

Larry sighed. "Adding two more steaks to the list."

"And potatoes. And another bag of salad, and—"

Larry grinned. "Calm down. I've got this."

"Do we have gas for the grill?"

"Yes, got that, too," Larry said.

"Yay! I'm so excited!" Karen said, and bounced out of the room carrying her phone.

"Me, too," Larry said, curious to see what kind of man Hunter Knox had turned out to be.

———————

It was a little before noon when Harold Franklin from the flower shop showed up in the ER carrying a vase of red roses.

"Delivery for Ava Ridley," he said.

"I'll call her up," the receptionist said, and then got on the PA system. "Nurse Ridley, please come to the front desk."

Harold turned toward the door leading into the ER, and a couple of minutes later, Ava walked through.

"What's going on?" she asked.

The receptionist grinned and pointed.

"Morning, Ava. These are for you," Harold said and handed them over.

Ava's eyes widened. She set the vase on the desk, then pulled the card.

All my love, Hunt

She smiled, slipped the card into her pocket, and carried the roses back to the nurses' desk. She knew they'd tease and grill her incessantly, but she wasn't giving up anything but the name. And she was right.

"Oh my gosh! Ava! Are those yours? Who sent them? Is it your birthday?"

"They're from Hunt," she said, and set the bouquet out of the way on the desk and then went back to work.

But every time she walked by, she saw them and smiled. Hunt Knox loved her. All was right in her world.

CHAPTER 12

Danny Wilson, otherwise known in Blessings as Melvin Lee's daddy, was the newest employee at Forbes Plumbing and glad to have the job at home rather than the pipeline jobs he'd been doing for so long. He had too many kids, and another one on the way, and was grateful to be working at home.

"That about does it for the day," Danny said as he gathered up his tools. "When you get ready to install sinks and new fixtures, just give us a call."

"Will do," Hunt said.

The house was immediately quiet now that Danny was gone, but Hunt was satisfied by the work they'd done. The roofer and his crew would be here tomorrow to put on a new roof. It was ironic that his brother Ray worked for this roofer and would be part of the crew redoing his own mother's house.

While the roofers were working, he and Billy Younger, the carpenter he'd hired, would begin tearing up the kitchen floor to fix whatever made it sag.

But that was tomorrow.

This evening was about going to dinner at Larry and Karen's house with Ava, and Hunt hurried to get ready. Even though he'd known them all his life, he was going to have to look at Larry and Karen with new eyes, too. They were no longer just people he knew. There were the parents of the woman he was going to marry. He wasn't expecting problems, but thoughts of the dinner made him a little anxious just the same.

He locked up the house before leaving, and then drove a few blocks over to get Ava. She answered the door in black slacks, red flats, and a cherry-red sweater. But the light in her eyes and the way she looked at him were what stole his heart.

"You look beautiful," Hunt said as he helped her on with her coat.

Ava paused, giving him a long, studied look from head to toe, and then sighed.

"So do you."

Hunt grinned. "I need to look my best. I've never had a meet-the-parents dinner before."

Ava rolled her eyes. "You have known my parents your entire life. Likely longer than I have."

"Yeah, but then they were just Ava Ridley's mom and dad. Not the parents of the woman I love."

"But they've known you forever…and they've known all my life that I loved you madly. Even when it was just a childhood crush, so this won't be a surprise. Just a relief that I won't be pining needlessly anymore for the man who got away."

He laughed. "Pining needlessly? Where do you get all your drama?"

She grinned. "Oh, definitely from Mom. But I'm also hard-core and focused like Dad when it comes to what I want to do. I can't be bullied into doing something I don't believe in, and I won't be threatened by anyone and let them get away with it, either."

"Might that be a reference to the old boyfriend?" he said.

"It might," Ava said.

"Fair enough," Hunt said. "But I can't be blamed for missing what you think was obvious back then. You were only thirteen years old when I left Blessings. You were jailbait. Now get your cute little backside out the door or we're going to be late," Hunt said.

Ava sighed. He'd just told her she was beautiful and that her backside was cute. And they were going to break the news to her parents tonight that he loved her and wanted to marry her. This was a grand way to end a day.

Larry had the barbecue fired up on the back patio and steaks on the grill. Karen had baked potatoes in the warming oven and a big tossed salad in the fridge, waiting for dressing.

Karen had made her famous ginger carrots for a side, and Larry had picked up a chocolate cream pie from Granny's for dessert.

She was curious to see Hunt again. Even though she remembered Marjorie and Parnell losing their first child at an early age, Hunt had, by order of birth, become the oldest child, the responsible child, the one Marjorie always depended on. And their daughter had always been enamored of the babysitter's oldest son. But now Ava was all grown up and bringing him to dinner. Karen had suspicions, but she wasn't going to get her hopes up until she saw them together. She'd know then if they were serious.

It was straight up six o'clock when their doorbell rang. Larry was still outside at the grill, so it was Karen who went to the door. There was a smile on her face as she opened it, and then her breath caught in the back of her throat.

Hunt Knox had turned into one very good-looking man. Even the too-long hair brushing the collar of his jacket fit his persona. He was a good four inches taller than he'd been at eighteen, and his blue eyes were hard and piercing now, until he looked at Ava. That was when she saw them melt, and she knew.

Thank you, Lord.

"Come in, the both of you!" Karen hugged her daughter, then gave her a quick kiss on the cheek. "We missed you so much when we were in Vegas," she said.

Ava laughed. "Oh, Mom, you are so full of it. You and Dad didn't miss me for one second."

Karen giggled and gave Hunt a quick hug. "It's wonderful to see you again. You grew up into a handsome young man. We're so sorry about Marjorie. You know how much we thought of her."

"Yes, ma'am," Hunt said. "Thank you."

"Where's Dad?" Ava asked as they took off their coats and hung them in the hall closet.

"Out back grilling steaks. Follow me," Karen said.

Ava reached for Hunt's hand and held it all the way through the house and then out onto the patio.

"Larry, they're here!" Karen said.

Larry Ridley was smiling as he turned around, and then he saw Hunt and blinked.

"Uh…"

Ava laughed. "Dad! If the mere sight of Hunt leaves you speechless, that means Mom's gonna have the floor all night."

Larry put down his tongs and shook Hunt's hand.

"Well, we can't have that," he said. "Forgive me, Hunt, but you changed so much from the kid I remember that it took me aback. It's good to see you again. I can't wait to hear what you've been doing, but right now I need to know one thing from you."

"Yes sir, and what would that be?" Hunt asked.

Larry grinned. "How do you like your steak?"

Hunt relaxed. "Anywhere between medium and medium rare."

"A man after my own heart!" Larry said, and then winked at Karen. "Sugar, why don't you and Ava bring us something cold to drink while I finish up these steaks."

Ava gave Hunt a questioning look.

"You know what I like. I'll take anything you bring me," he said.

She smiled and followed her mother into the house.

Karen opened the refrigerator. "I'm taking your daddy a beer because you know he thinks he has to have beer when he grills. What do you think Hunt wants?"

Ava didn't even hesitate. "He wants me, Mama. And I want him. When he leaves Blessings, I'm going with him. Be happy for us, because I have never been so happy in my life."

Karen squealed, then hugged Ava over and over, laughing and crying.

Unaware of the revelation, Larry was moving steaks around to make sure they didn't overcook, when Hunt walked up beside him.

"Sir...I'm gonna marry your daughter."

Larry blinked again, and then grinned. "Okay, then you need to drop the 'sir' and call me Larry. I have to say, that's an interesting conversation opening, but I was beginning to think I'd never hear those words come out of any man's mouth. Welcome to the family, Hunt! Proud to have you!"

Hunt exhaled softly. He'd done the hard part. Loving Ava for the rest of his life was going to be easy.

Karen came bouncing out of the house carrying a longneck bottle of beer, and Ava had one for Hunt.

The smiles on their faces said it all.

Larry elbowed Hunt. "It appears that Ava might have just told her mama what you told me. As you can tell, we're very happy for the both of you," Larry said. "Now, out of curiosity, where the hell have you been all these years, and what do you do for a living?"

It wasn't something Hunt wanted to repeat, but they deserved to know why he'd disappeared from Blessings.

"I flew choppers for the army for seven years. Now I fly choppers for an oil company out of Houston, mostly ferrying roughnecks back and forth to offshore drilling rigs up and down the Texas and Louisiana coast."

Karen gasped, and the smile slid from Larry's face. "Holy shit, son. You went to war, didn't you?"

Hunt nodded.

Larry swallowed past a sudden lump in his throat.

"Then, thank you for your service."

Hunt pointed at the steaks. "Looks like your steaks are about done."

And just like that, Larry knew talking about that was off-limits.

"Whoops, you're right! If you'll grab that platter, I'll get them off the grill."

A couple of minutes later, they all went inside with the steaks. Ava and Karen already had everything else on the table, and when the men came in, Karen turned around and gave Hunt a big hug.

"Welcome to the family, sugar!"

Hunt smiled. "Thank you, ma'am."

Karen frowned and poked him in the chest.

"You can't start calling me 'ma'am.' You're gonna make me feel old now. Call me Karen, or whatever feels right to you, but save the 'ma'am' for strangers."

"Yes, ma'am," Hunt said.

They laughed, and Ava sighed. This was the best.

Hunt and Ava stayed later at her parents' house than she'd intended. By the time Hunt was walking her up the steps at her house, it was close to eleven. He went inside with her to make sure everything was okay, then hugged her.

"You know I want to stay with you again, but you need to rest. What you need to know is that this was one of the best evenings I've spent in a long time…except the times I spend with you."

Ava leaned back in his arms. "They love you. I love you. You can do no wrong."

Hunt grinned. "If only the rest of my life was this easy."

"Sometimes easy gets boring," Ava said.

"I don't know about that. Loving you is the easiest thing I've ever done, and you're too ornery to ever be boring," Hunt said.

She sighed. "I have a couple of days off coming up. I'll make it up to you then."

Hunt cupped her cheeks. "Honey…there are going to be times when I'll be just as tied up with my job as you'll be with yours. But as long as I have you to come home to, it will be worth it."

Then he settled his lips on hers and kissed her—slowly, then harder—until they both groaned.

"I give," Hunt said. "Night, sweetheart. Love you."

"Love you, too," Ava said, and watched him leave before she locked up and went to bed.

Hunt was up by daylight and ready when the roofing crew pulled up. His brother Ray wasn't sure how to approach a relationship that was no longer there.

"You climbing today, too?" Ray asked.

Hunt shook his head. "Obviously, I'm fine with heights, but only when I'm flying. I'll leave all this to the experts."

Ray nodded, then began helping unload their equipment while Hunt went back inside to wait for Billy.

The carpenter pulled up about an hour later, and soon he and Hunt were pulling up the old flooring in the kitchen. Once the tiles were removed, the sag in the subfloor below was more obvious.

Hunt stood with his hands on his hips, surveying what looked like the beginnings of mold and rot.

"Birdie said this house didn't flood inside during the hurricane, but there was water under the house."

Billy nodded. "It happened to a lot of houses here. We had to shore up Mom and Dad's back porch after the water receded. So, let's get a few of these boards up and see what we're dealing with below."

Hunt got a pry bar and a hammer and began working on one of the blackened areas. The board came loose and then broke off.

"Rotten," Billy said.

Hunt nodded and pulled up a few more—enough so that Billy could shine a light down into the opening.

"Well, right here's your problem," Billy said. "A couple of floor joists are broken, and two or three more look about as rotten as this subfloor. I'll make a quick run to the lumberyard and get the material we'll need. In the meantime, why don't you go ahead and pull up the rest of the subfloor just in this area so we can get into the space."

"Sure thing," Hunt said, and when Billy went out the back door to get in his truck, Hunt began prying up rotting wood and tossing it aside.

And so the morning passed, with roofers stomping and hammering above their heads, and Hunt and Billy sawing and nailing on the floor. Billy left to get the plywood to patch the subfloor, leaving Hunt outside putting new treads on the back porch steps.

When the workers took a lunch break, Hunt stayed home and made a sandwich, grateful for the momentary silence within. While he was eating, someone knocked on the door, and then he heard a voice call out.

"Hunt! It's me, Emma! Okay if I come in?"

"In the kitchen!" When she walked in, he pointed at the floor. "Sidestep the hole. We've been replacing floor joists, but we'll have subfloor back down before quitting time."

Emma glanced down, remembering the sag, and once again felt guilty that none of them had thought to address the issue.

"I can't stay, and I know I'm probably the last person you want to see, but I brought something I want you to have."

"What's that?" Hunt said.

Emma took a small ring box out of her pocket and opened it, revealing a ring with a gold band and a ruby setting.

"This was Mama's engagement ring. She gave it to me when Gordon and I got married. It was my something borrowed, and then she told me to just keep it. But Birdie said you and Ava were seeing each other and that it might be serious."

"It is," Hunt said.

Emma nodded. "I want you to have it for her. Even if it's not the engagement ring you give her, you'll both have something of Mama's."

Hunt saw the tears in her eyes and felt a sadness for what they'd lost, and then she put the box in his hand and he got his first good look.

"Lord…I remember this ring, but I never knew it was her engagement ring. Are you sure you want to give this up?"

"I'm sure. If Ava is the woman you love, remember Mama helped raise her, too. She will love it, and I'll bet she remembers it, too."

Hunt closed the box. "Thank you for thinking of her."

"I was thinking of you, too," Emma said. "Mama would be really happy to know it was being passed on to another member of the family."

"Then, I thank you, and this is so going to be Ava's engagement ring. Next time you see it, it's going to be on her finger."

Emma sighed. "I'm glad you approve. Now I'm going to get out of here so you can finish your lunch. I can't wait to see what this place looks like when you're through with it, and I keep wondering who'll live in it next."

"It needs to belong to new people who'll put good energy into it," Hunt said.

"Agreed," Emma said. "So, Birdie said we were all coming over soon to get what we want of Mama's stuff before the auction."

"She said something about coming this Saturday," Hunt said.

"Then Saturday it is. You and Birdie are the only two take-charge, organized people in the family."

Hunt walked her to the door, then after she was gone, took the ring and put it in an inner pocket of his duffel bag. Now he needed to figure out the perfect way to give it to Ava tonight.

———

A new shipment of cattle cubes had just come into the store, and Arnold Hollis was getting ready to move pallets to the far end of the building. But when he got on the forklift and started it up, the lift wouldn't work. He got off, saw oil leaking out of the hydraulics, and sighed, then went looking for Dub.

Birdie was coming up the hall and Arnold waved her down.

"Hey, Birdie. Have you seen Dub? The hydraulics are out on the forklift, and we just got in a new shipment of cubes that need to be moved."

"He's out back, I think. Want me to go get him?" Birdie asked.

"Just tell him the forklift is leaking fluid. I'm gonna go start moving the cubes by hand."

Birdie eyed the stoop to Arnold's shoulders and knew he was already depressed about his boys being in jail.

"Why don't you just wait a bit, or get some of the guys to help you?" she said.

"I need to stay busy," Arnold said, and then winked at her. "Keeps a man out of trouble when he stays busy, you know," and then walked back into the storage end of the building.

Birdie smiled, thought nothing more of it, dropped off the paperwork Dub wanted, and went back to her office.

Arnold stood for a few minutes, eyeing the setup and trying to figure out what would be his best option, then walked all the way down to the far end of the building to see how much room they had there.

A couple of sacks had slid sideways off their stack, and he crawled up onto the pile to straighten them. When he did, a big rat leaped out, hitting him square in the chest before running off into the shadows.

Startled, Arnold lost his footing. He knew as he was falling backward that it wasn't going to be a good landing because there was nothing back there but concrete. He hit the floor on the back of his head, then his body followed. His chin popped forward against his chest as his neck snapped. It was the last thing he heard.

The sacks started falling then, slowly sliding down from the pile onto Arnold's body, and onto the frayed wiring that the rats had been chewing. One wire sparked, and then another, and then it flared. Sparks landed on the paper sacks and began to smolder.

It wasn't until actual flames began rising that one of the employees smelled smoke and ran back inside.

"Fire! Fire!" he yelled, and grabbed his phone and called 911.

It was midafternoon, and Hunt was nailing down loose boards on the front porch when he heard a siren. He paused, then stood up and looked toward the sound.

All of a sudden, Ray was standing on the edge of the roof above him shouting and pointing.

"Something is on fire! It looks like it's up by the feed store, and Birdie's not answering her phone."

That was not a good sign, and Hunt was worried.

"I'm going to see," he said, and ran back into the house long enough to get his bike helmet and the keys to his Harley. Moments later, he shot out of the driveway and disappeared up the street.

Ray was still on the roof and hitting Redial on Birdie's number over and over, but now it was going to voicemail.

Hunt wasn't thinking past getting to the site of the fire. He wouldn't let himself consider Birdie being in danger, but someone was or this wouldn't be happening.

Police cars were speeding up Main Street as he turned at the light. He could see the smoke now, a boiling pillar of black rising high into the sky. People were running up the street, while others like him were coming out of side streets onto Main.

It wasn't until he passed the hardware store that he saw the actual structure fire and knew it was, in fact, the place where Birdie worked. The fire appeared to be confined to the east end of the building where the loading dock and the feed and seed were stored, but he didn't know where she was.

He wheeled in to the curb a short distance away, parked the bike, hung his helmet on the handle, and got off running.

A crowd was already gathering, and the police had formed a barricade to keep back the onlookers. He was frantically searching the faces of the people pouring out of every exit when he saw Birdie come staggering out of a side door and stumble to her knees.

He jumped past the barricade and ran toward her. She was coughing and choking from the smoke and trying to get up when Hunt reached her and pulled her back up to her feet.

She looked up. "Hunt?"

"I've got you, honey," Hunt said. He picked her up in his arms and carried her away from the smoke and the flames.

Two ambulances were already on scene, treating people for smoke inhalation, and as soon as Hunt got her there, they began giving her oxygen and checking her vitals.

"Call Emma," Birdie begged, and Hunt reached for his phone.

Emma answered abruptly, almost as if she'd been waiting for the call.

"Hello? Hunt?"

"Yes, it's me. Truesdale's is on fire. Birdie is out and safe, but she got a lot of smoke. They're giving her oxygen on scene, and she wanted me to call you."

"Oh my God! I heard the sirens. I saw the smoke. And she didn't answer her phone. Tell her I'll be right there."

Hunt caught Birdie's eye and gave her a thumbs-up, then settled down near her to wait.

Emma arrived minutes later, horrified by what was happening, and gave Birdie a quick hug, then sat down beside Hunt and stared at the fire.

"This is so awful. Is she okay?"

"Some smoke inhalation. The oxygen will help. She can't get to her car and is in no shape to drive it anyway. And I'm not putting her on the Harley. When they let her go, will you take her home?"

"Of course," Emma said.

Hunt watched the firemen in action, and within the hour, they had the main part of the fire knocked down.

Hunt and Emma were still waiting with Birdie when her boss, Dub Truesdale, approached.

"Hey, Birdie, I have everyone accounted for but Arnold. By any chance, did he go to lunch late or go home early?"

Birdie glanced toward the burned end of the building and then moaned.

"No. Arnold was moving that new shipment of cattle cubes. He said the forklift was leaking fluid, and he was going to do it by hand."

Dub paled. "Oh hell. Are you serious? Why didn't he let me know?"

Birdie's eyes welled. "The last couple of days he's been kind of down. He said his boys got arrested, and he and Donna were thinking of moving home to West Virginia. He said a man needed to stay busy to stay out of trouble."

All of a sudden, there was a shout at the doorway near the loading dock, then a flurry of people began going inside the burned area. Dub took off running.

Hunt's heart sank. He had a bad feeling about the missing man's welfare. But before they could learn the outcome, Birdie was released with a caution to go to the ER if she experienced any trouble breathing.

Hunt followed Emma and Birdie home and helped get Birdie inside before leaving them on their own. It wasn't until he got back to the house that he realized he had a text from Ava.

Heard about the fire and that there was a death. Is Birdie okay?

He sighed. That explained what happened to the missing man. He stopped and returned the text.

Yes. A little smoke inhalation. Emma took her home. I need to see you tonight. Are you free?

He sent the message, then waited. When her text came back, he grinned.

I always charged before, but you get a deal. For you, I'm always free. My house. Six p.m. I'm cooking.

He laughed and sent one last text.

You're not just cooking. You're smokin' hot, lady, and you're mine, all mine. See you at six.

———————————

The firemen had been inside the loading area checking for hot spots when they found a partially burned body trapped between the outer wall and what had been a large stack of bagged cattle cubes.

At that point, Chief Pittman and a couple of EMTs were called to the scene. But it was Dub Truesdale who identified the body by the unburned part of the man's jacket and the fact that he only had one employee unaccounted for.

Lon was sick at heart. The last time he'd seen Arnold had been in his jail, witnessing the heartbreaking conversation between him and his sons, who were awaiting transport to county. Now he was going to have to notify Donna Hollis that her husband had died in the fire and tell the boys as well. This was one of the times in his job when he wondered why some people suffer such tragedies.

He left an officer on guard at the scene and went back to the office to notify the county coroner. The body couldn't be removed from the scene until it was determined there was no foul play. After that, Lon went to notify Arnold's wife.

He drove across town to their home, but when he pulled up in the driveway and saw Donna sitting out on the front porch staring in the direction of the fading smoke, his heart sank. She'd either already heard or suspected, and it was no wonder. The sirens. The smoke. And she probably tried to call Arnold without getting an answer, and since there was no other car in the drive, Arnold must have driven their only vehicle to work.

She was already crying as Lon came up the steps.

"He's dead, isn't he?" Donna cried.

Lon sat down in the chair beside her.

"Yes, ma'am. I am so sorry. They found his body in the warehouse."

Donna covered her face and began to wail. "Oh my God! Why is this happening? Wasn't it enough that I lost my sons? Why did I have to lose my man?"

Lon stood. "I don't know, Mrs. Hollis, and I'm so sorry. But it's chilly for you sitting out here. Will you let me help you inside?"

Donna let Lon walk her into the house, then settle her on the sofa.

"Is there anyone I can call for you?" he asked.

She shook her head. "All I had was Arnold and the boys. We were going to move home to Bethlehem. That's in West Virginia, where I grew up. I got my mama's house, and we were gonna live there for free. Only now I don't have any way to get there and no money to hire it done. I don't know why I don't just die, too. This isn't right. This just isn't right," she said, and then leaned back against the sofa and closed her eyes.

Lon didn't know how he was going to make it happen yet, but this was a situation he couldn't ignore.

"We'll help you, Mrs. Hollis. The people here in Blessings help each other when the need is great, and this is one of those times. We'll figure it out, and we'll get you home, I promise. Do you have family there?" Lon asked.

"Yes, my sister and two brothers," Donna said.

"Then you get on the phone and you call them right now. You don't need to be dealing with this alone. Just have a little faith in us. You tell them we'll get you home."

Donna looked up then, her eyes red-rimmed and swimming in tears.

"You can do that for me?"

"Yes, ma'am. Even if I have to drive a U-Haul all the way to West Virginia and back myself, we will get you there."

"How do I get our car back? It's at the store," Donna asked.

"We'll get it back to you as soon as the fire department clears the area. Right now, they're waiting for the coroner."

She was quiet for a few moments, and then looked up at him. "Have you told my sons?"

"No, ma'am. Not yet. I wanted to tell you first. I'm going back to make the notification now, unless you want to tell them yourself. I can take you, if you do."

"You tell them. Right now, I don't feel like I'll ever want to see them again."

"Yes, ma'am, and again, I'm so sorry for your loss," Lon said, then left the house and headed back to the station.

He wanted this day over with. He wanted to go home and see Mercy's beautiful face and laughing eyes and hear stories about her day at Granny's. This day had been a kick in the gut.

His feet were dragging when he pulled in at the back of the jail and got out. It wouldn't be long before they'd serve supper, but he was about to ruin Teddy and Brian Hollis's appetites, and hated like hell that it had to be said.

He entered the booking area, and then opened the door into the jail and walked down to their cells.

Teddy stood.

"When are they coming to move us?" he asked.

"Tomorrow," Lon said. "But that's not why I'm here. I'm afraid I have bad news about your dad. There was a fire at the feed store today, and he didn't make it. I'm really, really sorry, boys."

Brian leaped off his bunk and grabbed the bars, screaming, "No! No! Oh my God!"

Tears were rolling down Teddy's face. "Does Mama know?"

"She does now."

Teddy staggered back to his bunk and dropped.

"We don't have family here. What's going to happen to her?" he asked.

"She wants to go home, and we'll get her there because that's what we do here in Blessings. We take care of our people. We don't rob them. We don't hurt them. We don't steal what is theirs," Lon said.

Then he walked out and went back to his office and called Mercy because he wanted to hear her sweet voice and be reminded of good in this world.

While Lon was calling his wife, Donna Hollis was calling her sister. She was trembling so hard it was difficult for her to hold the phone, and then she sat listening to it ring and ring before it went to voicemail.

Donna took a deep breath, then started talking.

"Joy, this is Donna. Something terrible has happened. Call me."

CHAPTER 13

An hour later, Lon Pittman was still at the station, waiting for the coroner. But his thoughts were on the promise he'd made to Donna Hollis. It was going to take the cooperation of everyone in Blessings to raise enough money to get Arnold Hollis buried and Donna back home, and he knew exactly who to contact to get the ball rolling—Ruby Butterman.

Peanut Butterman's wife was the hub of charity events in town, and she would be the one who could help him with this tragedy.

He glanced at the time, took a chance that the Curl Up and Dye might still be open, and called there first. The phone rang a few times, and then he got a breathless answer.

"Curl Up and Dye, this is Ruby."

"Ruby, this is Lon Pittman. Can you talk, or do you want to call me back?"

"I'm closed, so I can talk. It took me a minute to get to the phone because I was mopping. What's up?"

Lon began to explain, and by the time he was through, Ruby was in tears.

"Bless her heart," she said. "I can't imagine how broken she must feel. I'd heard the boys were in jail, but didn't know why. And I knew there'd been a fire, but we've been slammed today and no one ever mentioned there was a casualty. So, what are we aiming for? Raising enough money to get Arnold buried and her back home? Or adding some to that so she'll have something to live on until Social Security gets her widow's benefits started?"

"Yes, the latter. I'm thinking Dub Truesdale should have insurance to cover his employees, so she might even get an insurance settlement from that. We'll have to find out."

"Just leave it to me," Ruby said. "First thing I'll be doing is going to see her and find out what her wants and wishes are. We'll go from there, okay?"

Lon sighed. "Yes, very okay, and thanks."

"Always," Ruby said.

Lon hung up, and then Avery buzzed his office.

"What's up?" Lon asked.

"The coroner is on the scene," Avery said.

"Thanks," Lon said. "I'll be at the feed store and then going home from there. Call if you need me."

"Yes, sir," Avery said.

Lon grabbed his hat and once again left through the back of the station to get to his car.

While the chief was still tending to death, Ava was at the nurses' station monitoring patient calls and tending to life.

She had just come out of a patient's room when she heard a commotion out in the lobby, and then a man came into the ER pushing a very pregnant woman in a wheelchair. He was obviously pale and shaken, and the woman was crying and moaning and appeared to be in serious distress. When she realized the man was her ex, Vince Lewis, she was shocked.

When Vince saw her, he started pushing the wheelchair toward her, talking frantically, trying to explain.

"We were on our way home from Florida when she went into labor. I took a detour off the main highway because this was the closest hospital I knew of. She's eight months pregnant and bleeding."

"Roll her into room four," Ava said, and then called out to one of the other nurses. "Page Dr. Quick, ASAP."

Within seconds, Vince had his wife in the exam room with Ava right behind them.

"It's okay, honey, it's going to be okay. This is my friend, Ava. Ava, this is my wife, Carly."

Ava reached for the young woman's hand and gave it a gentle squeeze.

"Hello, Carly. It's nice to meet you. Let's get you up on the bed and see what's going on, okay?"

Vince helped Carly out of the wheelchair and up onto the bed. "We're going to need you to put on this gown," Ava said.

Carly was crying. "I'm scared. Am I losing the baby?"

"Just take deep breaths and stay as calm as you can," Ava said. "Your husband brought you exactly where you need to be."

At that point, two more nurses came in and began helping Carly out of her clothing. Dr. Quick arrived and began an immediate examination, talking calmly and quietly to both the husband and wife as he did, until he had all of the information he needed.

"Ava, notify surgery we're bringing a patient up for a C-section."

"Yes, Doctor," Ava said, and hurried out of the room.

A few minutes later, orderlies wheeled Carly Lewis out of the exam room and up the hall, with Vince walking along beside her, holding her hand.

Vince came back later, pale and shaking and apologizing.

"I'm sorry. This was the closest place I could think of. She means the world to me. This is our first child. Thank you for being so kind to her."

Ava frowned. "Why wouldn't I be kind to her? She's a patient in need. Go back to the surgery waiting room and just be the husband and the man you're supposed to be. I don't need thanks. I was just doing my job."

Vince nodded, and then hurried away.

Ava sighed. What were the odds?

Then she said a quick prayer for both mother and baby and went back to work.

———————

When Hunt returned to the house, Ray stopped what he was doing and ran to the edge of the roof to question him.

"Is Birdie okay? She wasn't hurt?"

"She's okay. Got some smoke inhalation. She was on oxygen for a bit, and then Emma took her home."

"Thanks, Hunt. Thanks for checking on her," Ray said.

Hunt frowned. "I don't need thanks for that. She's my sister, too."

Then he picked up his hammer, staring at the front porch and trying to remember what it was he'd been doing, and then got back to work. But he couldn't stop thinking about the man who'd died. One morning you wake up, kiss your wife goodbye, and go to work. And then never make it home.

He didn't know the Hollis family. They must have moved here after he was gone, but he'd heard what Birdie told her boss. Both of his boys in jail. And now Arnold was dead. His poor wife. Her whole world had blown up in her face.

Bless her heart. Bless her heart.

━━━━━━━━━━

Lon was at the feed store with the coroner. It appeared Arnold had been trapped by the fire, but they wouldn't know how he'd died until the autopsy.

When the coroner finally finished his initial examination and all the photos were taken, they removed the body and drove away. The damaged side of the store was roped off, and the inventory inside declared a total loss.

Dub Truesdale would have to remove all of the soaked and burned inventory from the premises, then tear down that side of the building before it could be rebuilt.

It was a hard hit to take at the beginning of a new year, but he was insured. The hardest part was losing Arnold. Dub dreaded talking to Arnold's wife, but it was a phone call he had to make.

Finally, everyone was gone, and he went to the privacy of his pickup and called her number. The phone rang and rang, and he didn't think she was going to answer. Then he heard a shaky voice.

"Hello?"

"Mrs. Hollis, it's me, Dub. I can't tell you how sorry I am that this happened. We still don't know what caused the fire. Only that he was unloading sacks in the area where it broke out."

"Thank you for calling," Donna said.

"Of course, but that's not all. I want you to know that I'm covering the funeral expenses, and it is part of my policy to have a hundred thousand dollars of life insurance on every employee, if their death happened on the job. I don't know how long it will take the insurance company to pay up, but that money will be yours. I wanted you to know this now for your peace of mind. I'd give anything for this not to have happened, but it did. I've never understood the workings of God's ways, only that we have to find a way to deal with them."

Donna was crying openly now. The relief of knowing she could bury Arnold in dignity—and she wasn't going to be destitute and trying to live on widow's benefits—was huge.

"Thank you, Mr. Truesdale. God bless you," she said.

"Yes, ma'am. If there's anything I can do for you, don't hesitate to ask. I'm serious. If you're planning on moving and need help getting furniture out of the house, all you have to do is call. Oh…do you have extra keys to your car?"

"Yes, here at the house."

"We'll be needing those to get the car back to you. If I come by your house to pick them up, then I'll get someone to help me get your car back to you, okay?"

Donna sighed. "Yes, I sure would appreciate that. I'll have them ready," she said.

"I'll be right there," Dub said, then he hung up, put the phone down in the seat beside him, and covered his face. He didn't want anyone driving by to see him cry.

But his news had drastically changed Donna Hollis's needs. Chief Pittman had been talking about helping her out, and she wanted him to know that wouldn't be necessary now, so she called the police station and asked to speak to the chief.

"Hold a moment, please," Avery said, and put the call through to Lon's office.

Lon was typing up the last bits of the case, mentioning the arrival of the coroner and the time of the removal of the body, when the phone on his desk rang. He swiveled his chair around and answered.

"Chief Pittman."

"Chief, this is Donna Hollis. Do you have a minute?"

"Yes, ma'am. What do you need?" Lon asked.

"The reason I'm calling is because of what I no longer need," she said, and then relayed the information Dub Truesdale had given her.

"Under the circumstances, that's good news," Lon said. "I thought that might be the case. Dub's a good man. But that money won't last you forever. We're still going to help you. Don't think for a minute that you're going to have to deal with all of this on your own, okay?"

Donna was in tears again. "Yes, okay. Blessings has such good people in it. It's why we moved here. But I want to go home now, and as soon as I can make it happen, I'll be leaving."

"Just so you know, your sons were transferred to county today. They've both pled guilty and will be sentenced whenever their court date is set."

"That's all on them," Donna said. "I have no intention of being 'that mother' sitting in the courtroom bemoaning their fate. Whatever sentence they get is what they deserve. They shamed themselves, and they shamed their father and me."

"Yes, ma'am," Lon said. "In the meantime, don't worry. We're still going to be doing what we do to make your transition home a little easier."

"All right then," Donna said, and hung up.

She sat there in the silence of the house with the phone in her lap, wondering about the hand of fate. It had certainly given her a slap-down she didn't deserve. But like Dub said, she would just have to make the best of it. Then she thought of the car keys and ran to get them before Dub showed up. Solving one small problem at a time was how she was going to get through this.

———————

Knowing what he did now, Lon called Ruby and updated her on Arnold Hollis's funeral expenses being covered, so the immediate need to pay for that had been alleviated, and there was life insurance money coming to Donna as well.

"That's good to know," Ruby said. "But there's no telling how long it will take for all of that to happen. Donna wants to go home, and we need to help her make that happen. I think our best bet is a notice in the paper about some money-raising event that will get everyone out. I'm still working on it. Don't worry. We'll get Donna some cash to get a moving van and get her on home."

"Thanks, Ruby. You're the best," Lon said.

"Peanut thinks so," Ruby said, and then giggled and disconnected.

She grabbed her purse and locked up the shop on her way out. It was time to pay Donna a visit. She'd already called Dan Amos for an address, so instead of crossing Main to go home, she came out of the alley behind her salon and headed north into the residential area there.

———————

Dub Truesdale and one of his employees had just delivered the car to Donna's house. She thanked them for their trouble, and then after they left she dropped the car keys in her purse and sat down, unable to think what to do next.

There was no funeral to plan. The coroner would have Arnold's body for autopsy. And since she was moving back to West Virginia, she didn't want to leave Arnold here. It made her feel better to think about taking his ashes back with her and scattering them there.

She was just now realizing how insulated her little world here had been. With only the one car, she'd never had outside interests beyond home and family. Wherever they had gone, they'd gone together. She had friends at church, but not close ones. Not the kind she would have gone to lunch with because their budget did not accommodate lunches with friends.

Her sister still had not returned the call, and so she sat, uncertain what, if anything, she needed to do next. Weary and heartsick to the bone, Donna leaned back in the chair and closed her eyes.

The next thing she knew, someone was knocking at her door. She got up, smoothing her hair as she went, and opened the door.

"Donna, I apologize for stopping by without calling first. Is it okay if I come in a moment?" Ruby asked.

"Of course," Donna said. "Please come in. I'm just passing the time here in the living room, waiting for my sister to call. Have a seat."

Ruby sat, then leaned forward, her elbows on her knees as Donna sat back down in her chair.

"I want you to know how sorry I am for what happened to Arnold. You have my deepest sympathies," Ruby said.

Donna nodded. "Thank you, Ruby."

"Of course," Ruby said. "But I'm here about you as well. Chief Pittman called me about your situation…about wanting to go home, and I want you to tell me, in your own words, what you need for us to get you there."

Donna's eyes welled. "I honestly don't know, except that I'm not burying Arnold here."

Ruby nodded. "Then you intend to wait until the coroner releases the body and have it transported to West Virginia?"

"We always said we didn't want to be buried, so I reckon I'll take his ashes back with me," Donna said.

Ruby's focus shifted. "You do know that funeral homes can ship ashes to you?"

Donna wiped her eyes, then shook her head. "No, I don't think I did."

"Well, they can, so don't let the unknown of when his body is released be the deciding factor in your decision of when and how you want to leave, okay? Just so you know, the funeral home here can receive Arnold's body from the coroner, follow your wishes, and ship the ashes at a later date to your new address. Chief Pittman also told me about Dub's phone call, but there's no way to know when any of that will go into effect, so we want to have a couple of fund-raisers here in Blessings to give you the freedom to make your own choices…if that's all right with you?"

Donna covered her face and burst into tears.

Ruby jumped up and went to her. Within moments she was down on her knees in front of Donna's chair, patting her arm.

"I'm so sorry, sugar. I'm so, so sorry. Cry all you want. I'm a good listener, and we'll get this figured out together, okay?"

Donna nodded. But the relief was huge. She was no longer trying to figure this out alone.

Junior was at the pharmacy when he heard about Birdie and the fire. At first he was shocked, and then sad no one in the family bothered to tell him. Then when he found out Arnold Hollis had died in that fire, he was sad all over again.

Arnold had always been friendly to Junior and had even taken him home one night during a downpour when his car wouldn't start. Junior remembered the man's kindness and his gentle spirit, and now he was gone.

Junior left the pharmacy with full intention of going home, but the thought of going back to nothing was suddenly more than he could bear. In a spur-of-the-moment decision, he made a U-turn in the street and drove out to Grey Goose Lake, then parked and got out.

Back when he was little, Hunt used to bring him and Ray out here to fish. Hunt had always baited their hooks and taken the fish off the lines. He was a good big brother, and what they'd done was unforgivable.

He walked down to the edge of the water, then paused, staring out across the water and watching the sunlight sparkling on the surface. A flock of Canada geese was swimming in the middle of the lake, and there was a big, gray crane standing in the edge of the water just down shore from where Junior was standing. There was so much beauty here…and such peace. Junior squatted down at the water's edge, picked up a couple of rocks, and gave them a toss.

The ripples spread out from the point of contact like an echo… going farther and farther…growing bigger and bigger, like the lies that had destroyed his family. If he could do it over, he would never have kept the secret. Even though the consequences would have taken them down, Hunt would not have felt so betrayed. Instead, he'd paid the price for their sins.

Junior was still watching the geese when his phone suddenly rang. When he saw it was Ray, he answered.

"Yeah, what's up?"

"Hello to you, too," Ray said. "Did you hear about Birdie?"

"Yes, I heard about Birdie, but not from any of the family. Thank you for calling," he said, and hung up.

Ray called back.

Junior answered angrily. "What?"

"What the hell's wrong with you?" Ray asked. "Where are you?"

"Grey Goose Lake."

There was a long pause, and then Ray asked, "What are you doing out there?"

"Remembering how Hunt used to bring us fishing when we were kids. He was a good big brother. What we did to him was bad."

Ray sighed. "I know, but there's no going back. What's done is done."

"I don't like myself," Junior said. "I am a loser. We failed Hunt. Then we failed ourselves. And we failed Mama. I don't even matter enough to any of you to let me know Birdie escaped a fire today. I disgust me."

"Come by the house," Ray said. "We'll talk."

"I don't want to talk, and I don't want to get blind, stinking drunk again tonight," Junior said.

"Then what do you want?" Ray asked.

"Just for all this to be over. For Hunt to leave town so I don't have to remember what we did to him."

"Come back into town," Ray said.

"I'm not ready to come back into town," Junior said. And the more he talked, the louder he got until he was shouting. "What do you think I'm going to do out here? You're talking like I'm going to do myself in or something, and that's not gonna happen because I'm also a coward. I'm out here because it's beautiful and quiet and I don't want to talk to anybody. Just leave me the hell alone."

He disconnected, then dropped his phone in his pocket. Even though it rang again and again, he ignored it.

Emma was beginning the preparations for their supper when her doorbell rang. She wiped her hands and went to the door.

"Hi, Ray. Come in."

"Emma, I just talked to Junior. He's out at the lake and talking all crazy. I'm worried."

Emma frowned. "What do you mean, talking all crazy? And what is he doing at the lake?"

"I don't know...but he said he was remembering how Hunt used to take me and him fishing and what a good big brother he was. Then he said he hated himself, and what we did was a bad thing. He's hurt because none of us called him about Birdie, either."

Her stomach suddenly knotted. "Do you think he's—"

"No. Oh, I don't know. He told me to leave him alone and that he wasn't out there to hurt himself because he's too big a coward. I'm freakin' out. What if he goes and tells Hunt?"

Emma dropped onto the sofa. Ray sat in a chair beside her. They stared at each other in silence—each waiting for the other one to answer that question. What if?

Finally, it was Ray who broke the silence.

"What do we do?"

Emma shrugged. "Nothing. Whatever happens happens. If I could do it over, I wouldn't make the same choice. But nobody can change history. Go home to Susie. Live your life. It's all we can do."

Ray sighed, his shoulders slumping. "I feel kinda like Junior. I don't like myself, either."

Emma's eyes narrowed. "Life isn't a popularity contest. Go home."

Ray got up and walked out.

Emma rolled over onto her side, curling up on the sofa and staring dry-eyed at the wall.

But Ray still wasn't satisfied with leaving Junior out at the lake like that. Emma hadn't heard the hopelessness in Junior's voice, but she knew why he was the way he was. It was Ray's opinion that she should be more sympathetic. After all, she was a part of it, too.

They'd just buried their mother, and he didn't want to have to bury his brother because he'd ignored what felt like a cry for help. But the only other person he could call was Birdie, and he didn't know how she was going to react. She was pretty upset with all of them and, with the fire at her work and Arnold dying, likely more upset.

But she was still their baby sister, and Junior loved her a lot. Maybe she could convince him to come home. So Ray got in his car and then gave her a call.

CHAPTER 14

Unaware of the family drama, Hunt was getting ready to go pick up Ava. He had the ring in his pocket and was going to play the rest of the evening by ear.

Blessings was limited in choices of places to eat out, but not in food. Granny's menu was varied enough to suit most every palate, and the barbecue joint and Broyles Dairy Freeze took care of everything else. But the way he felt, he could put ketchup on cardboard and make it work if making love to Ava was on the menu for dessert.

He gave himself the once-over in the bathroom mirror and frowned. He still needed a haircut. Maybe another day, he thought, then put on his leather jacket, got the car keys, and left the house. The roofers would be back tomorrow, and so would the carpenter. They had the floor joists fixed and the subfloor patched in the kitchen, but there was still a place in the bathroom floor to repair as well. But that was tomorrow. Tonight was for the woman who'd put the light back in his life.

When he pulled up in her drive, the anticipation of just seeing her face made his heart skip. God. He was so far gone.

He got out and was on his way to the front porch when Ava came bouncing out of the house, waving.

He laughed. "I'm glad to see you, too," he said, then walked her to the truck, helped her in, and kissed her square on the mouth. "You look beautiful."

Ava sighed. "Drive, or take me back in the house."

"One thing at a time, love," he said, and got in. "Talk to me about your day," he added as he started the truck and drove away to Granny's.

"Well, you won't guess who showed up in the ER."

"Who?" Hunt asked.

"Vince Lewis and his wife, who was eight months pregnant. Supposedly, they were on their way home to Atlanta when she went into labor. I don't know exactly what route they were on, but he detoured and came straight to Blessings Hospital."

"Was she okay?" Hunt asked.

Ava nodded. "The baby was in distress, so they took his wife to surgery. One C-section later, they are the proud parents of a baby girl. He apologized for coming back, but it was the closest place he knew to bring her. Anyway, she's here for a while until she and the baby are able to travel, or until they're stable enough to Medi-Flight them back to Atlanta. Either way, his fleeting interest in me has shifted to more important things in his life."

Hunt heard the satisfaction in her voice and knew that whatever had transpired, she was good with it, and that's all that mattered to him. Then he turned off Main and into the parking lot at Granny's and parked.

Ava suddenly pointed. "Oh look! There are Peanut and Ruby."

Hunt frowned. "Ruby as in Ruby Dye…who owns the hair salon?"

Ava nodded. "She and Peanut got married a while back. They had quite a story making it happen, too. Her ex-husband showed up, kidnapped her, and there was quite a race to run him down and rescue her."

Hunt's eyes widened. "In Blessings? In my head, bad things like that never happen here."

"There have been all kinds of family dramas happening in Blessings through the years. Some of them tragic, like what happened today to Mr. Hollis, and some of them heroic, like Johnny Pine rescuing Lovey during the hurricane. Even when we mess up, somehow we find a way to come together in the end."

"Good to know. I like happy endings," Hunt said. "Are you ready to go inside?"

She leaned across the seat and kissed him.

"Yes, please."

Hunt felt the kiss all the way to his bones, then got out of the truck and helped her down. They went in hand in hand, and from the look on Hunt Knox's face, the diners were no longer in doubt about where Hunt and Ava's relationship was going.

Lovey greeted them, grabbed a couple of menus, and was leading them to an empty booth when Hunt saw Birdie sitting in a booth by herself. She looked so lost and forlorn.

"There's Birdie," Hunt said.

Lovey stopped. "She's eating alone. You two want to sit with her?"

"Of course," Ava said.

Lovey led them over. "Hey, Birdie, want some company?"

Birdie looked up. "Yes! Please! After everything that happened today, I didn't want to spend the evening alone."

They sat down, and then Ava reached for Birdie's hand.

"I heard about the fire. I'm so sorry about Arnold," she said.

Birdie's shoulders slumped. "I was so scared. All of the power went out inside the building, and my office is down a hallway with no windows. It was pitch-dark and the smoke was so thick I was choking. I couldn't find my phone and didn't want to take time searching for it. I finally found my way out of the building, and then dropped." Then she looked across the table at Hunt, and there were tears in her eyes. "The next thing I know, my big brother is picking me up and carrying me to one of the ambulances. I was never so glad to see anyone in my life."

Ava looked at Hunt. "You didn't mention that when you told me Birdie was okay."

He shrugged. "Because I didn't do anything but show up and take her to the ambulance. They lined her up with the others they'd put on oxygen and kept her there until they were sure she was okay. Emma took her home."

"Because you called Emma, and then followed us and helped get me inside," Birdie said. "Stop playing down the fact that you were there when I needed you."

Hunt grinned. "Yes, ma'am."

Birdie sniffed. "Thank you."

"You're welcome," Hunt said. "So what's the special tonight?"

"Meatloaf," Birdie said. "I love it, but never make it just for myself."

"Sounds good. That's what I'm having," Ava said.

They ordered without looking at a menu, and while they were waiting, more than one diner came up to grill Birdie about the fire. She was too rattled to answer, so Hunt fielded their curiosity. And then their food arrived and that ended the visits.

Two young men stopped by their table while they were eating to say hello, but their attention was on Birdie. After they left, Hunt teased her.

"Which one do you like best?" he asked.

"I don't know what you're talking about."

"Come on, little sister. Yes, you do. You're pretty, young, and single, and they were slobbering a little around the mouth. That's always a dead giveaway," Hunt said.

Birdie frowned. "You're lying."

Ava laughed out loud. "Yes, he's full of it."

Hunt grinned. "Okay, so they weren't slobbering. But one was sweating a little, and the other one kept stuttering. Have you ever gone out with either of them?"

Birdie sighed. "No."

"Why not?" Ava asked.

Birdie shrugged. "The spark's not there, and I'm not the kind of person to lead someone on just for fun."

"Good for you, kid," Hunt said.

Ava nodded. "I understand about that spark. If it's missing, then it's all a waste of time."

Hunt glanced at her, and then reached across the table and squeezed her hand.

"Your hesitation was my blessing," he said.

Birdie grinned. "What don't I know?"

Ava glanced at Hunt and nodded.

"That Ava is going with me when I go back to Houston," Hunt said.

Birdie gasped. "As in…forever?"

"As in forever," Ava said.

Birdie's eyes welled. "This is awesome, and Mama would be so happy. I told Emma I thought you two were hitting it off, but I didn't know this was happening."

"Thanks," Hunt said. "I think it's pretty awesome, too."

"This makes me even more determined to wait for my Prince Charming to come find me…whoever he may be," Birdie said, then her cell phone rang. She glanced at the caller ID, then looked up. "It's Ray. He never calls."

"Then answer it," Hunt said. "If it's not important, just tell him you'll call him back in a few."

She nodded and picked up the call, speaking in an undertone so as not to disturb other diners.

"Hello."

"Birdie! It's me. I already talked to Emma but she acts like it doesn't matter, and I'm worried. I don't know what to do but I can't just leave him out there in that shape."

Birdie was frowning and starting to panic.

"Wait! Ray! You're not making sense. What's wrong, and leave who where?"

"Oh. Right! Junior disappeared. I couldn't find him. I called and he finally answered. He's out at Grey Goose Lake. He won't come back to town. He kept talking about what a good brother Hunt was to us when we were little…how he took us fishing out there and all. He sounded all sad and said he was a loser. I got scared. He told me he wasn't going to hurt himself—because he was too big of a coward to kill himself—but I don't know if… He sounded lost. Emma acted like she didn't care. But I care. What do you think I should do?"

Hunt could tell by the changing expressions on Birdie's face that something was wrong.

"Oh my God, Ray. I don't know. Do you think he's suicidal?"

Hunt's heart skipped a beat. "What?"

Birdie covered the phone. "It's Ray. He's in a panic. Junior went out to Grey Goose Lake because it's where you used to take him and Ray fishing. Junior was talking about what a good big brother you were. He's depressed and maybe suicidal, and Ray doesn't know what—"

"Give me the phone," Hunt said.

She handed it over.

"Ray, it's me. Do you really think Junior is capable of that?"

Ray was startled that Birdie and Hunt were together. "Uh…I don't know. But I'd never be able to live with myself if I ignored what feels like a cry for help."

"I'll take her out there. We'll go talk to him," Hunt said. "Here's Birdie."

Birdie took the phone. "We are all at Granny's having supper. We're leaving here as soon as we can pay."

"Then I'm coming, too," Ray said.

Birdie's thoughts were spinning. This was the opportunity she'd been waiting for, to get everyone together to deliver her mama's message, and a crisis situation might be the perfect time.

"Leave Susie at home, but get Emma and bring her with you."

"She won't come," Ray said.

"You tell her I said she has to, that I have an important message for all of you," Birdie said, and then disconnected. "Thank you, Hunt. The trip out there is going to mean more to you than you can imagine."

"If this is a family meeting, then I think you need to drop me off at the house," Ava said.

"Uh…no," Hunt said. "If we're going to be partners in life, there aren't going to be secrets between us, remember?"

Hunt waved their waitress down, got their ticket, and left in haste. Sundown wasn't far away, and he was worried about finding Junior before it got dark.

"Get in with us, Birdie. I don't want you driving around out at the lake by yourself. I'll bring you back to your car later."

She didn't argue and piled into the truck with Ava in the middle as Hunt took off out of town.

Ray was already on his way back to Emma's house, and when he knocked on her door again, she was surprised and then angry.

"I already told you I—"

"Hunt and Birdie are on their way out to the lake right now. Birdie said to tell you that you have to come, that she has an important message for all of us. So if I have to drag your hateful ass out to my car, I'll do it."

Emma sighed. "Whatever," she muttered. "I'll need to leave Gordon a note to—"

"Just get your jacket and your dang phone and call him on the way."

Emma ran to the coat closet, grabbed her coat, and pocketed her cell phone on the way out the door. Maybe if they all showed up together, it would keep Junior from saying anything to Hunt about their secret. It was old…in the past…and she wanted so much to forget it had ever happened.

———————

Junior was sitting on a rock overlooking the lake, watching the sun moving slowly toward the horizon. He'd been out here after dark plenty of times, but usually drinking beer with a bunch of guys.

He remembered once when Hunt brought them out that they'd stayed after the sun went down and had a wiener roast down by the shore. Hunt built a little fire right by the water and then cut them green sticks to use to roast their wieners.

Junior remembered the elation of hanging out with his big brother, and what fun they'd had—Hunt telling ghost stories while he and Ray huddled on either side of him eating their hot dogs and sharing that one bottle of root beer because it was all Hunt had the money to buy.

The hurt of knowing what they'd done to Hunt after all the love he'd given them was killing Junior. He wished to God he would just hurry up and die, because most days he was so sad it hurt to breathe.

The sun was sitting on the tree line now. If he squinted just right, it almost looked like it was floating on a sea of green loblolly pines. The breeze finally laid, and the last rays of sunlight were melting like butter on the glass-smooth surface of the lake.

He heard the sound of cars driving up back in the parking area and hoped they didn't come his way. The sound of voices carried in the stillness, but they were just murmurs. Even though they were coming closer, he still couldn't hear the words.

He kept watching the curve on the path, and when he saw Ray and then Birdie, he sighed. He should have known Ray would panic. But then he saw Hunt and Ava.

"Dammit, Ray, what did you do?" he mumbled, and started crying.

And in that moment, Hunt saw him as the little brother he'd been. The gentle one. The quiet one. Whatever the hell he'd done that changed him, it hurt Hunt to know how broken he'd become.

He walked up to Junior and put his arms around him.

And that's what Emma saw when she came running up the path. "Junior! Junior! What did you say?" she cried.

Ray turned, frowning. "He didn't say anything, Emma. He's crying. That's all."

Emma's legs were shaking. She was so relieved that she dropped down onto the rock where Junior had been sitting and stared at all of them, wondering what fresh hell was going to happen next.

But none of them were prepared for Birdie's ultimatum.

"I've been waiting for the right moment to get us all together but never imagined it would be like this," she said.

Hunt still had his arm around Junior's shoulder as they turned to face her, but then he reached for Ava and pulled her close. "What's going on, Birdie?"

"Do you remember Elliot Graham?" she asked.

Hunt frowned. "Yes. I used to mow his yard. What does he have to do with us?"

"In the past few years it's become known around town that he's something of a psychic. He won't claim it. He just says that he knows stuff. Anyway, he came to the funeral home the night we had Mama's viewing, said he had a message for me from Mama, and asked if I would step outside where it was quiet, so I did."

At that point, no one was moving. No one was asking questions. They were riveted to Birdie's story.

"Hunt, he told me that Mama wanted you to know she was sorry. That what happened to you wasn't fair, and what our family did to you was unforgivable, but that she didn't know the whole truth until she was shown it on the other side."

Junior moaned, and Hunt tightened his hold on him as Birdie continued.

"Elliot said he had no idea what any of it meant, but he was just supposed to deliver Mama's message. So here's the message. Mama said it starts with Emma, and Daddy did it. She said Junior and Ray knew and said nothing because Daddy demanded silence from all of them."

Hunt remembered that paper he'd found behind the picture in Junior and Ray's room.

"He made you all sign some kind of an oath, didn't he?" Hunt asked.

They looked at him in shock.

"What are you talking about?" Birdie asked.

"I found it behind a picture in the boys' room," he said, and pulled it out of his wallet and handed it to Birdie.

Birdie read it, then looked up at them, frowning.

"What does this mean?"

Emma stared off across the lake.

Ray couldn't look at Hunt.

But Hunt felt like he'd been gut-punched.

"Birdie, you said Dad did it? Are you saying Dad took my money?"

Birdie nodded. "That's the message Mama sent. I guess she wanted Elliot to deliver the message to me because I'd had no part in any of it and wouldn't be inclined to continue the secret."

Hunt's arms dropped to his sides, but when Ava grabbed his hand, he held on and started asking questions.

"Why? Emma? What did you do that started it? Junior…how did it involve you? Damn it, Ray, what the hell did they do that was so bad that you would lie to me, too? Why did Dad steal from me?"

When no one talked, he turned loose of Ava and stepped into the middle of them, his fists doubled up in anger. And he began to talk, and the more he said, the louder he got until at the end he was shouting.

"For the love of God. Mom had to die to know the truth, and one of you better start talking. You've had fifteen years of grace with no recourse. I'm the one who got hurt. Isn't that enough? I'm not going to do anything to anyone…but I deserve the truth."

"I'll tell," Junior said.

Emma looked at Ava, and then stood.

"No. It began with me. It's my story to tell."

Hunt turned to face her. "Then start talking, sister."

She lifted her chin in defiance, but her voice was trembling.

"I got pregnant, but I was scared and didn't tell anyone—not even my boyfriend. I threw up almost every morning after Mom left to take Birdie to school. But then Dad hurt his hand and was off a whole week. He figured it out and had a fit. I begged him not to tell Mama. He asked me who the father was, and when I told him, I thought he was going to kill me. He told me to call him right then and there and get him over to the house. I called him, but I didn't tell him why."

Birdie sighed. "Oh, Emma."

Emma shrugged. "I had just turned sixteen. I thought I was a big deal. My boyfriend showed up, and Dad told him what I'd revealed, grabbed him by the arm, and said he was going to have him arrested for rape. My boyfriend looked at me, and then laughed and said rape had nothing to do with it, that I did what I did with a smile on my face."

Hunt shuddered, remembering his father's trigger-quick temper.

"What happened?" Birdie asked.

Emma looked at Junior, and then back at Hunt. "Dad doubled up his fist and hit him so hard he flew backward, hitting the back of his head on the corner of the kitchen table. It split like a ripe melon, and blood went everywhere. He dropped and didn't get up."

Hunt's heart was pounding now. He knew before she said it what was coming, and it was still a shock to hear the words.

"Daddy killed him. Junior saw it happen. I saw it happen. Daddy made Junior help carry the body to the truck bed. They covered it with a tarp just as Ray came into the kitchen. He saw all the blood and freaked. Dad came in, told me and him to clean it up before Mama got home and then get ourselves to school. He'd drop Junior off later."

"Lord have mercy," Hunt whispered, and turned and looked at Junior. "What did you two do with the body?"

Junior wiped his hands across his face, as if trying to wipe away the memories.

"Daddy drove up to the swamplands and then up into a bayou. We carried the body to the water's edge and left it for the gators. Daddy drove me back to town and got me a permission slip for being late to school."

Hunt frowned. "Okay, he killed the boy, but why did he need the money?"

"Because of me," Emma said. "School was just about over, remember? A few days after you were gone, he sent me to Florida to a home for unwed mothers. Mom thought I had a summer job there. But I was going to have the baby and give it up for adoption. He stole your money to fund that."

Hunt shook his head in disbelief. "It was your mistake. He made me pay for your mistake? Why?"

"Because I wanted to keep the baby, but he killed the father. He said he wasn't going to raise a kid and look at it every day and be reminded of what happened. He didn't have the money to send me, so he took yours. I didn't want to give up my baby, but he made me go, and we were all guilty of his death by participation in one way or another."

Birdie was in shock. This was the last thing she would ever have expected to hear.

"Did Mama know all of this?" Hunt asked.

"Not to my knowledge," Emma said.

"What happened to the baby?" Birdie asked.

Emma shook her head and started crying. "Oh…that was karma coming back to bite me. I miscarried in my seventh month and it died. It was a little boy. I can't have any more."

Before Hunt could react, Ava was beside him. And when she slid her arm around his waist, the rage within him began to fade, and the longer she held him, the quieter he became.

Then he looked at Junior.

"You were fifteen, right?"

"Barely," Junior said.

Hunt's eyes narrowed as he looked at Ray. "And you…how old were you, thirteen?"

Ray nodded. "The same age as Ava."

Hunt took a deep breath and pulled Ava closer.

"And I had just turned eighteen. We were kids…just kids. He was our father, and he screwed all of us, not just me. He involved you in a murder. No wonder you were afraid to tell. I'm sorry I was so angry at you. I'm sorry that I carried such hate with me for so long. I'm sorry Mama was caught in the middle of this nightmare."

"This is what Mama wanted," Birdie said. "She wanted us to make peace. I just know it. Thank you, Hunt. You were always a wonderful big brother, but you have turned into one amazing man."

Junior reached out to shake Hunt's hand, and Hunt shook his head and hugged him. Then Emma was in his arms, too, sobbing and begging forgiveness, and Ray added his apology to the others, and then they all turned, opened their arms, and pulled Birdie into the mix.

Ava stood aside with tears in her eyes, so happy for Hunt, and yet horrified about that boy's body being dumped in the swamp.

"Emma...I have a question," Ava said.

Emma turned around. "Ask."

"I don't remember you dating anyone at that time, and no one was ever reported missing. Who was it?"

Emma closed her eyes, remembering his face and how much she'd loved him, then she looked at Ava and sighed.

"Mark Ryman."

Ava frowned. "The Rymans who lived up in the hills west of Blessings?"

"Wait. What? The one they called Tall Man?" Hunt asked.

Emma nodded.

Hunt shook his head. "That's not right."

"What do you mean, that's not right?" Emma cried. "I guess I know better than you who I was in love with."

"That's not what I meant," Hunt said. "I knew Tall Man. He was a year older than me."

"Yes, yes," Emma said. "So what?"

"So, Tall Man was in Iraq. We were both in the army and on the same base for a couple of months before his unit shipped out to another base. He didn't die in our kitchen...but he did die. About two years before I was shot down. He was a foot soldier. His truck drove over an IED. He was one of three who died that day. I saw his name posted. Dad didn't kill him. Junior, you didn't help hide a body. Ray, you cleaned up his blood, but he shed a lot more fighting a war before he died. Emma lost a baby. But you all lost what was left of your childhood because our father was a coward. Instead of assuming Tall Man was dead, he never checked to see if he was still alive, and made all of us pay so he could hide what he'd done. There is no secret to hide. And as far as we're all concerned, Emma ever being pregnant was her business…and none of ours. Understood?"

They all nodded, including Emma.

Junior dropped to his knees and started rocking back and forth, shaking his head in disbelief.

"This secret nearly killed me, Hunt. Thank you for coming home. Oh my God…I am free."

"And me," Ray said.

"We should have defied Daddy and told you that day," Emma said.

"But he said he'd go to prison, and Mama would lose the house, and we'd all be homeless, maybe even go to foster care," Ray said. "He said we had to protect Birdie from winding up in foster care."

At this point, Ava spoke up.

"I know I'm not family, but I'm going to be. I'm going to Houston with Hunt after the house sells. And being family gives me a little leeway to say something, too. I saw a side of your father that none of you saw. Ray and I were still too young to go to school, and Birdie wasn't even born, but I remember things that I thought were mean."

Hunt was horrified. "Like what, Ava?"

She shrugged. "Well, for instance…he would eat the last piece of pie in the house and blame it on me or Ray. He took money out of Marjorie's purse and told me if I told, he'd say it was me. Your daddy was a liar and a manipulator, and none of you need to feel guilty another moment. You were kids, and he used you to suit his needs. All of you were victims. You just never knew it. And Hunt had the answer you needed, and he never knew it. I know one thing for certain, and that is right now your mama's spirit is so happy that the truth is out… that there's no more secret to be kept."

Hunt was shocked. "He did that…even to you?"

Ava shrugged. "It's how I knew him. He didn't scare me, and he was hardly ever there when Marjorie was babysitting me. But I didn't want anything to do with him. And I think it's time we all went home. Each of you is going to need time to process this. But you need to remember that tomorrow is the first day of the rest of your lives, and you need to find a way to be happy. I know I'm going to spend the rest of my life making sure Hunt is as happy as I know how to make him. And as soon as Hunt has honored his promise to Marjorie, we're going back to Houston, and you'll always be welcome visitors."

"There's something we need to do before we leave here," Hunt said, and pulled out that paper he'd found—the one their father made them sign.

"Any one of you happened to have a cigarette lighter on you?" he asked.

"I do," Junior said. He took it out of his pocket and handed it to Hunt.

Hunt got down on his knees at the shore, wadded up that oath Parnell Knox had made them sign, and set it on fire.

They stood in silence, watching the last bit of the secret going up in smoke.

When there was nothing left of it but ashes, the brothers and sisters shared one last embrace, and then got in their cars and went their separate ways. Birdie caught a ride back with Emma, who took her to get her car, leaving Hunt and Ava to go home on their own.

Hunt could hardly grasp what had just occurred, but like Junior, the truth had set him free.

"Thank you for being there," Hunt said. "You added that last bit of confirmation to Dad's real personality. He was a sonofabitch, and none of us are responsible for that."

"I think of Marjorie…living with all that anger," Ava said. "I never said anything to any of the others after she was hospitalized. But at first, she was really resentful that she had gotten lung cancer because she never smoked."

"But Dad did," Hunt said. "She was a victim of secondhand smoke."

"And your daddy's mean streak," Ava said. "I saw him blow smoke in her face all the time and then laugh when she coughed."

Hunt paled. "Did we just not see that, or were we so used to it we didn't see it for the subtle abuse that it was?"

"I don't know. Maybe I noticed it because neither of my parents smoked. You know?"

Hunt nodded. "Yes, that makes sense," and then he reached for her hand, lifted it to his lips and kissed it as he drove. "Ava Ruth, you are my saving grace."

She shivered from the feel of his lips on her skin, remembering.

CHAPTER 15

IT WAS FULL-ON DARK BY THE TIME HUNT AND AVA GOT BACK TO town, but the streetlights lit the way home. Hunt pulled up into her driveway.

"After all that's gone on, do you still want to come in?" Ava asked.

The ring in his pocket was a reminder of what was yet to come.

"After all that's gone on, you are still the light in my life. I feel like I have a bad taste in my mouth, and I need a taste of something sweet to take it away."

"I have pie," Ava said, and got out.

"That's not what I had in mind," Hunt said.

Ava laughed as they got out and went inside, but the moment the door closed behind them, Ava wrapped her arms around his neck and kissed him.

"Was that sweet enough?" she asked.

"Always," Hunt said. "How do you feel about a sleepover?"

Ava smiled. "I feel good about that. I have new toothbrushes, but do you need to go home and get your jammies?"

"I don't own any," he said.

"My kind of man," Ava said. "Follow me."

"To the ends of the earth," Hunt said, turning out lights as they went.

When they reached the bedroom, Hunt took off his jacket, got the ring out of the pocket, and turned around.

Ava was sitting by the window, the blinds already drawn, taking off her boots one at a time. As she leaned over, her hair fell forward, momentarily hiding her face. It wasn't until she straightened up that she realized Hunt was watching her.

She smiled.

"You look like a man with a secret. What's going on?"

He shook his head. "No secrets between us, remember? I never said the actual words 'marry me,' but I'm saying them now. Ava Ruth Ridley, I love you to forever and back. Will you marry me?"

Ava sighed. She'd heard Hunt say these words a thousand times in her dreams, but never awake and aloud. When he got down on one knee in front of her chair, then opened the box, she gasped.

"Yes, yes, a thousand times yes! Oh, Hunt, it's beautiful."

Hunt held his breath as he began to put it on her finger, and then relaxed when it slid right on.

Ava smiled. "It fits! How did you—" Then she stopped and looked at it more closely. Tears welled. "Oh, Hunt. This was Marjorie's ring, wasn't it?"

He nodded. "Emma had it. She gave it to me this morning. She knew we were serious, but she didn't know about you going to Houston with me until you told them. She said Marjorie loved you like a daughter. It was time to pass it on."

Ava leaned forward, wrapped her arms around his neck, and kissed him.

"I keep reminding myself this is no longer a dream. This is my reality. I never thought I'd see you again, and now I'm going to spend the rest of my life with you. I am blessed."

"I'm the one who's blessed," Hunt said. "You took the loneliness out of my life with your love and laughter. I can't wait to get you to Houston and show you my world."

Hunt stood, then pulled her to her feet and began undressing her, then himself. When he stretched out beside her in bed, all she was still wearing were the ring and a smile.

———

At Ruby's request, Peanut brought a hamburger and fries to Donna's house while Ruby was still there, and as soon as he brought it to the door, Ruby began gathering up the notes she and Donna had made.

"You go sit down and eat something. Even if it's only a few bites, you'll feel better," Ruby said. "In the meantime, I'm going to get busy on all of this, and I'll keep you in the loop. When you get a firm date for leaving Blessings, let me know, okay?"

"Yes, I will, and thank you for all the help, and thank Peanut for the food. You don't know how much I appreciate it," Donna said.

Moments later, they were gone, leaving Donna with a sack of food and the silence of her house.

She went to the kitchen, put her food on a plate, and sat down to eat. A short while later, her phone rang. She took it out of her pocket, saw who was calling, and pushed her food away.

"Hello? Joy?" Donna said.

Her sister's voice was high-pitched and frantic. "Honey, I was fretting all day because I forgot my phone when I went to work. Then I get home and hear this message, and I'm just sick that I wasn't here when you need me! What's wrong?"

"Oh, Sister, the worst. Today, there was a fire at the feed store where Arnold works. Somehow he got trapped. He's dead, Joy."

Joy wailed. "No, no, I'm so sorry. This is horrible, terrible. What can we do to help? Are the boys okay?"

And that's when Donna lost it.

"No, they're not okay. They got arrested last week, attempting to rob a man and steal his car. It nearly killed me and Arnold, and they're gone. Transported off somewhere today."

Joy gasped. "What? You aren't serious?"

"Yes, I am, and we never saw this coming. I've never been so disappointed in them in my life. And then today this happened. I want to come home. I can't be here alone. I just want to come home."

Joy burst into tears, crying now along with her sister. "We'll all get together and clean up Mama's empty house and make sure everything is in order…nothing leaking…and we'll chip in and get the utilities turned on for you."

"I can pay you back for that," Donna said. "The people here in

Blessings are raising some money to help me get home. There are good people here, but without Arnold, I won't stay."

"What about the boys? Where will they take them?" Joy asked.

"I don't know and I don't care. They were already running away from home when they got arrested, so as far as I'm concerned, they were the ones who left us. I'll call you again when I know more, but I just wanted you to know about Arnold."

"I'm so sorry. I wish I was there to help you," Joy said.

"I'm not going through this alone here, but I want to be with my family when this is done. I'll call you soon," Donna said.

"We love you, Donna. We'll be happy to have you home. Take care of yourself."

"I will," Donna said, and disconnected.

Hearing her sister's voice had given Donna a measure of peace, and for today, it was enough.

She threw away the food that was left, then locked up the house. And for the first time in the twenty-two years of her married life, she went to bed alone.

———————

It was the weight of Hunt's arm across Ava's waist that woke her to the fact it was morning and her alarm hadn't gone off. She hadn't remembered to set it.

Panicked, she opened her eyes, glanced at the time, and then relaxed. It was exactly 5:00 a.m., and the beautiful man behind her, holding her close, was still sleeping. She glanced at the ring on her finger and sighed.

Then Hunt's hands moved from her waist to her breasts, and she knew he was awake. Lust stirred, and she rolled over onto her back and closed her eyes as he moved between her legs.

What an absolutely perfect way to wake up.

They made love with a slow, perfect passion, and then later parted company in haste, with Ava speeding to the hospital and Hunt going back to the house. Things were moving at a steady pace, but still not fast enough for Hunt. He wanted this over. He was ready to take Ava home.

Hunt and Ava weren't the only people in Blessings who were having a good morning.

Junior Knox woke up happy. Last night's revelation at the lake had changed his world. The moment the alarm went off, he jumped up and hurried off to shower and shave, then made himself some breakfast. He had places to go today and wanted to look his best.

Because of the fire, he didn't know if Birdie would be working, but he gave her a call anyway, knowing she would always take time to talk to him.

She answered on the second ring.

"Hello? Junior? Is everything okay?"

"Hi, Birdie. Yes, everything is fine. I wasn't sure if you would be home or back at work."

"No, we're closed down for a few days until Dub can get everything cleaned up and get in some new inventory. We're moving things around inside the main building to make room until the warehouse can be rebuilt."

"I'm sure sorry about all that," Junior said.

"I am, too," Birdie said. "So what's going on?"

"I have a couple of questions and thought you might know how to get me started. Do you know if there's any place here in Blessings where a guy could go to classes to get a GED?" Junior asked.

It was the last thing Birdie expected to come out of his mouth, but the best news ever.

"Junior! I'm so proud of you! Yes. Go to the library. Talk to the librarian. I know they have classes there, but I'm not sure how it all works. I don't know whether you have to wait and start with a new class or if you can just start at any time."

"Do you know what it costs?" he asked.

"I think they're free. And I think they're online. The library has a couple of meeting rooms, and I think the people meet in one of those."

"Thanks. Oh… If you hear of any jobs in town, let me know. I'm going to apply at the Crown first. I don't care if all I do is sack groceries. I got a lot of catching up to do."

"I will, Junior. I promise. Good luck, and keep me posted."

"I will, Sister. Love you."

Birdie sighed. "Love you too."

While Junior was on his way to the Crown, Ray was already on the roof at his mother's house, laying new shingles with the crew. This would be their final day of work and he wanted to do it right.

Every now and then he caught a glimpse of Hunt moving in and out of the house below and thought, *When I grow up, I want to be like him.*

It was a fact that the Knox brothers had aged after Hunt was gone, but emotionally, they were all still back in their teens and in the trauma of that day, still the scared and horrified kids caught up in the sins of their father.

Only now, after the secret had come to light and the truth was known, were they finally free to heal. And in that moment, standing on top of the house that had harbored the secret and looking up at the clear blue sky, Ray felt all the possibilities life had waiting.

Emma was going through an evolution of her own. She had decided last night as she was watching Gordon sleep that she was taking the secret of her baby to the grave. He didn't need to know, and Hunt had already declared that as far as her siblings were concerned, that was her story, and hers only, to tell.

Finding out that Mark Ryman did not die in their kitchen had been the release she'd needed to forgive herself. God would do the rest. All she knew, and would be forever grateful for, was that Hunt and Mama had saved them all.

———————

It was just after 10:00 a.m. when Junior walked into the Crown and headed straight for the customer service desk.

Wilson Turner, the manager, was back on duty sporting a swollen nose and two black eyes, but he was alive to tell the tale of how it happened, and he would heal.

"Morning, Wilson," Junior said. "Heard about your accident. Good to see you back on the job."

Wilson grimaced. "Thanks, Junior. It was quite a wild ride. What can I do for you?"

"I'd like a job application, please."

"For yourself?" Wilson asked.

Junior nodded. "Yes, sir. And I don't mind what I do. I just want to work. I'm going to be going to night school to get my GED, so I'll need daytime hours, wherever I work."

Wilson turned around and got an application out of a drawer behind him, then handed it over.

"It appears you have a purpose in mind," Wilson said.

Junior nodded. "Yes, sir. If it's okay with you, I'll be bringing this right back as soon as I get it done."

"Sure," Wilson said, and then watched him leave. He didn't know what had transpired to make it happen, but Junior Knox had obviously experienced some kind of revelation.

Maybe it was the loss of his mother that had prompted him to change, but whatever it was, he wanted to be the first person in Blessings to give the young man a chance.

About thirty minutes later, Junior came back in with his application and met a young woman carrying a baby, who was going out.

"Morning," Junior said.

The young woman looked startled that he'd spoken, and then nodded shyly and kept walking.

Junior didn't know her name, but he knew she lived in the Bottoms and had been part of the big renovation that had happened there.

He hurried back to the service desk and handed the application to Wilson.

"Here you go, Wilson, and thanks."

"Sure thing," Wilson said.

"Oh, who was that young woman who just left? She was carrying a little boy. She lives in the Bottoms."

"Oh, you must mean Barrie Lemons. She has two kids. One school age, and then the little guy. She was having a rough go of it until Cathy Terry rebuilt all those houses."

"Yeah, my brother Ray helped roof some of those houses," Junior said. "Well, I'd better get going. Thanks again."

He started to walk off and Wilson called him back.

"Hey, Junior?"

Junior stopped and turned around. "Yes, sir?"

"Can you start work tomorrow?"

Junior's eyes widened. "Yes, sir!"

"It's stocking shelves and sacking groceries. Forty-hour week. Pay is ten-fifty per hour. Payday is every two weeks. Two days off. Time and a half for overtime…if you want it."

Junior felt like crying.

He walked back to the customer service desk, his voice shaking.

"I didn't expect this, but I sure appreciate it," he said.

Wilson shrugged. "I'm taking a chance here and we both know it. Don't let me down."

Junior kept nodding. "I won't, sir. I won't let you down."

"From 6:00 a.m. to 3:00 p.m., with an hour off for lunch. We'll go through the routine tomorrow morning after you clock in. Just come to the service desk first and we'll get you started."

"Thank you, Wilson. Thank you so much. I won't let you down, I promise."

Junior walked out in disbelief. It was a sign. This was it. The chance he'd been waiting for. He had a purpose. And he had a freaking job. By the time he got back in his car, he felt like crying, but he laughed instead. Next stop, the Blessings library to find out about classes for getting his GED.

He pulled up in the parking lot, then sat for a couple of moments, thinking about how hard this was going to be. He hadn't studied anything but the bottom of a beer bottle since dropping out of school, but getting a high school diploma was something he wanted to do.

He pocketed his keys as he got out, and started walking toward the steps of the library. There was sunlight in his eyes, and for the first time in fifteen years, there was peace in his heart.

"I'm doing this, Mama. I'm going to make you proud."

───────

Ava's engagement ring was the new talk of the ER, and as word spread throughout the hospital, the questions about her relationship with Hunt Knox began to change.

Rhonda Bailey, one of the nurses she worked in the ER with, was the first one to ask.

"Where are you and Hunt going to live? Are you living in his mother's house? Is that why he's fixing it up?"

Ava shook her head. "No. It was in her will that they sell it and divide the money among all five of the kids."

"Ah, so where are you going to live, then?" Rhonda asked.

"Houston. When Hunt leaves, I'm going with him."

Rhonda's expression fell. "Oh…I was afraid you were going to say something like that. You know I wish you guys all the best, but I sure am going to hate to see you go. I love working with you."

"And I love working with you. I love Blessings. It will always be my hometown, but my home is wherever Hunt is. I've loved him forever."

Rhonda smiled. "Then I'm happy for you, but you better be telling the powers that be that you're leaving so they can start interviewing for replacements. With both you and Hope Talbot gone, we could find ourselves shorthanded in emergencies."

"You're right, and I will," Ava said. "I'll check in with personnel during my lunch hour and let them know."

"What do Larry and Karen think about you leaving?" Rhonda asked.

Ava grinned. "Oh, you know how Mom and Dad are. They're happy for us, and they love to travel. Houston will just be one more place they have an excuse to visit."

While news about Ava's imminent exit from Blessings began to spread through the hospital, there was also good news spreading through Blessings regarding Davey Randolph, the little boy Hunt had flown to Savannah. He had been taken from the critical list and moved from the ICU into a regular hospital room, and with permission from his parents, his first visitor was Richard Borden—penitent and begging forgiveness.

CHAPTER 16

THREE DAYS LATER, THE KNOX FAMILY HAD FINALLY REMOVED the keepsakes and pictures they wanted from the house, and the roofers had long gone.

The new roof made the house look good, like a woman with a new hairdo. Hunt felt good about the progress. A lot had been done in a short time, and the painters were due tomorrow. Once they had come and gone, the old house would have a new face to go with the new hair.

Hunt had spent days cleaning up and covering up everything that didn't need painting. All of the hardware was removed from drawers and cabinets. The doorknobs were covered up, and windows taped and covered to keep paint off the panes. He'd done everything he could think of to speed up the process, and now it was up to the professional paint crew who would begin work tomorrow.

But today was the yard sale, and there was a line of cars on both sides of the street, with locals digging through what was left of Marjorie Knox's life.

Junior was at his new job, so Emma and Birdie were taking the money, and Ray and Hunt were loading up purchases for the buyers.

There wasn't a thing left inside the house now, and Hunt's bag with his clothing was in the truck. The truck would sell at auction on the same day that they auctioned off the house, so he still had it for now. And at Ava's invitation, he was moving in with her until he was done.

Days ago, Emma had put up signs about the yard sale all over town, and the response today was steady and productive.

The furniture Hunt feared wouldn't even sell went first. Dan Amos bought almost all of it and, with Hunt and Ray's help, loaded it up in a small moving truck and took off to Savannah to have it refinished and reupholstered. He would use it to furnish another rental house.

As for the rest of the items scattered about the yard, they were quickly disappearing.

Once Hunt saw Emma and Birdie in tears, and knew how they felt. It was hard to see people going through their mother's things, talking about the condition, bargaining for a better price, and tossing some of it aside. It felt like they were judging Marjorie, and it hurt. But it was life, and they were doing what she wanted.

By the time Ava got off work at three and came by to check on the progress, everyone had gone home and there wasn't anything left. Hunt was sitting on the tailgate of the truck when she drove up, and got off and came to meet her.

"Hi, darlin'," Hunt said as he gave her a quick hug. "Did you have a busy day?"

"Oh, always," she said. "But it appears you guys did, too. I can't believe it's all gone."

"Dan Amos bought most of the furniture. The rest of the stuff went pretty fast after that," Hunt said.

"Oh, for his rental properties! I never thought of that," Ava said. "So, what's the plan? Do you want to bring your Harley and the pickup to my house, or what?"

"Since you offered, I'll follow you home on the Harley, then when you bring me back, I'll get the truck and stop by the bank to deposit the money from the yard sale before I come back to your house."

"Sure thing," Ava said. "I'll go home and open the garage. I never park in it because I use it for storage, but there's plenty of room to park the bike."

"Great," Hunt said. "I'll just lock up the house and be right there."

Ava got in her car and headed home. A couple of minutes after her arrival, Hunt pulled up and rode the bike into the garage, then they went back to get the truck.

As soon as Ava stopped in the drive, Hunt leaned over and kissed her.

"See you in a few."

"I can't wait," Ava said. "Finally, we'll be living under the same roof."

"Practicing for the real thing," he said, and then he was out and striding toward the truck.

Ava began her usual ritual once she was home, stripping off the work scrubs at the washer and going to shower.

By the time Hunt arrived, she was in old jeans and a long-sleeved T-shirt and barefoot. Her long hair was clipped up on the top of her head, and she was at the kitchen table having pop and cookies and going through her mail.

He came in the back door, pausing in the doorway to admire the view. When she looked up and caught him watching her, she waved toward the refrigerator.

"Beer and pop in the fridge, and I saved you some cookies."

Hunt was still in awe that this beautiful woman not only loved him but was going to marry him. He wanted to pick her up in his arms and take her to bed. Instead, he got a Coke and grabbed a couple of cookies as he sat down.

"What was your take at the yard sale?" Ava asked.

Hunt unscrewed the lid from his pop and took a drink. "About fifteen hundred dollars, which was surprising considering how old and worn out the stuff was, but you know what they say… 'One man's trash is another man's treasure.' What about your day?" he asked.

She shrugged. "The normal ER stuff: stitches, staples, and broken bones. Oh… But there was one positive development. Vince Lewis and family checked out today. They airlifted the mother and new baby back to an Atlanta hospital, while he had to finish the trip home alone."

"He didn't cause any more trouble for you?" Hunt asked.

She shook her head and brushed the cookie crumbs from her hands.

"No, but I'm glad he's gone. His wife seemed really sweet and totally oblivious to what a jerk he is. I hope he straightens up and treats her right, but I sure wouldn't bet my life on that happening." Then she picked up a cookie and gave Hunt a bite. "I would, however, bet my life on you."

That vow was so touching, and so unexpected, that it was all Hunt could do to chew and swallow, and then he reached for her hand.

"I would never betray you."

Ava started to smile and then saw the expression on his face.

"Oh, honey." She got up and plopped down in his lap and put her arms around his neck. "I know that. I know you. Remember? I've been in your corner for as long as I can remember knowing you existed. I love you. So much. I know how hard it was for you to come back. To face the rejection of your family. To bury your mother. To keep a promise that was hard to make. You are, to me, what being a man is all about. And you're mine. Okay?"

She made him want to cry. Instead, he kissed the length of her neck, from the hollow at the base of her throat to her chin. Then he cupped her face with his hands and leaned forward until their foreheads were touching.

He could feel the warmth of her breath and the flutter of her eyelashes against his cheeks.

"Lord, woman. I thought flying was the closest I would ever be to God, but loving you tops it all," Hunt said, and then he kissed her.

———————

Hunt and Ava spent a quiet evening at home. Without the pressure of wanting to be in two places at once, he was at peace. Ava was watching TV and reading the local paper while Hunt was in the shower, and when he came back to the living room minus a shirt and wearing his old sweatpants, she looked up and smiled.

"Squeaky clean and sexy as hell. If you could bottle that, you'd be rich," she said.

Hunt grinned. "It's a thought. So what's in the paper?" he asked.

"Um, for starters, it appears there's going to be a dance and a silent auction at the country club to raise money for Arnold Hollis's widow. She wants to go home to West Virginia. That's where the rest of her family lives."

Hunt was silent for a few moments, thinking. "Isn't it weird what death does to us? I came back to where I was born because of a death, and Mrs. Hollis is doing the same thing, going home to where she was born because of a death. Some people think of home as the house they live in, but it's always been about the people to me, and it appears Mrs. Hollis feels the same way. My home will always be with you, no matter where we are in the world."

"Thank you, darling," Ava said.

Hunt smiled. "You're welcome. And on another note, I forgot Blessings even had a country club."

Ava laughed. "I know. It's to go with the golf course. Really, the only difference between them and us is the amount of money in their pockets. And for the rest of us, Ruby Butterman has also organized what sounds like a fun event that's happening on Sunday after church. She's calling it Potluck at the Park. You buy tickets ahead of time, and then everyone brings covered dishes. They'll be laid out buffet-style all over the park. Turn in your ticket and you get a plate and eat to your heart's content. I'm off on Sunday. That's where we need to go to eat dinner."

"I'm in for that one," Hunt said. "The dance at the country club, not so much."

"Why? I know you can dance. I've seen you," Ava said.

Hunt grinned. "Teaching Emma how to dance with a boy does not constitute being a good dancer. She kept trying to lead. Mom made me teach her."

Ava nodded. "I know. I saw part of it. Then my mother came and picked me up and I had to go home. I was jealous of Emma for days because you danced with her and not me."

Hunt's eyes widened. "Good lord. First of all, you can't be jealous of my sister, and at that point, how old were you anyway?"

Ava grinned. "Not nearly old enough for the thoughts I'm sure I had."

"But you're old enough now," Hunt said. "And I'm so going to take advantage of that."

———————

The next morning, Ava left for work with the smile Hunt had put on her face, and Hunt felt like the luckiest man in the world as he went to meet the painters. He was sitting on the porch steps when they drove up.

The PaintByNumber.com logo on the side of the truck made him smile because their phone number was included within the design. A sense of humor was never a bad thing.

Their long ladders were fastened onto the racks over the truck bed, and paint sprayers, equipment, and cans of paint were in the bed beneath it. While they were getting out, another truck with two more men pulled in behind them.

"Morning," Hunt said, eyeing the paint-speckled coveralls the men were wearing.

"Morning. I'm Bill Smith. These are my sons, Herman, Carl, and Glen. Are you Hunt Knox?"

Hunt nodded. "Yes, sir, I'm Hunt. Want to do a walk-through before you start unloading?"

"Absolutely," Bill said. "Come on, boys. Let's go see what we need to do to make this old girl pretty again."

Hunt liked the way Bill said that. It made him think they took pride in what they did, and when they followed him inside, they listened intently to everything he said, nodding and taking notes as they went.

When they went up to the attic, Hunt paused. "This was once my bedroom, so I want it finished out just like the rest of the other rooms, even though there's no bathroom up here."

"But there's sure room for one if a person was a mind to add one," Bill said, eyeing all of the work Hunt had already done. "You prepped this up pretty good. It will make our job go faster."

"That was my intent," Hunt said as he led them back downstairs.

Bill waved to his boys. "You know the drill. Start unloading. And leave the paint on the front porch for now. I want Hunt to verify we picked up the right colors before we start work."

"Yes, Daddy," they echoed, as Bill popped the lids on the paint cans.

"This is the exterior color, and this one is for the exterior trim, and the small can is the door color, right?" Bill said.

Hunt checked his order sheet against the color numbers on the paint cans. "Yes."

"And these over here are interior paints. This is for the ceilings and woodwork, and this is the color for the walls. Am I right?" Bill asked.

"Confirmed," Hunt said, and then put his order sheet away. "There's nothing I can do here today except get in the way. If you need me, you have my number. I'll swing by later and see how everything is going."

"Okay," Bill said. "And just so you know, we're starting with the exterior because we have good weather in the forecast."

"You're in charge. Do your thing," Hunt said, and then got in the truck and drove away.

He'd been needing a haircut ever since he rode into town, and now that he was at loose ends for the day, he thought he'd stop by the Curl Up and Dye and see about getting it trimmed.

———

Ruby Butterman had gone in to work early to receive some deliveries and had already turned the Closed sign to Open. She'd taken a load of shop towels from the dryer and was in the act of folding them when the bell over her front door jingled.

Thinking it might be the expected deliveries, she set the basket of unfolded towels aside and started up to the front of the shop, then realized who'd just come in.

"Good morning, Hunt!"

"Morning, Miss Ruby. I was wondering if you had time to trim up my hair a bit sometime today."

"Oh, no more Miss Ruby. That was when you were a boy. From all I've heard about you, I think you've earned the right to be called a man. Just Ruby."

"Yes, ma'am," Hunt said.

She smiled. "As for the haircut, I can do it right now, if you want. I came in early because I'm expecting deliveries and don't have appointments beginning for at least another hour and a half."

"Yes, I do, and I appreciate you working me in," Hunt said.

"Take off your jacket and come on back. You can hang it on that coat-tree there in the corner."

Hunt did as he was told and followed her into the salon area.

Ruby waved at her styling chair. "Sit here long enough for me to get a cape on you so we won't get you all wet, and then we'll move to the shampoo station. After that, you can tell me how much you want cut. And please don't tell me you want all of that pretty dark hair buzzed off, because I think it might make me cry."

Hunt laughed. "I haven't had it buzzed off, as you called it, since basic training."

A couple of minutes later Ruby was washing his hair. Later, they moved back to her chair, and after a few directions from Hunt she began to comb and snip, talking as she worked.

"Did y'all see the notice in the paper about the country club dance?" Ruby asked.

"Yes, Ava told me, but I'm not much of a dancer. I am, however, a really good eater, and that Potluck in the Park sounded like it was right up my alley. I hope the weather holds for you. January in Georgia is iffy."

Ruby laughed. "Oh… Me and weather have an understanding when I need something done. Everyone told Peanut and me not to have our wedding in the park because it might rain. Even Peanut was a little anxious. But I knew it would be okay and did it anyway. Weather was perfect, and it's going to be again."

Hunt grinned. "So you're saying never underestimate the power of a woman with a purpose?"

"Something like that," Ruby said.

"Then I'm going to assume it's perfect weather, too," Hunt said.

Ruby combed and snipped. "Awesome!" she said. "I have some tickets here at the shop. If you want, you can buy them today."

"Yes, I want," Hunt said. "Don't let me forget them before I leave."

"I won't," Ruby said.

A few minutes later, Vera and Vesta Conklin came in the back door, fussing about which one of them was at fault for forgetting the lunches they'd packed, when they saw Hunt. And just like that, the frowns on their faces slid off like butter on hot bread and they were all smiles.

"Well, hello there," Vesta said.

"My good morning just got better," Vera added.

Hunt grinned. He remembered the Conklin twins.

"Morning, girls. It's nice to see you again," Hunt said.

"It's nice to see you, too," Vera said. "You were always a cute boy, but you grew up to be a fine-looking man. We're real sorry about your mama."

"Yes, ma'am. Thank you," Hunt said.

They just stood there staring, admiring his dark hair and blue eyes, although they couldn't help but notice how fine his body had filled out in the years he'd been gone.

Ruby paused. "Girls, I didn't get that last load of towels folded. Would you mind finishing them up for me?"

They both blinked and then realized they'd just been redirected.

"What? Oh! Sure thing, Ruby. We'll get right on that," Vesta said.

They gave Hunt one last lingering look, and then took off their jackets and went to work.

Ruby was still cutting his hair when the delivery man showed up, and the twins immediately switched focus from folding towels to another man on the premises.

When they went up front to sign for the deliveries, Hunt glanced at Ruby.

"I take it the girls are still single?"

She rolled her eyes and lowered her voice. "Yes, they are, and I know it shows, but there's not a thing I can do about their blatant admiration for the opposite sex."

Hunt grinned. "Not a thing wrong with that. I admire the opposite of my sex, too."

Ruby giggled. "Like maybe Ava Ridley?"

"Like Ava," Hunt said. "I put a ring on her finger and I'm taking her back to Houston with me."

Ruby squealed. "Are you serious? Oh, that's awesome! We will miss her, but she's such a sweetheart. I'm thrilled that she finally let somebody love her. God knows plenty of men in this town have tried, but she wouldn't give them the time of day."

Hunt smiled in all the right places, but it was relaxing to just sit and listen, absorbing all of the female chatter going on around him and remembering what it had been like growing up in his house. Between his mother, Emma, Birdie, and Ava, there'd always been chatter and giggles. What he didn't remember was any camaraderie between his father and the boys.

Why hadn't he noticed that then? Maybe it was because his mother more than made up for the lack of paternal guidance. Or maybe it was because that dissatisfied, sarcastic, begrudging man was the only father he'd ever known and he didn't know anything different. But he did now.

Then Ruby tapped him on the shoulder and turned him around to face the mirror.

"Okay, Hunt, what do you think? I'm calling it quits unless you want more taken off the length," Ruby said.

Hunt eyed the cut and gave her a thumbs-up.

"Nailed it," he said. "What do I owe you?"

Ruby grinned. "We'll settle up front, and I'll get you those potluck tickets, too."

Vesta and Vera were folding towels but looked up long enough to giggle and tell him goodbye.

Hunt nodded and smiled. "Ladies," he said, and grabbed his jacket on the way up front to pay for the haircut and tickets, and then he was gone.

Hunt checked his phone to make sure he hadn't missed a call or text from the painters, and then swung by the Crown to pick up some groceries for Ava. It would give him a chance to see Junior in action, and a little brotherly pat on the back for a job well done was always a good thing.

He pulled into the parking lot at the Crown and as he did, he saw Elliot Graham walking toward his car and jumped out to catch him before he drove off.

Elliot was putting groceries in the trunk of his car when he heard footsteps behind him and turned around.

"Hello, Hunt. It's good to see you again," Elliot said.

Hunt eyed the old man in disbelief. He hadn't aged a bit since he'd seen him last. Still a little on the thin side. Still had that thick shock of white hair and eyes with a hint of sparkle. And to Hunt, he still looked a little bit like a fairy king.

"It's good to see you, too," Hunt said. "I wanted to thank you for delivering that message to us from Mom. It has changed all of our lives for the better."

Elliot shrugged. "As I told Birdie, I did nothing but deliver a message, but I was happy to do it, and I am gratified to know of the impact it has had on all of you."

"Thanks again," Hunt said.

Elliot smiled. "You're most welcome." Then he paused. His eyes got a faraway look in them as he tilted his head sideways, then he blinked and looked back at Hunt. "She'll die and be reborn, so don't quit."

Hunt forgot to breathe, then took a step forward.

"What do you mean? Who dies? Reborn how? Quit on what?"

Elliot shrugged. "It's just what they told me to say. They said you'll remember it when the time comes, and you'll know what to do."

Then he smiled, patted Hunt's arm, and got in his car and drove away.

Hunt was too shocked to move and too afraid to acknowledge the scenarios running through his head. Then he saw Junior come hurrying out of the Crown to the cart stall, shook off the feeling of dread, and jogged across the parking lot as Junior began pushing a row of carts back inside.

"Hey, Hunt!" Junior said when his brother appeared beside him.

"Hi, Junior. Looks like you're doing a good job here."

Junior grinned. "You should know. You did this job all the way through high school, right?"

"Yes, I did. Keep up the good work. I've got to pick up a few things for Ava, and then go check on the painters."

Junior nodded, then pushed the carts back into place inside before pulling one off for Hunt.

"Here you go, and tell Ava I said hi."

"Thanks. I will," Hunt said, then took the shopping cart and headed to the dairy case at the far side of the store.

While he was shopping, he felt a tap on his back and turned to see Ava's mother with a big smile on her face.

"Hi, darlin'," she said.

"Hi, Karen. What's for supper?" he asked.

Karen giggled. "Anything you want. What time you want to come over?"

Hunt grinned and shook his head. "I was just teasing with you. I have no idea what time I'll be free this evening. I have painters at the house, and my day won't be over until they go home. I did, however, move into my future wife's house last night because we sold the bed I'd been sleeping in at Mom's."

Karen laughed. "That's a weak excuse to take my daughter to bed."

Hunt smiled. "At least I waited until she grew up. I honestly never knew any of this was going on when she was a kid."

Karen shook her head. "Larry and I thought it was funny…at first. We had no idea it was serious to her. And then the older she became, the more you mattered in her world. When you left, and then everyone shut down and wouldn't talk about you anymore, she grieved as if you'd died. We thought she would finally get over you, but she has proved us all wrong. The best part is finally getting you in the family."

Hunt was so touched, he hugged her. "Thank you, but I'm the lucky one. Tell Larry hi for me, and you guys will have to come over and see the house after it's finished."

"Can't wait," she said. "Love to the both of you."

"Thanks," Hunt said, and finished shopping with a smile on his face. It was amazing what being loved could do to a man.

He took the groceries back to Ava's and put them up, then went to check on the painters.

Satisfied that all was well, he sent Ava a text, told her he loved her, and he'd see her after work. He was headed downtown to gas up the truck when he began hearing the ambulance sirens and realized they were leaving town in the opposite direction. He said a prayer for whoever was in need and kept driving.

———————

Skipping lunch was a common occurrence in Ava's occupation, especially in a small hospital like the one in Blessings, and especially working the ER. Emergencies didn't have a schedule, and sick people in the beds upstairs didn't have a routine. So the job and the patients always came before a nurse's hunger pangs.

Ava had a candy bar she'd been eating for over two hours, taking a bite now and then when the free moments presented themselves. But she was thinking about what she would make for supper tonight and hoping Hunt got the hamburger meat she'd put on the grocery list because she wanted spaghetti and meat sauce.

She was entering some data into the computer on the patient they'd just dismissed and trying to finish the rest of her candy when they heard an ambulance coming in.

"Uh-oh," Rhonda Bailey said. "You better chew and swallow that fast. They're back from the wreck site at the two-mile bridge north of Blessings."

Ava quickly hit Save on her work and grabbed some wet wipes to clean her hands. She took a quick drink from her water bottle and then stood. Last they'd heard, there were multiple injuries, so everyone was ready and waiting when they began wheeling in the first of three victims.

The EMTs were rattling off the injuries and stats, and nurses were directing them to different exam rooms. They'd called down two doctors from upstairs to aid Dr. Quick, and Ava was serving as the triage nurse, getting pertinent info, assessing the symptoms, and directing the most seriously injured into exam rooms first. It was steady chaos but nothing they hadn't dealt with before, and then the victims' relatives began coming into the ER, getting in the way, arguing about who'd caused the accident, making it even more difficult for the ER staff to tend to the injured.

Dr. Quick stepped out of an exam room, saw what was going on, and called out, "Ava, call the police."

"Yes, sir," she said, and turned around to go to the phone when one of the men grabbed her by the arm and slung her around, shouting, "You ain't callin' no cops on us!"

At that moment, orderlies came running to Ava's aid.

CHAPTER 17

HUNT WAS AT THE GAS STATION, STANDING BY THE PUMP AND waiting for his tank to fill, when he heard ambulance sirens again. Wherever they'd gone, they hadn't gone far because they were already returning. He thought about Ava and all of the other medical personnel and how important they were to this little town. A part of him felt guilty that she was leaving because of him, but she'd chosen love over location and that was never a bad thing. The hospital could always hire more medical personnel, but there was only one Ava Ridley and she was his.

A man pulled up to the other side of the pumps and got out, nodded to Hunt, and then swiped his credit card and started pumping gas, while the woman with him went inside.

"You're Hunt Knox, ain't ya?" the man said.

Hunt nodded. "Do I know you?"

The man grinned. "Probably not. My name is Moss Payne. I used to play dominoes with your daddy at the Blue Ivy Bar. You have his dark hair, but you got your mama's blue eyes. She was a good woman. My sympathies for your loss."

"Thanks," Hunt said, remembering his daddy's days of coming and going at the Blue Ivy had ended as he got older. Likely because the kids kept coming, making it harder than before to stretch a dollar.

Then the pump kicked off. Hunt replaced the nozzle in the pump and was screwing the gas cap on when Moss's woman came hurrying out of the store, waving her phone.

"Moss! Moss! Willa Jewel, who works in the cafeteria at the hospital, said there's a big fight in the ER. The families of the people who were in the wreck out north of town got into a brawl. She said blood's flying everywhere."

Hunt's gut knotted. *Ava!* "Where are the police?"

The woman shrugged. "Maybe at the crash site. Sometimes it takes a while for the Georgia Highway Patrol to find places like this, and they help out."

Hunt jumped in the truck and headed back up Main, driving as fast as he dared. He didn't know if a hospital the size of Blessings had security officers or if the police were already on the scene, but he had to make sure Ava was okay.

It took him less than two minutes to get from the far end of Main to the ER parking lot, but when he drove up on a number of vehicles parked in all directions and didn't see any police cars on the scene, it made him uneasy.

Hunt jumped out on the run, and as he entered the lobby he could tell by the shouts and screams coming from the ER that the fight was still ongoing.

The receptionist at the front desk was wide-eyed and in a panic.

"Where are the police?" Hunt asked.

"They were at the wreck, all except for one officer who was already out on another call. He's on his way here now, and the others are coming in from out of town."

"What's the fight about?" Hunt asked.

"A boy from the Ryman family was running off to get married to a girl from the Dillon family. Pete Dillon took off chasing them, and that caused the wreck."

Hunt's eyes narrowed. Ryman? As in Tall Man's family? What were the odds? He didn't know what he was walking into, but Ava's welfare took precedence over any hesitance he had in interfering with police business.

He took off in long, angry strides, hit the doors with the flat of his hands, and walked right into a melee.

Orderlies were trying to keep the angry family members away from the exam rooms where doctors were tending to victims. Rhonda Bailey was behind the nurses' desk with blood on her cheek and a small cut over her eye, and another nurse was crying.

Two grown men were fighting with each other, and two females with them were screaming and cursing and pulling each other's hair.

Then Hunt saw Ava, pinned against the wall by another man. She was arguing with him and struggling, trying to get free. Every fighting instinct the army had instilled in Hunt kicked in, and he began wading through the melee, punching and shoving, trying to get to her.

One of the men turned to swing at him, and when he did Hunt hit him in the chin with an uppercut. The man's eyes rolled back in his head. He fell backward onto the floor and didn't get up.

The other man came at Hunt from the right, so caught up in the bloodlust of battle that it didn't even dawn on him that his "enemy" was now unconscious on the floor.

Hunt hit him in the nose with his first punch, and then the side of his jaw with his second. The man fell to his knees, both hands over his face, moaning, "You broke my nose!"

The women who'd been screaming and cursing were suddenly silent, standing there in shock and staring at Hunt.

The man who had Ava pinned became aware of the silence and turned around, saw his brother on the floor, and then shouted at Hunt.

"Who the hell are you?" he asked.

That's when Hunt realized who he was. Josh Ryman. Tall Man Ryman's brother. What the hell were the odds of their families butting heads like this again?

Then Hunt saw the fear on Ava's face and started walking toward her, his hands doubled into fists, his gaze fixed on Josh's face.

"I'm Hunt Knox, and you, Josh Ryman, have your hands on my woman. I'm going to give you about ten seconds to turn her loose or there won't be enough left of you for the doctors to put back together."

Ryman's eyes widened. "She was going to call the police!" he said.

Hunt was getting closer. "Three seconds, dammit, or let her go."

"For the love of God, Josh! We already called the police," Rhonda said.

"Fine!" Josh shouted, then turned Ava loose.

She staggered, trying to catch her balance, while Josh turned his rage on someone else and began cursing and shouting at the Dillon family.

Ava grabbed at the wall to steady herself and started running toward Hunt. All she wanted was to be out of this mess.

Ryman only saw the movement from the corner of his eye. In the heat of the moment, and thinking it was an orderly going to take him down, he turned and swung, hitting Ava in the chest so hard she flew backward into the wall.

Hunt saw her gasp, grab at her chest, and then she was down. And in that moment, Hunt remembered Elliot's message.

She'll die and be reborn. Don't quit.

"No! No, you stupid bastard! What have you done?" Hunt shouted, and ran to her.

Ryman was horrified and instantly abject and holding up his hands and walking backward. "I didn't mean to hit her! I didn't know it was her!"

Hunt pushed past him, and then dropped down beside Ava's body and rolled her over, frantically searching for a pulse. There was none.

"She's not breathing!" he shouted. "Is there a defibrillator?"

"Just one, and they're using it trying to keep the Dillon girl alive," Rhonda Bailey said.

"Jesus help me," Hunt muttered and started chest compressions. "Tell them we need it!" he shouted and kept pushing.

Josh Ryman was in tears, and the families who'd been fighting were staring in horror at what they had unwittingly caused. The brawl was over, but for the injured girl who'd just lost the baby she was carrying, the fight to stay alive was still ongoing.

Hunt was still doing CPR when Rhonda came running back. She dropped to her knees beside him and began to help.

When the police arrived, Hunt was barely aware of what was happening behind him. His focus was completely on Ava. Her lips were blue now. Her skin had no color. He hadn't been this scared the day he and his gunner were shot down, but he hadn't quit on life then and he wasn't going to quit on hers now.

Chief Pittman began arresting the people who'd been fighting, then hauling them out.

But Hunt kept hearing Elliot's warning.

Don't quit. Don't quit.

The words echoed in his head as he continued with compressions. One minute ran into two, then three, then four, and Hunt was too scared now to stop because that would mean giving her up to God.

Don't quit. Don't quit.

All of a sudden there was a rush of people coming out of ER, and Dr. Quick issuing clipped, decisive orders. They lifted Ava up onto a gurney and rolled her into the last empty exam room on the floor.

Nurses began cutting away Ava's clothing and attaching the leads to the electrodes that were connected to the heart monitor. Another nurse came running, pushing the defibrillator into the room, and moments later it was charging.

Hunt was shaking from the tension of what he'd been doing and panic was setting in.

Don't quit me, Ava. Please God, don't quit me, baby. Come back. Please come back.

"Clear!" the doctor yelled, and slapped the paddles to her chest.

Her body bucked from the shock, but the monitor still registered a flat line.

They charged it again, and again the doctor yelled, "Clear!" and hit her with the paddles one more time.

They stepped back, watching for a heartbeat, and then Ava gasped. The monitor registered a beep, and then a series of erratic beeps, and then all of a sudden there was a heartbeat, and all Hunt could think was *Thank you, God.*

"I've got a pulse!" Rhonda cried.

They put her on oxygen and started an IV, making sure that each heartbeat was followed by the next.

Dr. Quick turned to Hunt. Now that Ava had a heartbeat, he wanted to know what had caused it to stop.

"Somebody...just tell me what the hell happened?" he asked.

"She took a hard blow to her chest," Hunt said. "I saw her gasp, grab her chest, and drop. When I got to her, she wasn't breathing. I think the blow stopped her heart."

Quick began ordering X-rays to check for broken bones.

"When will she wake up?" Hunt asked.

"I don't know, but the important thing right now is that she has a heartbeat. I'll know more later."

"I need to call her parents," Hunt said, then took Ava's phone from the pocket of the scrub top she'd been wearing and stepped out into the hall to make the call.

Karen answered, thinking it was her daughter.

"Hi, honey!"

"Karen, it's me, Hunt. I'm calling to let you guys know there was a fight in the ER. Ava got hurt."

"Oh my God! Are you there?"

"Yes. We're still in the ER."

"Dear lord, what happened? Is she bleeding? Last time this happened she got stitches."

"No, ma'am. She's not bleeding. I'll tell you about it after you get here, okay?"

"We're on the way," Karen said.

Hunt put Ava's phone in his pocket and went back into the room. Dr. Quick was still checking vital signs and waiting for the portable X-ray to come in.

"Her parents are on the way."

Quick nodded. "Her blood pressure is coming up. Her pulse is getting stronger. Her pupils are reactive."

"This is good, right?" Hunt asked.

"Yes, this is good."

"She needed a defibrillator. Rhonda said you only had the one," Hunt said.

"Small hospital. Few luxuries here. We only have one and were trying to resuscitate one of the victims they brought in. Your CPR saved Ava's life," Quick said.

"What about your patient?" Hunt asked.

"We didn't save the baby she was carrying, but we saved her," Quick said.

"Then it happened the way it was meant to happen," Hunt said. "Will Ava stay here, or will she have to be transported somewhere?"

"She's stable here. Right now, we don't know what all we're dealing with, so moving her wouldn't be wise. I need to see X-rays and then we'll go from there."

"Then I'll be here with her," Hunt said.

Quick smiled. "I expected that. We'll be moving her upstairs soon."

"Her parents are on the way," Hunt said.

"They'll be fine. I don't expect them to cause a fight. And I understand we have you to thank for ending the other one. Our orderlies were having a terrible time keeping the families out of the exam rooms, too. That's what started the fight in the first place."

"I wasn't trying to be a hero. I was just trying to get to Ava. They were in the way," Hunt said.

"A little military coming out in a time of need?"

Hunt shrugged. "Maybe. It was a knee-jerk reaction to the fear on Ava's face. If that young couple that they brought in survives and gets married, they're both going to have the in-laws from hell."

"Maybe this incident gave all of them a reality check. Anyway, they can be mad all they want somewhere else, and tonight, that will be locked up beside each other in the Blessings jail."

Before Hunt could respond, Ava's parents appeared in the doorway of her room. Dr. Quick stopped them, then walked them back out in the hall. Two nurses were tending to Ava and monitoring her condition, so Hunt followed the doctor out into the hall and walked into the middle of the conversation with Ava's parents.

Karen Ridley was trying not to panic, but the fact that they hadn't let her and Larry see Ava had scared her.

"Dr. Quick! How is she?"

"She's alive but unconscious."

"What happened?" Larry asked.

Quick looked at Hunt. "You didn't tell them?"

"I was going to after they got here," Hunt said.

Karen's eyes widened in sudden fear. "Tell us what?"

"Ava was taken hostage during the fight," Hunt said.

Quick frowned. "I told her to call the police because the families were arguing loudly, disturbing the other patients, and then I went back to my patient, unaware that one of the men took her hostage to keep her from calling."

"But what happened to her?" Karen asked.

"I didn't see it. I'll let Hunt explain."

Hunt shrugged. "I was pumping gas when I heard there was a fight in the ER. I came to check on Ava and walked into a brawl. Josh Ryman had her pinned against the wall and wouldn't let her go. I sort of threatened him with dismemberment if he didn't turn her loose. He dropped his hold, and then the families began arguing again, and when Ava started toward me Josh thought it was someone coming at him from behind and swung his fist as he turned. He hit her hard...really hard...in the chest. She flew back. Hit the wall and then dropped. Basically, the blow stopped her heart. By the time I got to her, she didn't have a pulse. I did CPR. Scared the hell out of me. It was about four minutes of that before they had a defibrillator free, and then once they used it they got a heartbeat. She's breathing on her own, but they have her on oxygen."

Karen began to sob and threw herself into Hunt's arms. "You saved her life. Oh my God...Oh, Hunt. You saved her life."

"We all did," he said.

Dr. Quick glanced back in the room and then added, "We'll be moving her upstairs soon, but you can go in and see her now. There's no way to know if she can hear what's being said, so don't say anything that might frighten her."

They nodded in unison and went inside.

Hunt followed them into Ava's room and, once more, stood at the foot of the bed while her parents took up posts on either side.

Karen smoothed hair away from Ava's forehead, then leaned over and kissed her.

"Ava, darling, your dad and I are here, and so is Hunt. We just want you to know we love you, and that you're going to be okay."

Hunt stood without talking, listening to her parents' words of comfort, knowing that love would become part of what would heal her. He wanted to hold her in his arms until she opened her eyes and smiled at him—to hear her sass—to hear her laugh—to feel the warmth of her breath against his face as they made love.

He'd seen a lot of men die in the war, and when they quit breathing, they were gone. Ava had been dead in his arms, and he'd witnessed life returned to her. Hunt was so grateful to God for giving her back. He didn't know how all that worked in heaven, and right now he didn't care. All he knew was that his sweet Ava was alive again, and how much he loved her.

He glanced up at the clock over her bed and thought about the painters and the house, and how important that had been to him this morning, and how inconsequential it was now, and how fast priorities can change.

He had arrived in Blessings on New Year's Day. He'd been here less than two weeks, and in that time he'd buried his mother, learned the truth of the family secret that had driven him away, fallen in love, and been working diligently to fulfill that promise he'd made to his mother. Today had begun as just another day in the steps toward fulfilling that promise.

He couldn't know this would be the day Ava died, or that the CPR he'd learned in the military would be the difference it made in reversing her fate, but he was grateful.

Thank God. Thank God.

The Rymans and the Dillons were booked for disorderly conduct. The two women were released on their own recognizance because the only people they'd hurt were themselves. They apologized to each other in tears, then begged a ride from one of the officers to get them back to the hospital to check on their injured family members.

The two men fighting had not only hurt each other, but it was nothing to the hurt Hunt Knox had dealt. They'd caused considerable damage to property at the hospital. Caused injuries to hospital personnel because of flying debris, and they were sorely ashamed.

The two Hunt had taken down were patched up in the ER. One with a broken nose reset and taped up. The other one sent off to jail with an ice pack to his jaw.

But it was Josh Ryman who was in the most trouble. What he'd done to Ava Ridley was unintentional, but his irrational behavior and his rage and violence had caused it, and now all three of the brawlers would be facing a judge tomorrow. Bail would be set.

But there was nothing that was going to take away the shame of their behavior or the grief of knowing that their first grandchild was dead because of what they'd done.

While Ava was being moved into a bed upstairs, Hunt was on the phone with the painters.

"I'm sorry to hear your girl got hurt," Bill Smith said.

"So am I," Hunt said. "Don't worry about locking up. I'll have one of my sisters come by and give you a key. You can lock up this evening when you leave and let yourselves in tomorrow," Hunt said.

"That'll work," Bill said. "We're getting along fine. We'll put a second coat on the outside tomorrow morning. I've already got two of my boys working on the inside. They started in the attic, and they're working their way down toward the front of the house."

"If nothing happens, I'll be by tomorrow to see," Hunt said, and hung up. He didn't know if Birdie was back at work, but he knew Emma would be free and gave her a call.

———

Emma was coming out of Franklin's Florist when her cell phone rang. She put the flowers she was carrying on the hood of her car, then answered.

"Hello."

"Emma, it's me, Hunt. I need a favor."

The fact that he was asking was like a gift. She smiled.

"Sure thing. What do you need?" But when he began to explain, she was quickly horrified. "Oh my God! Is she going to be okay?"

"I hope so. I think so. But she's not conscious, and I'm staying in the hospital with her tonight."

"Of course," Emma said. "Where are you now?"

"They moved her to the third floor. Room 300."

"I'll be right there," Emma said. "And it's okay if the painters have a key? Because if it bothers you, I can easily meet them tomorrow to let them in."

"No, it will be okay, and thanks. I'll see you in a bit," he said, and disconnected.

He headed for the elevator, while Emma grabbed her flowers and jumped in the car. She'd deliver the flowers to the cemetery later. Right now, the living needed her more.

Karen and Larry were in Ava's room when he walked in.

"Any change?" Hunt asked.

"Her vital signs are all good," Larry said.

"Then why isn't she awake?" Hunt asked.

"I don't know. The doctor said it would happen when she was ready."

Hunt sighed. That sounded like doctor talk for they didn't have a clue, but Ava was alive, so he wasn't going to complain.

"I'm staying with her," Hunt said.

Karen glanced at Ava and then nodded. "We thought you would. We can stay if you need to—"

"Nothing in my world is more important than her," Hunt said.

Larry nodded. "Understood. And in ours…but they don't need all of us up here. We'll stay a while. You promise to call us if there's any change?"

"Absolutely," Hunt said.

"If she wakes up, you tell her we were here," Karen said.

Hunt nodded.

"And we'll be back in the morning anyway," she added.

Hunt hugged her.

"I'm so sorry this happened."

"You saved her life," Larry said. "You made the difference."

Hunt moved to the side of Ava's bed and slid his hand beneath her palm. Before, she would have clasped it immediately. The limp feel of it against his skin scared him, but Elliot said she would be reborn, and Hunt wanted to believe, so much, that she would wake up and be all that she had been.

CHAPTER 18

AVA WAS DRIFTING. SHE WAS SEEING AND FEELING AND HEARING, but in a place she'd never been before. Movement was without effort, like floating, and she was unaware of being in a body.

In this place, she understood.

Everything.

The why of it.

The how of it.

And that there was no end to it.

The beauty of it was beyond description, and the sounds…unexplainable, but mesmerizing…leading her, pulling her along by some invisible rope.

She was curious, and yet there was a sense of having left something undone.

She was surrounded by a blue so pale it almost looked white, and then it began vibrating, and the lights began to change into a thousand different hues of colors she'd never seen.

All of a sudden, there was a bright light before her, and within the light a voice—a voice so beautiful and so loving that she wanted to lie down within the sound of it and just be.

You came too soon. You are not at the end of your path. It is your choice…you can stay…or you can return. Look into the light and choose.

The light grew brighter and wider, and then she saw all that was before her, and the multitudes awaiting her, and it was so beautiful she could not look away.

Then the light flickered, and she was looking down into a room where a woman lay upon a bed. She saw two people standing beside the bed, and then recognized them as her mother and father, holding each other and crying. And then she saw a man holding the hand of the woman in the bed, but she could not see his face.

As Ava began moving closer, a terrible feeling of dread began sweeping through her. There was a familiarity in the long, dark hair strewn across the pillow, then the curve of the woman's cheek, and then the dark wings of her brows.

She was beside the man now. She could see his face. She knew him. She'd known him forever.

It's Hunt. And the woman in the bed is me! What's happening... What's happening? Why don't I wake up? No. No. No. I don't want to die.

And all of a sudden she was back in the body and struggling to find herself within it again. Arms...legs...a heartbeat...pain. Feeling lost. Feeling scared.

Then Hunt's hand slid beneath her palm and she remembered that. She was willing her fingers to curl around it, but they would not.

She heard his voice, but she could no longer see him.

Hunt! Hunt! Don't turn me loose. I don't know how to find my way back yet. Just don't let me go.

———————

Good or bad, news always spread fast in Blessings, and this was no exception. Within hours, everyone knew about the Ryman boy trying to elope with the Dillon girl, and about Pete Dillon, the girl's daddy, chasing them down and wrecking all of them on the two-mile bridge north of town.

Everybody knew about the family brawl that had ensued in the ER after the victims were brought in from the wreck. They knew the Dillon girl had been hurt the worst, and that she'd lost the baby she was carrying, and after that her heart had stopped two times. People said it was because her soul didn't want to give her baby up. They said it was a mother's instinct to stay with her child, but that she was finally stabilized enough to take to surgery.

They knew the Dillon boy had a broken arm and a concussion, and that Pete Dillon was released with nothing more than a broken nose.

But it was what Josh Ryman did to Ava Ridley that sent shock and disbelief throughout the community.

It was all over town, and the gossip was spreading.

They said Josh Ryman hit Ava so hard it stopped her heart.

They said she dropped dead on the hospital floor.

And that's when the storylines began straying from the truth.

According to some stories, Ava's fiancé, Hunt Knox, had waded through the brawl, laying Dillons and Rymans on the floor to get to her. The fact that there was only one Dillon and one Ryman fighting each other didn't matter. The story sounded better their way.

The story continued with Hunt and a nurse doing CPR for nearly an hour (although it was barely four minutes) until the only defibrillator in the hospital was freed up to shock Ava's heart back into a normal rhythm.

They knew she was alive now, but they were grieving that she still had not regained consciousness. So the next step in Blessings when things went wrong was to either feed people or pray for them. And since food wouldn't help, prayer vigils were starting up all over town.

Emma updated her brothers and sister that evening, telling all of them what had happened. It was a mutual decision when the Knox siblings all gathered together and made a beeline to the hospital.

———

Hunt's chair was right beside Ava's bed, close enough that he could hold her hand and angled so that he had a clear view of her face. He was watching for the signs her doctor had mentioned, like eyelids fluttering, fingers twitching, any shift in breathing patterns, any body movement at all. The X-rays had revealed a slight fracture in her sternum, which would raise other issues as she began to heal, but those were possibilities, not certainties, and Hunter Knox had survived a war because of possibilities, so he wasn't giving up on a total healing.

It was nearing 7:00 p.m., and even though Ava's room was quiet except for the continuing beep of the heart monitor and the intermittent sound the blood pressure cuff made as it inflated to take a reading, he could hear activity beyond the door.

He'd been talking to her for hours, because he remembered hearing voices and people talking after he'd been hospitalized, even before he'd been awake enough to respond. He wanted her to know that wherever she was, she wasn't alone.

Suddenly, something crashed to the floor out in the hall, and he saw her flinch. He jumped to his feet and moved closer.

"Hey, darlin', it's me, Hunt. I know you heard that, so I know you can hear me. I love you so much, Ava. I need you. Please come back to me."

Silence.

He reached for her hand, then gave her fingers a gentle squeeze.

"Can you feel that? You don't have to answer…just squeeze my fingers so I'll know you heard me."

Nothing.

He groaned and then sat down, ignoring the lump in his throat. Then he dropped his head and closed his eyes.

Don't you do this, God. Don't do this to her. Don't do this to us. I'm begging you. Please…give her back.

Then there was a soft knock at the door behind him.

"Come in," he said, and got up, thinking it might be her parents. When he realized it was his family, the lump in his throat turned to tears. "Come in," he said again, and when Birdie walked up and hugged him, he held her like he'd never let her go.

"We gotta stop meeting like this," Birdie said, and it made him smile, remembering that he'd walked in on them at their mother's bedside.

Emma hugged him, then Gordon shook his hand. Junior gave him a quick hug and a pat on the back. Ray did the same, then they all glanced toward Ava's bed.

"How's she doing?" Emma asked.

"Vitals are good. She's reacting to sound. It's just a matter of her deciding to wake up," Hunt said.

"You're both in our prayers, but that's not why we've come. What can we do for you so that you won't fret about what's happening at Mama's house?" Emma asked.

"I can meet your deliveries and let them in anytime you want," Ray said. "Emma's got a key. All you have to do is give me your schedule."

"I'll gladly take off work to do the same," Gordon offered. "Whatever you need done, we're ready to help."

"We don't want you worrying about your promise to Mama when you need to be focused on Ava," Junior added.

Hunt sighed. All of the stress he'd been feeling about that just disappeared.

"That would be awesome," he said. "Ray, I'll text the schedule to you. As soon as the painters are finished, a new kitchen stove is due to be put in, then kitchen and bathroom counters go in, but everything is already on order with delivery dates. So all you need to do is be there to make sure they are installed properly, then new faucets go in after that. The only thing that's not already paid for is installing the new cookstove."

"We let you down once, Hunt, but that will never happen again," Emma said. "Trust us. We want this to look as good as you do. I'm just sorry that it wasn't done *for her* when she was still here…but we can do it now, *for you*."

"Thank you. All of you," Hunt said, and after quiet goodbyes, they were gone.

He pulled up the schedule in his notes, then forwarded it to Ray. It was a relief to know the schedule wasn't going to be messed up.

A nurse came in to check Ava's stats and adjust the IV drip, and then she was gone, too, and once again Hunt and Ava were alone.

He sat back down beside her bed and reached for her hand. He wasn't expecting a response. He just needed to touch her.

"I'm here, Ava. You and me forever, right?" he said and gave her fingers a slight squeeze.

Between one heartbeat and the next, her fingers curled.

He gasped. Was that an involuntary motion, or did she mean to do that?

Testing her, he slowly tried to pull his hand away, and when he did, she tightened her grip.

"Ava? Is that you?"

She squeezed.

Breath caught in the back of Hunt's throat.

"Welcome back, baby… Welcome back," he said, then rang for a nurse and sent a text to her parents.

It was the voice—Hunt's voice—that led Ava back. The love in it was its own tone, a whole octave above fear and uncertainty. She knew it. It was that voice she'd slept with for all the years of her life, the one she heard in her dreams. The one belonging to the boy she'd adored—to the man he'd become—the man who held her heart.

She could hear him talking to other people now, and heard the excitement in their voices. But it was his voice that held her… anchored her. Before, she'd seen tears on his cheeks. Now she needed to see that smile.

When she finally opened her eyes, his face was the first thing she saw.

"Hey, baby…welcome back," Hunt said, and then leaned down and kissed her.

"Love—"

Hunt's eyes welled. "Love you, too. Your mom and dad were here, then left. But they're on the way back right now."

Ava clutched his hand, then licked her lips. "You…stay?"

He kissed her forehead, then whispered in her ear.

"Yes. Relax. I am within the sound of your voice."

"Mine," she said, and then closed her eyes.

"Forever yours," Hunt said, then sat down and reached for her hand, and this time when he did, her grip was strong.

———————————

The good news about Ava Ridley's resurrection spread through Blessings as fast as the news of her death had done, but there was one person who knew before all the others, and that was Elliot Graham, the man who'd delivered the warning that saved her life.

The satisfaction of knowing his warning had been heeded was enough. And to acknowledge the spirits who continued to send him messages, he lifted a glass of wine that night in their honor.

While Elliot was in his home drinking wine, Hunt was sitting near the window in Ava's room downing a burger and fries that Karen and Larry brought him.

Ava woke a couple of times while her parents were still there—long enough to satisfy them with her continuing recovery—and after she fell back asleep the third time, they left her in Hunt's care.

———————————

The floor was quieter at night. Enough so that Hunt dozed off now and then. Once he'd fallen asleep leaning forward in the chair with his forehead on Ava's bed, and woke up with her fingers in his hair.

The next time he dozed off, he went to war, then woke up with a jerk when the nurses began changing shifts. He hadn't dreamed like that in quite a while, and the only times he went back there in his sleep were in times of stress. What had happened to Ava fell into that category and then some.

They woke Ava up taking vitals, and the moment she opened her eyes, she was looking for him.

"I'm here, baby, but I'm kind of in the way. I'm going to get a cup of coffee and then I'll be right back, okay?"

"Yes, okay," Ava said.

A few minutes later, the nurse was leaving as he walked in with his coffee. Ava was awake and in a reclining position.

"I remember stuff," Ava said. "Can we talk?"

"Absolutely," Hunt said, then put the coffee aside and sat down on the side of her bed. "You talk. I'll listen."

"There was a fight in the ER. Did I dream that?"

Hunt remembered the doctor telling them not to lead her memories, but if she was asking, he could answer.

"No. That happened," he said.

She nodded, then put a hand on her chest. "My chest hurts. It hurts to take a deep breath. Why am I here?"

"What do you think happened?" Hunt asked.

"That I got hit by something. Is that right?"

"Yes. That's right. But you're healing, and you're going to be fine."

Ava nodded. "I thought it was something like that," she said, then closed her eyes.

Hunt thought she was going back to sleep when she suddenly opened her eyes and clutched his hand.

"I need to ask you something and then tell you something."

"Okay," Hunt said.

"Did I die?"

Hunt was shocked by the question. "Why would you ask that, honey?"

"Because I was in light…and colors in hues I've never seen, and there was a voice within the light that told me I'd come too soon. The voice said I could stay or I could go back, but I had to be the one to decide. And then I saw two visions within the light. In the first one, I was standing at the threshold of what I would call heaven. And it was so beautiful and the voice was pure love and I didn't want to leave."

Hunt shuddered. Hearing how close he'd come to losing her was frightening.

"Then the light shifted, and I saw another vision. I think I was in this room but I was looking down. I could see a woman in a bed. I saw two people standing by the bed crying. They were my parents. I saw a man holding the woman's hand but I couldn't see his face, and I came closer. Then I was beside the man and I saw it was you. There were tears on your cheeks, and then I saw the woman in the bed was me, and I was thinking over and over that I didn't want to die. I wanted you."

Hunt swallowed past the lump in his throat and held onto her hand, but she kept talking.

"As soon as I thought that I didn't want to die, I think I went back inside my body. But the moment I did that, I couldn't see, and I couldn't remember how to make anything work. But I could feel your hand. I tried to make my fingers work, but they wouldn't. After that, I just remember waking up and sleeping and waking up and sleeping, and always, always, trying to find my way back. I want you to know that every time I found the strength to surface, it was because I was following the sound of your voice. I chose you, and that's why I'm still here."

There were tears on Hunt's face again, but he didn't care.

"I'll be thanking God every day for the rest of my life for giving you the choice, and I'll be thanking you every night when I hold you in my arms that you chose to come back to me. I love you, Ava."

She sighed, and then closed her eyes again. "Love you too," she mumbled.

Hunt slid off the side of her bed, raised the guardrail back into place, and then pulled up the covers.

Her eyes opened.

"You'll stay?"

"Right here," Hunt said. "Close your eyes. I've got you."

Hunt took Ava home two days later. Getting hurt had hastened the end of her job. Even though she and Hunt weren't leaving for Houston just yet, she wasn't strong enough to return to work.

When he got her back to her house, she took a deep breath as she entered.

"Home never felt so good." And then she glanced at him. "Or looked as good. You plan on keeping that three-day beard?"

"No. It makes me look too much like Dad. Are you doing okay? Where do you want to land, sugar? On the sofa in the living room, or do you want to lie down on your bed?"

"I think I just want to prowl the house for a couple of minutes. You know…make myself a glass of tea. Sneak a cookie or something. I was an impatient patient. I admit it."

Hunt grinned. "I don't know about that. I like your sass. But I'll turn the bed back just in case, and then I'm going to shave."

"Make yourself pretty for me," Ava said, and turned to walk away.

Hunt stood, watching the way she was moving. She walked a little hunched over, favoring the pain in her chest, but she was steady on her feet. He started to leave, and then waited a couple of minutes until she came back. Once she was settled in her chair with her feet up, he kissed the top of her head and left her alone.

He got out his electric razor, turned it on, then frowned at his reflection.

"I see you, Parnell Knox, but I'm nothing like you," Hunt muttered, and ran the razor straight up the side of his cheek, leaving a streak of smooth skin within the whiskers, then kept it up until they were gone.

After that, he showered and changed into clean clothes, then went to check on Ava. She was kicked back in the recliner with her feet up, eating a cookie and talking on the phone.

All was well in his world.

He called Ray to check on the progress at the house, as he had every morning, and was pleased to learn that the painters were gone, and the crew from the granite company in Savannah was coming to install new countertops in the kitchen and bathroom.

"I got this," Ray said. "You just stay home with Ava today."

"Yeah, thanks," Hunt said. "I'll get her mom to stay with her tomorrow, so if your boss calls, don't turn down any jobs, okay?"

"Okay," Ray said. "Give Ava my best. Talk to you later."

Hunt dropped the phone in his pocket, poured himself a Coke, snagged a couple of cookies from the cookie jar, and went back to the living room with Ava.

"Everybody is going to Potluck in the Park today," Ava said.

"I know. Birdie was going, so I gave her our tickets and asked her to get us some stuff to go."

Ava sighed. "I was so looking forward to going, but now, not so much. I'm not ready for all that and I know it. I hope the turnout is good so Mrs. Hollis can get home. Do you think she'll be there?"

"She's going to be the guest of honor. It will be her chance to thank everyone. Birdie said Dub got all of the damaged goods hauled off and the burned part of the building cleared away. He's opening the store back up tomorrow, so she'll be back at work."

Ava picked a raisin out of the oatmeal cookie she was eating and put it in her mouth, talking as she chewed.

"Rhonda came up to tell me goodbye when you were checking me out this morning. She said the Ryman boy went home yesterday, but that it will be another couple of days, at least, before the Dillon girl is released."

Hunt glanced at her, and then focused on the look on her face. Either someone said something to her about that day or she was remembering more.

"Good to know they're healing," Hunt said.

Her eyes narrowed, studying his expression. He gave away nothing.

"She said Josh Ryman's charges were more serious than the others."

"Oh yeah? I hadn't heard anything about their charges, but I knew the Blessings police hauled them out of the ER and took them to jail," Hunt said.

"They have security cameras in the ER," Ava said.

Hunt sighed. "I would have assumed that. What are you trying to say, Ava?"

"The crew who works in the ER kept saying that you saved my life."

"Honey, I haven't said much about that because Dr. Quick told us not to tell you anything, that you needed to remember it by yourself."

"Oh." She put both hands on her chest. "Am I sore because of CPR?"

"Maybe, but that isn't what hurt you," Hunt said. "You got hit in the chest. It cracked your sternum. After that, we did CPR."

"I know I died, Hunt, so stop skirting the issue, okay? How did it happen?"

"To keep a long story short, Josh Ryman hit you in the chest so hard it stopped your heart."

"Oh my God. Did they use the defibrillator?" she asked.

"Not at first. They were already using it on the Dillon girl. I did CPR until they freed it, and then Dr. Quick shocked your heart into a normal rhythm."

Ava got up and sat down in Hunt's lap and put her arms around his neck.

"You saved my life."

"A whole bunch of people saved your life. I was just in on it. And on Ryman's behalf, I will say he was horrified at what he'd done. I wanted to break his damn neck, but you mattered more than revenge."

"This is the second time I've been physically hurt working in an ER. I thought coming to a small town would be safer, but I was wrong."

"Fear makes good people do crazy things. Sometimes bad things," Hunt said. "You don't have to go back to nursing until you feel ready.

You don't have to go back at all if it bothers you. I make enough money that you wouldn't have to work at all unless you want to."

Ava nodded. "There are lots of things I can do with my nursing degree, including teach. I won't waste it, and I love the work. But right now, I'm seriously reconsidering my options. I know one thing. I'll never work ER again."

"Then so be it," Hunt said. "Now let all that go. What can I do to entertain you until Birdie shows up with our food from the potluck dinner?"

"I don't know," Ava said and buried her face against his neck.

"I think you need to stretch out in your bed for a bit, okay?"

She nodded, then slid out of his lap and let him walk her to her room. She sat down on the side of her bed long enough for him to pull off her shoes, then she eased down on her back and stretched out. Hunt pulled up the covers.

"Close your eyes, darlin'. Let all this shit go and just rest. Your mom and dad will probably be over this afternoon. You need to rest up for them."

"Love you," Ava said.

"Love you," he replied, and walked out, leaving the door open so he could hear if she called.

CHAPTER 19

RUBY BUTTERMAN WAS IN HER ELEMENT. THE PARK WAS PACKED. Tables were filling up with food faster than she'd expected, and every eating establishment in town had not only shut down for the day to ensure anyone wanting to eat out today would be doing it here, but also had donated food from their businesses to share.

Ruby delegated Peanut to get the tables and chairs from the school cafeteria to the park and back, and the local churches had brought their tables and chairs from their dining halls to add to the seating. There were quilts spread out on the ground for some people to sit on, and portable picnic tables and folding chairs scattered about the park.

For Ruby, it was a re-creation of their wedding reception all over again, only this time the weather was cool and there was no threat of rain.

Donna Hollis had a seat of honor in the gazebo and was in disbelief at what was being done on her behalf.

Ruby had styled Donna's hair, and Donna was wearing a new dress. It was the first time in years she'd felt pretty, and sad Arnold wasn't alive to see her this way.

There was a constant stream of people coming up to pay their respects, and more than one person had put an envelope in her lap as they were leaving. "Just a little something extra," they would say. Or "Safe travels," they might add. All she could do was thank them and try not to cry.

When Ruby came up to get the dinner started, Donna had a lap full of envelopes. Ruby locked them up in her car, then came back to the gazebo.

"It's time to get this party started," she said. "Are you ready for this?"

"I think so," Donna said, and then let Ruby lead her to the

microphone. It was her chance to say thank you and goodbye, but she was nervous.

"You'll be fine," Ruby said.

Donna took a deep breath, then moved closer to the microphone and quietly cleared her throat.

"First of all, thank you. All of you. On the worst day of our lives, Arnold and I thought we would never be able to hold our heads up in this town again. After what our boys did, I was so ashamed that I wanted to die." Her voice began to shake. "But God took Arnold instead. I'll never understand why. All I know is that everything and everybody I loved in this world is gone, and my only solace—the only thing I could think was that I wanted to go home…back to Bethlehem, West Virginia, where I was born and raised. But the likelihood of that happening was slim to none until all of you began offering help, giving me hope.

"Now, because of your generosity, I'm that much closer to going home. I love Blessings so much. I thought we would live here forever. Be buried here, even. But I guess God had other plans. So thank you for caring enough to help. Thank you so, so much. I don't know what else to say but God bless you."

The applause that followed was loud and fervent, and then a pastor from the Methodist church stepped up and said a prayer, and as soon as he said, "Amen," someone in the crowd shouted, "Let's eat!"

Food and laughter ensued.

Birdie had turned in her tickets, but instead of eating there, she got three plates to go, one for her and one each for Hunt and Ava, along with a separate box with three desserts. She was struggling toward the car with her load when a young man came running toward her.

"Hey, Bridgette! I haven't seen you in ages. Looks like you could use some help."

Birdie stopped. She couldn't remember the last time someone had called her by her given name, and she was still trying to place him when he smiled. It was that one dimple in his right cheek that gave him away.

Wade Montgomery!

She hadn't seen him since their junior year of high school.

"Wade! What on earth are you doing back in Blessings?"

"I came back to help Uncle Dub."

Birdie stared. "My boss, Dub Truesdale, is your uncle?"

Now he looked as surprised as she felt.

"You work at the Feed and Seed?" he asked.

"Since straight out of high school."

"Then we'll be seeing more of each other, I guess. So, will you let me help carry this for you?"

"Yes, and much appreciated," Birdie said, and handed the stack of boxes over, then took the smaller box with the desserts off the top and carried it.

"Where are we going?" Wade asked.

"To my car. I'm going to eat with my brother and his girlfriend. She just got out of the hospital."

"Which brother?" he asked.

"Hunter, the oldest one."

"Good dude," Wade said. "You lead. I'll follow," he added, and then disputed his own words and walked beside her all the way. As soon as the food was in her car, he gave her a quick pat on the shoulder. "Enjoy, and I'll see you tomorrow."

Birdie blinked. "Wait. What?"

"At work. I'll see you at work," he said.

"Oh, right. Tomorrow. Yes, I'll see you tomorrow," and then she sat in the car without starting it up, just so she could watch him walk away.

Tall, dark, and handsome. Check.

Friendly and personable. Check.

Worked in the same business. Check.

But she hadn't thought to inquire about the important stuff, like was he married? Did he have a girlfriend? Where was he living? And exactly what was his job description going to be at the Feed and Seed?

After he disappeared within the crowd, Birdie started up her car and drove to Ava's house. She got out carrying the desserts and knocked on the door.

Hunt opened it, smiling. "Hey, kid, come on in."

"The dinners are still in my car. I brought mine here, too, if that's okay?"

"Of course it's okay. I'll get the food. You can find your way to the kitchen."

"Is Ava awake?" Birdie asked.

"She's waking up. I saw you drive up and woke her. She'll be here shortly. Go on in."

A few minutes later, they were seated around Ava's kitchen table, talking about Donna Hollis's thank-you speech, the huge turnout, and everything but Wade Montgomery's sudden reappearance in Blessings. Birdie didn't want to hear Hunt start teasing her about another guy.

———

Peanut and Ruby took Donna home after the potluck was over, then Ruby walked her back to the house.

"I'll call you tomorrow. I know we sold almost six thousand dollars' worth of potluck tickets, plus a few donations added in. That's already been deposited into your bank account. There's the silent auction at the country club tomorrow night, so there'll be more. And whatever else is in the envelopes you were given today. We'll see what kind of a total you come up with. Hopefully it will be enough to get you home, and a little nest egg to carry you over until your benefits start coming in."

"I'm so grateful," Donna said. "I'll count up what they gave me today and take it to the bank in the morning, too. Thank you for everything."

"You're welcome, sugar," Ruby said. "Now go inside and get your shoes off and get comfy."

"I will, and thank you again," Donna said, and went inside, put up the food she'd brought home, then carried the envelopes into her bedroom and laid them aside until she had changed her clothes. Only after she was comfortable did she sit down on the bed and begin opening them up.

The first twelve all had cash ranging from $20 to several with $100 bills, and a few with even more. The next envelope she picked up had $1,000 in cash. She gasped. She'd never held that much cash money in her hand at once, and she added it to the stack.

The next couple of envelopes had checks, and the next five had more cash. The stack was growing, and she was crying now.

"Oh, Arnie, would you just look. I never knew people could be so kind and giving. I'm just so sad you had to die for this to happen."

Finally, there were seven envelopes left, and Donna was so blinded by tears that she kept wiping her eyes just to be able to see what was inside.

More cash. A hundred dollars in tens and twenties. Fifty dollars in ones. Two $20 bills.

She was down to two envelopes. One was long. One was small. She opened the long one first and pulled out another $100 bill.

"Lordy be," Donna sighed, and added it to the pile. Then she opened the last envelope and pulled out a check. She stared at it for a moment, telling herself that she wasn't reading it right, and then read aloud.

"Pay to the order of Donna Hollis. Ten thousand dollars and no cents."

It was written on a joint account owned by Duke and Cathy Talbot, and signed by Cathy Talbot. Donna frowned, trying to remember why she knew that name, and then it hit her. This was the woman who rebuilt the Bottoms! And she'd just given Donna the last push she needed to rebuild her life.

She turned around, laid it on the stack with the checks, and then began counting the cash. There was a total of $6,720 in cash. Then she picked up the checks and started counting those amounts. Thirteen thousand one hundred dollars.

"Oh my God. That's almost twenty thousand dollars right here, and Ruby said she'd already deposited six thousand, and there's still the silent auction. This will get me home, with money left over."

Donna's heart was pounding as she gathered up the cash and divided it between two envelopes. Then she put the checks in another envelope, put all three inside her purse, and stuffed it under her pillow. She was sleeping with this tonight and taking it straight to the bank in the morning.

───────────────

Ava's parents came over late Sunday afternoon and had more stories to share about the potluck in the park. Without even asking, Karen told the both of them that she'd be over in the morning to stay with Ava so Hunt could finish up with Marjorie's house.

"I appreciate that," Hunt said.

"She's my baby, too," Karen said, and patted Ava's hand.

Hunt grinned. "Point taken."

Ava leaned against Hunt's shoulder. She was listening to them talk and thinking about the time when her parents would be too far away to drop in, and closed her eyes.

She didn't know when they left, or when Hunt carried her back to bed. And when she woke up later, she showered, put on a nightgown, and crawled back into bed.

"Do you want anything to eat or drink?" Hunt asked.

"No. All I want to do right now is sleep."

Hunt sat down on the side of the bed. "I think that's understandable, honey, considering how far away you were when you decided to come home."

Ava frowned. "I never thought of it that way."

"I probably took a few trips when I was healing from the chopper crash, too."

"Do you remember all that?" Ava asked.

"Only parts of it. They kept me knocked out for quite a while because of the pain. But I slept a lot then, too. So being tired from what happened to you is your body telling you to slow down because it's trying to heal." Then he leaned over and kissed the side of her cheek. "And by the way, since you're a nurse, I shouldn't have to remind you of that."

Ava sighed. "Duly noted, Dr. Knox. If you need me, I'll be right here."

Hunt waited until she closed her eyes, then went back into the living room. But instead of turning on the television, he sat down within the silence.

It took a few moments for him to realize how he was feeling. His knuckles were sore and skinned from the fight. He was shaken to the core by how close he'd come to losing her, and all it had done was shift him back into a kind of PTSD.

He took a few cleansing breaths, and then he closed his eyes and began focusing on one small sound at a time until he had identified each one. It was something he'd done often after they'd finally released him from the hospital and mustered him out. When he'd been alone and still gaining strength. Before he'd found the job he had now. Then, the fear within him was so strong. Everything had made him jumpy. He was convinced he would never be the same.

So he had created this game. Each time he heard a sound, he had to sit and listen to it over and over until he had it identified, and once he knew what it was, it was no longer an unknown, so he was no longer afraid—like he had defeated an enemy.

It was his subconscious reminding him that if he knew what it was, it no longer held any power over him. And so he began it again now, listening, identifying, defeating the unknown—until he could feel the calm settling within him.

And it was good.

———————

Karen was at the house early the next morning. She was carrying a plate of hot cinnamon rolls when Hunt opened the door.

"Morning, Karen. Ava is just now getting into the shower. She's moving a little slow."

"These will perk her up," Karen said. "They're her favorite. I don't suppose you'd want any before you leave?"

Hunt grinned. "If you're willing to share, I'm not going to refuse."

Karen took them to the kitchen, wrapped up a couple in tinfoil and then handed them to him as he picked up his coffee.

"Call if you need me…for any reason," Hunt said. "My number is on the counter and in Ava's phone."

"I will, honey. Don't worry. I've got this," Karen said.

"I'll swing by here at noon to check on you two. Let me know if there's anything you need me to bring."

"Thank you for loving our girl, and for taking such good care of her," Karen said, and then hugged him.

"It's totally my pleasure," Hunt said. "Thank you for her, and the cinnamon rolls."

And then he was gone.

Karen could still hear the shower running and went back to Ava's bedroom to let her know she had arrived.

———

Birdie had never really looked forward to going to work before today. She went because it was her job and she liked her job. But today Wade Montgomery would be there.

She didn't know if he'd just come to help Dub get set back up after the fire or if he was here to stay. And she was curious.

She showed up for work at 8:00 a.m., although the Feed and Seed always opened by seven. It felt strange to drive up and see one whole end of the building missing. But there were now two small portable buildings on-site, and she was guessing they were where the sacks of feed and seed would be stored until Dub could rebuild.

She parked, and as always went in a side door and straight into the end of the building where her office was located, turning on lights as she went.

The scent of burned wood permeated everything. It was going to take a long time and a lot of airing out before that faded, and even longer to accept that a friend had died on the premises.

She put up her things and turned on the computer, then went up front to find Dub. He was usually behind the counter, talking to customers as they came up to pay. But today, both he and Wade were behind the counter, and Dub was obviously giving his nephew a rundown on how everything worked.

Dub saw Birdie approaching and smiled.

"Good morning, Birdie. Do you remember my nephew, Wade?"

"Morning, Dub. Yes, I know Wade, but I don't think I ever knew he was your nephew until yesterday when I saw him at the park." Then she smiled at Wade. "And a good morning to you, too."

"Morning, Bridgette."

Dub looked at him and grinned. "Don't nobody call her anything but Birdie."

"I never called her that," Wade said. "Bridgette is a pretty name. I'll stick with that."

Birdie smiled, and hoped her cheeks hadn't just flushed, because she was suddenly hot under the collar just looking at him.

"So, is there anything new I need to know today?" Birdie asked.

"One thing. The fire marshal said the fire started from an electrical short. We found signs of rats when we were clearing up. Damn things probably gnawed to raw wire, and something sparked it. We'll never know. But Arnold was just a victim, not the cause. And before you ask, we put out live rat traps."

"You need cats," Birdie said.

"And that, too," Dub said. "You saw the portable buildings. Feed will be in one, seed in the other until we rebuild. Cats are welcome. But the rebuilding is part of why Wade is here. He's going to be running the general end of the store so I can devote my time to the redesign and rebuilding. He'll be doing the ordering and most of the customer service, so you'll work with him like you worked with me."

Birdie nodded. "Got it, and my first question is where have you been putting the mail? There will be invoices to post and bills to pay."

"Oh…it's all on my desk. Holler if you have a question."

"Will do," Birdie said. "Happy first day at work, Wade," she added, did a quick little pivot, and went to work.

Wade watched her exit with more than a little appreciation.

Dub saw him staring and grinned.

"I'm just warning you now. She's a firecracker."

"Is she married?" Wade asked.

"Nope. And no boyfriends, either. She isn't a player, Wade, so don't mess up and hurt her."

"Aw, come on, Uncle Dub. I am not a player, either. One girlfriend in college, and for the past three years I've been living alone in an apartment in Boston, snowed in up to my eyeballs for what felt like six months out of every year and longing for the South. Your call rescued me. I'm so happy to be back. I don't ever want to leave again."

"This job isn't as cushy as the one you had," Dub warned.

"I know that. But there's rarely ever snow, and it never lasts. I missed Blessings. I'm happy to be back. Now stop worrying about Bridgette Knox and teach me what you want me to know."

Dub grinned. "Then follow me, boy."

———

Donna Hollis barely slept a wink for thinking of all that money underneath her pillow, and as soon as it was daylight, she was up to begin her day.

Once she got that money in the bank, she was going to start pulling everything out of drawers and closets that she wasn't going to take back with her and have a yard sale.

Before she could move forward, she had to let go of the past, no matter how exhausting or painful it might be.

———

Hunt's first impression upon driving up to the house was delight. The new roof with pale-gray shingles blended perfectly with the fresh white exterior and pewter-gray trim. It had updated the look of the house without losing any of its cottage charm, but it was the dark-blue door with brass fittings that made the house stand out on the block.

Inside, the white ceilings, the pale-gray walls, and white trim were stunning. The electrician had come and gone, and the small chandelier in the living room gave it a little elegance, as did the new light fixtures throughout the house.

Hunt started in the attic and walked from top to bottom, from back to front, imagining a new family coming in and making new memories—happy memories—here.

The old countertops were gone, and the new, reinforced framework was waiting for the new ones to be installed today. They'd had a delay yesterday in coming, so they would be here today. But that meant that this afternoon would be about installing the new kitchen and bathroom sinks and fixtures, so the countertops had to be in before noon.

Tomorrow, they'd deliver and install the new gas cookstove, and the day after that begin refinishing the old hardwood floors. It was going to look good. So good.

He was still in the kitchen when he heard trucks driving up. Countertops were here, and it was none too soon. One week from today, Marjorie's house and truck would go up for auction.

———

The glossy white countertops, with their faint hint of gray and silver marbling, had been installed, as had the kitchen and bathroom sinks and the new faucets to go with them.

Hunt walked through the house, checking to make sure everything was locked up for the night, and then went out the front door, locking it behind him. As he was getting in the truck, his phone signaled a text. It was a confirmation of tomorrow's delivery and installation of the cookstove.

This day was over, and now that his attention wasn't pulled in other directions, all he could think about was getting home to Ava.

Larry's car was also in the drive when he arrived, and he guessed a family supper was in his future. He walked in to the scent of chili and cornbread, and little bursts of laughter beneath the undertone of voices.

Ava was at the kitchen table. Larry was chopping onions at the kitchen counter, and Karen was at the stove giving a big pot of chili a quick stir.

Hunt leaned down and kissed Ava on the back of her neck.

"Hey, baby."

She looked up at him and smiled. "Hey, good-looking. We're working on a little chili party here."

"Sounds and smells good to me," Hunt said. "Give me a few minutes to clean up, and I'll be right back."

"You're good. Cornbread still has about ten minutes," Karen said.

Hunt gave her a thumbs-up and hastened his steps. He got out of his dirty clothes and washed up. It occurred to him how glad he'd be to get home and back to the wardrobe in his closet. His choices of clothing here were limited to what he'd brought with him. He dressed in clean ones and went back to the kitchen and sat down beside Ava.

"How are you feeling, honey?"

"I'm feeling good. I slept a lot today, as you know. I missed seeing you when you came by at noon because I was still sleeping then, too."

"That's what you needed to be doing," he said.

"How did it go at the house today?" she asked.

"Good. A lot done. We're almost finished, and the auction is set for a week from today. My boss is being understanding, but he sent me a text today asking when I thought I'd be returning. I told him I'd be able to let him know in a few days."

"I won't be a holdup," Ava said. "I'll be back to my normal self within a couple more days."

"We're not putting you on a deadline, and we're not leaving Blessings until you are a hundred percent."

Ava nodded. "Mom and Dad made a very generous offer that will take the pressure off of me and what to do with my house."

"What do you want to do with it?" Hunt asked.

"Sell it. Mom and Dad offered to handle that for me."

"But what about your things? You don't have to give up the furniture you want to keep, or anything else you want to take. I don't have an attachment to anything in my house. It's just stuff I picked up here and there. Nothing matches or coordinates."

She laughed. "None of that matters, but we'll fix it together, okay?"

Hunt stroked the side of her cheek. "Together sounds perfect. So, how about we get a moving van to load up what you want to keep, toss my Harley in with it, and they can bring it to us. In the meantime, we'll drive your car to Houston. If I'd known I was going to be bringing back the love of my life, I would have driven the Hummer, not the Harley."

Ava's eyes widened. "A Hummer? What else do you have that I don't know about?"

"A house with a pool?" he said.

"Oh my gosh! Jackpot, Hunter Knox! You are just full of surprises, aren't you?" Ava said.

"Maybe," he said, and then grinned.

"Cornbread's done," Karen said. "Bring your bowl. I'll fill it with chili from the stove. Everything else will be on the table."

Ava started to get up, when Hunt stopped her with a touch.

"You sit. I'll get yours."

Ava sank back into the chair and waited, thinking how close she'd come to losing all this.

They sat down together, and as they ate, plans for their future continued to unfold.

Later that night, after her parents were gone and Hunt was stretched out in bed beside her watching TV, he kept thinking of taking Ava up in one of the choppers, wondering if she'd love it as much as he did or if she would freak. Only time would tell.

When she finally fell asleep, he eased his arm out from beneath her neck and pulled up the covers. It hurt her to lie on her side, so until the fracture in her sternum healed, she would be sleeping on her back. He was afraid to get too close for fear he'd bump something and hurt her, but she didn't want him to sleep anywhere else. So he lay on his side with a pillow between them, making quiet promises to God that she would never hear.

All Hunt wanted in life was to keep her safe, but he was going to need help making that happen. Every pilot he had ever known claimed God for a copilot, so he was talking to The Man about watching out for Ava when he could not.

CHAPTER 20

THE SILENT AUCTION AND DANCE AT THE COUNTRY CLUB NETTED a little over four thousand dollars for Donna Hollis. The autopsy on Arnold's body had finally been released. Chief Pittman called her to let Donna know that he died from a broken neck, likely from a fall considering where they'd found the body, and that he would not have been alive by the time he was burned.

Of all the things that Donna had been going through, knowing her Arnie hadn't suffered in that inferno was the gift. And once the coroner released the body, the funeral home in Blessings picked it up. His cremation was scheduled, but it would be some days before ashes would be available. So Donna had taken Ruby Butterman's advice and asked them to ship the ashes to her new address. They readily agreed, again extending their sympathies for her loss.

Now all Donna needed was get home. Her little yard sale had netted a few hundred dollars to add to the account. The hardest things she'd had to part with were Arnold's clothes. But she kept telling herself that it would be better that they went to someone who needed them rather than turning them into a shrine.

Two days ago, she'd gotten a phone call from Ruby, asking when she wanted to move.

"I'd go today if I could," Donna said. "In reality, it'll take me a couple more days to get my stuff packed up."

"Then be ready," Ruby said.

"But how will—"

"Just be ready," Ruby said. "All will be revealed."

And so Donna packed up everything she was going to take, and now here it was, two days later, and she was sitting in her kitchen among boxes and bags when someone knocked.

Was this it what Ruby told her to be ready for? But who was going to take her home, and how was it going to happen? She opened the door, took one look at the couple on the doorstep, and burst into tears.

Her sister, Joy, rushed in, grabbed her sister into her arms and began hugging her, while her husband, Burl, stood on the threshold, grinning from ear to ear.

"Come in, come in!" Donna cried, and grabbed him by the hand. "What on earth? How did you—"

Burl pulled her to the doorway and pointed at the big U-Haul truck sitting in the drive.

"Did you drive this all the way from Bethlehem?" Donna asked.

"Nope," Burl said. "Somebody sent us plane tickets to Savannah. We flew in last night, stayed in a motel, and rented this here truck this morning. We're ready to load you up and take you home."

"I can pay you back for the truck," Donna said. "My friends here raised some money to help get me home."

"Well, some of those same friends must be responsible for the truck rental, too, because the contract for the truck rental was in the FedEx packet with the tickets. All we had to do was present the contract and my driver's license and car insurance and we were good to go. They even gave us directions on how to get to Blessings from the U-Haul place. I was supposed to tell you to call Dub when we arrived so he and the boys can move your stuff into the truck. So, who's Dub?"

Donna wiped her eyes, then blew her nose. "Arnold's boss. I'll give him a call."

Within an hour, five grown men arrived at Donna's house and came to the door. "Mrs. Hollis? We're here to help you load. Just tell us what you need us to do."

Donna waved her hand in the air. "Everything left in the house goes with me, except the appliances. They stay with the property. These are my sister and brother-in-law, Joy and Burl Davis. Burl is driving me home, so I'll let you men figure out how to load it up."

Burl had already done a walk-through at the house and knew what needed to be done.

"We need to start with the beds," Burl said. "There are twin beds in here, and then a queen-size bed in the master. Let's get them taken down and loaded, then the mattresses and dressers before we do the living room and dining table."

"Yes, sir," Dub's men said, and they went to work.

"Let's go sit in the porch swing," Joy said. "We can watch what they're doing and still be out of the way."

"I'm so glad you're here," Donna said as she and Joy sat down in the swing.

Joy patted Donna's knee. "I'm glad we're here, too, sugar. Family has to stick together, right?"

"Yes, that's right, but I need to call Ruby."

Joy smiled. "You go right ahead and talk. I'm just gonna sit here and swing the both of us."

Donna made the call, hoping she wouldn't be interfering with Ruby's work. It rang several times, and then Ruby answered.

"Hello."

"Ruby, it's me, Donna. I wanted you to know my sister and brother-in-law are here, and Dub sent some men to help load up my things. I know I've said thank you a thousand times already, but I'm gonna say it again. Thank you for helping me through the worst days of my life. I will never forget all the kindnesses and the blessings I have received since Arnold died. I won't see you again, but I will never forget you."

"You're welcome, Donna. I'm glad we could help. Safe travels, and when you get a chance, just text me and let me know you all arrived safe and sound," Ruby said.

"Yes. I'll do that," Donna said, and hung up. Then she leaned a little closer to her sister, letting the love and the swing lull the ache in her heart.

It took a mere three hours for six men to remove the Hollis

presence from the house. Donna called her landlord, Dan Amos, to let him know she was leaving.

"We're really sorry to see you go," Dan said. "But we understand your need. Safe travels, Mrs. Hollis."

"Thank you. I'll leave the key on the kitchen counter and turn the lock on the door as we leave."

And then Donna hung up, knowing she had just ended her last connection to Blessings.

"Do you have everything?" Joy asked.

Donna nodded. "Yes, I walked through the house twice. I'm good to go."

"Then hop in and we'll be on our way," Burl said.

"How long do you reckon it'll take to drive home?" Donna asked.

"Once we hit I-77 North out of Savannah, it's about an eleven-hour drive. We'll likely stop about halfway and spend the night somewhere, and then drive the rest of the way home in the morning. Safer that way," Burl said, and started up the truck and rolled out of the drive and onto the street. "West Virginia, here we come," he said.

Joy reached for her sister's hand and held it all the way out of town. She knew Donna was hurting for the sons she'd lost and the husband who'd died. She would always be sad for what had been, but in the years to come, maybe she'd find a new normal and a new life among her people again. When one thing dies, a new thing grows in its place. That's how life works.

Wade Montgomery made every excuse he could to place himself within Bridgette's presence at work at least three times a day. He liked her. He always had. He would like to get to know her better, but she didn't seem to be the least bit interested in him. Oh, she was nice and polite, even friendly. But he didn't think she was attracted to him at all. He hadn't yet decided if she just didn't like him or she was playing hard to get, but there was a possibility that she could very well break his heart.

It was just by chance that he saw a sign for the auction of Marjorie Knox's estate and pulled it off the bulletin board at the feed store and took it to Bridgette's office.

Birdie was entering invoices into the computer when Wade knocked, then walked in.

"Hey, Bridgette, is this where you grew up?" Wade asked.

Birdie glanced at what Wade was holding.

"Yes, why?"

"Uh…I didn't know your mother had passed. I'm really sorry."

Birdie sighed. She was going to have to stop ignoring him. It was getting too hard to be cool about it, because he distracted her to no end.

"Yes, and thank you. It was very recent…on New Year's Day."

"Oh. Wow. So you're selling the property, house and all?"

"It's what she wanted," Birdie said. "There are five of us kids, so whatever we get from the sale will be divided among us. Hunt has been remodeling it. It looks really nice now."

"Do you think I could take a look at it?" he asked.

"You mean like go inside and really look…as in a prospective-buyer kind of way?" she asked.

"Yes. I'm making Blessings my home. I can't stay with Uncle Dub forever."

"Where were you before?" Birdie asked.

"Boston. I moved there straight out of college."

Birdie frowned. "What did you do there?"

"I was in advertising. I'm good at it. But I'm a southerner at heart, and Boston has too much snow," Wade said.

"Do you have a girlfriend?" she asked.

He grinned. "No. Do I have to have one to go look at your house?"

"Don't be a smart-ass," Birdie said, and wadded up a piece of paper and threw it at him.

He laughed. "If I have to be accompanied by a member of the opposite sex, will you volunteer?"

Birdie rolled her eyes, and then glanced at the clock. "Let me call Hunt. If he's still there, I'll take you by on my lunch hour."

"Thanks," Wade said.

"You're welcome," Birdie said. "Now please hang that back up on the bulletin board when you go by. We need all the prospective buyers we can get."

"Yes, ma'am. Just don't forget to let me know if we have a date."

"Oh, we won't be having a date. We will be taking a ride and that is all," Birdie said. "Now scoot. I need to call my brother."

"Scooting," Wade said, then smiled all the way back to the front desk.

———————

Hunt was on the downhill slide of being done. The floors had been sanded and stained, and tomorrow the sealant would go on. He was running a dust mop over the floors to get rid of footprints when his phone rang. When he saw it was Birdie, he smiled.

"Hey, little sister."

"Hi, Hunt. Are you at the house?"

"Yes, why?"

"Oh, I have a maybe-possibly-prospective buyer who just saw the auction sign and wants to come look. I told him I'd bring him by on my lunch hour, but only if you were there."

"Well, I'm here, and it's ten to twelve. Are you coming now?"

"I guess," Birdie said. "I'll get him and head that way."

"You don't sound very excited," Hunt said. "A buyer is a buyer."

"I don't know whether he is interested in the house or in me. There, I said it. Just don't you dare tease me about it later."

Hunt laughed out loud. "Bring him by anyway. I might need to check him out."

"Lord," Birdie muttered. "See you soon."

"Oh…who's the buyer?" Hunt asked.

"Wade Montgomery. He's my boss's nephew."

"Bring him on. I'll know if he's serious about you or the house when I see him."

Birdie hung up, then grabbed her purse and jacket and headed up to the front of the store.

The last customer was walking out of the door when she walked up to the counter.

"Hunt's there. It's now or never," Birdie said.

"Now," Wade said, and then called out to one of the employees who was stocking shelves. "Hey, Eddie. You've got the register until I get back."

"Yes, sir," Eddie said and headed for the desk.

Wade walked out behind her, then as they started down the steps, he offered to drive.

"We can take my car if—"

"You're riding with me or you can follow me. It's your call," she said.

Wade frowned. "Don't you trust me?"

"Not yet," she said. "What's it gonna be?"

He sighed. "I'm riding with you."

She aimed the remote and unlocked her car. They got in and rode to the house in silence, and then as they were pulling up, Birdie saw him lean forward and smile.

"So far so good," he said. "Nice paint colors."

Birdie pulled up and parked. "Hunt picked them out."

She got out, then walked Wade inside, calling out as they entered.

"Hey, Hunt, we're here!"

Wade was already admiring the room size and the light fixtures, and he could smell the fresh paint. Then he heard footsteps coming up the hall from behind him and turned, then hoped to hell he was hiding his shock.

He'd grown up idolizing Hunt Knox, the high school quarterback, the boy who mowed their yard and sacked their groceries. But he would never have recognized him now.

So tall and muscular, and that dark, brooding face was nothing like the teenage boy with the sunny disposition.

"Hunt, it is good to see you again. You used to mow my parents' yard…Bill and Bonnie Montgomery? Remember them?"

And just like that, Wade saw recognition dawn and the smile was there again.

"Yes, I do remember them. You were just a little kid."

"I'm the same age as Bridgette," Wade said. "I'm really interested in this house. I don't want to take up too much of your time, but would you mind giving me the grand tour?"

Hunt glanced at Birdie and winked. "I don't mind at all. The only thing we have left to do is put the last coat of sealant on the floors, and that happens tomorrow. But everything else that we planned to remodel is done."

"You talk. I'll follow and listen," Wade said, then followed Hunt and Birdie through the house, listening to them talk and watching the way Bridgette's eyes lit up as she ran her hand across the new countertops and remarked about how beautiful the little house was now.

They went all the way to the attic and down again, then ended the tour on the back porch.

"I'd forgotten this backed up to the park," Wade said. "What a perfect place to raise a family."

"Do you have a family?" Hunt asked.

"Of my own? Not yet," Wade said. "I'm holding out for 'the one,' if you know what I mean."

Hunt glanced at Birdie. Her eyes narrowed warningly, so he said nothing, but he was feeling good about this guy.

"I know exactly what you mean," Hunt said. "So, you're planning on making Blessings your home?"

"Yes. Uncle Dub needs help at the store. That fire took a lot out of him, and I grew up here. I missed it. This is my chance to put down new roots. I sure appreciate you giving me the tour, but I'd better let you get back to work. Bridgette, I'm ready to leave when you are."

"Then let's go," Birdie said. "I'm starving, and we still have time for me to get food to go from the Dairy Freeze."

Hunt stood in the doorway watching them leave. He could tell by the side-glances Wade was giving Birdie, and the stiff set of her shoulders, that there was something happening between them. But whatever it was, it was theirs to explore.

He went back inside, finished up the floors, then locked up and went back to Ava's.

Wade and Birdie got back to the store with minutes to spare. She ate at her desk while she worked, and Wade sat out on the dock and downed his food before going back inside.

He'd already made up his mind about the house, but there was nothing to do but wait for the auction.

It was the day of the auction. Ava was feeling good—like a woman who was ready for hot Texas days and even hotter Texas nights, and she was dressed and going to the sale with Hunt. It would be her first appearance in public since the report of her death and resurrection. There would be comments about how she looked, if she'd seen "the light," if she'd talked to God, and variations on all of the above, and there was nothing she could do to stop them.

Junior traded days with someone at work so he could attend. Ray and Susie were going, and Gordon had taken off work to be with Emma.

Birdie was taking off work long enough to attend the auction. Even though she'd come to terms with what was happening, no matter who bought it, it was going to be sad because it would no longer be home.

The sale was to begin at straight-up noon. First they would sell the old black truck, and then the property. The auctioneer was on-site early, verifying that he had the correct description and plat number of the property, and the siblings were there early as well because the house would be open for prospective buyers to see the updates that had been made.

There was a steady stream of people coming and going through the house right up until the time for the sale to begin, and when it did, the black truck came up first.

The opening bid was $2,000, and after that it went up in increments until the bidding was down to two men. One wanted it for an extra farm truck, and the other wanted it for his teenage son to drive.

Hunt stood with his hands in his pockets, watching the bidders' faces. It was all the way up to $3,500, and the auctioneer was asking if there were any other bidders…that it was going, going…

All of a sudden, the parent with the teenager shouted, "Four thousand!" and the crowd gasped. He'd upped it $500 more in one bid.

The other bidder shook his head. "I'm out," he said.

"Sold!" the auctioneer cried and slammed the hammer down.

Ava leaned against Hunt and slipped her hand beneath his arm.

"Look, honey. I think that boy just got his first car."

Hunt smiled. "And I think you're right."

Then the auctioneer tapped the microphone to make sure it was still live and started off again.

"All right, ladies and gentlemen. We'll be auctioning off this house and the property it sits on next. You've all had a chance to see the updates. You have before you the legal description and location of this house as it sits within the township of Blessings, Georgia. The opening bid on this house is $180,000, and it's worth every penny and more. So do I have an opening bid? One-eighty, one-eighty, do I hear one-eighty?" he called.

"One-eighty!" someone shouted and raised his card with the number under which he'd registered.

After that opening bid, it started a flurry of bids, each raising the next and the next a couple of hundred dollars at a time.

Birdie wondered if Wade Montgomery was in the crowd, but she hadn't seen him, and as the bidding continued she decided he'd blown it off or changed his mind. A part of her was disappointed but she didn't know why, and then she let it go and refocused, only to realize the bidding had just passed the $200,000 mark. That was pretty pricey for Blessings. Especially in this neighborhood. She craned her neck, trying to see who was bidding now, but all she could hear was the auctioneer shouting as the bids continued to rise.

Hunt was surprised, and Emma was getting excited. Mama would be so proud that her little house was getting this kind of attention.

Like before, the bidding came down to two buyers bidding against each other in $1,000 increments. Two hundred thousand five, two-six, two-seven, and then a man shouted, "Two-ten." And the crowd went quiet, waiting to see if the other bidder raised that $210,000 bid.

But no one did.

The auctioneer started calling… "Two hundred and ten thousand dollars for this little beauty…with the entire city park for your backyard. What a bargain! What a bargain! Going once. Going twice. *Sold* to number thirty-one," he shouted.

The people began clapping and then parting to let the buyer through. Birdie could see movement but she still couldn't see who was coming through the crowd, and then the man emerged, smiling.

Her face flushed…then her heart skipped a beat.

It was Wade.

He hadn't just been playing her. He really wanted the house. And at the same time, now she wanted to cry. So he hadn't been interested in her after all. She'd just been a means to an end. So much for knights in shining armor. When was she ever going to learn?

She got in her car a much sadder and wiser woman, and drove back to work.

Late the same evening, Hunt was sitting on the back porch thinking about the day. He'd honored his mother and kept the promise he'd made. His job here was over. This was the longest he'd been grounded since he'd been shot down, and he missed being up in the air.

Ava came out and sat down beside him, then laid her head on his shoulder.

"Tomorrow you go to the lawyer's office for a final settling of the estate, right?"

"Yes. And I want you to know that extra eight thousand dollars I'm supposed to get from the estate? I'm donating it to the hospital in your name to buy more defibrillators. I nearly lost you because of the lack. I wouldn't want that choice to be taken away from someone else."

"Oh, Hunt. That is the most wonderful, generous thing you could ever do for me! Thank you," Ava said.

He reached for her hand and threaded her fingers through his, absently rubbing the ring he'd put on her finger, then glanced down at her. Her face was in the shadows, but he saw the glitter of excitement in her eyes.

"How fast can you be ready to leave for Houston?" he asked.

"All I'm taking are my clothes. I can pack them in a day. How about day after tomorrow?"

"Really?" Hunt asked.

"Yes, really," Ava said.

"We never managed to get married here," he said.

"I already have you and the ring. We can figure that out there."

"You don't want a big wedding? And have your daddy walk you down the aisle?" Hunt asked.

Ava laughed. "I'm almost twenty-nine years old. I left my mother and daddy's home years ago. All I need is you."

Hunt turned and took her in his arms.

"I don't know how I got so lucky. The loneliest times in my life were after I left home. Then, all I ever wanted was somebody to love…who would love me, too. And all that time you were here, just waiting for me to come back and get you."

Ava sighed. "I'm so ready to begin our life together. We've already done the hard part. We can tie up the loose ends later. I say day after tomorrow."

"And I agree," Hunt said. "There's just one thing."

"What's that?" Ava asked.

"I hope you're not afraid to fly, because I want to show you what I see every time I go up."

Ava shivered with excitement.

"What do you see, Hunt?"

He was quiet for a moment, and then he turned to her in the darkness.

"I see the heavens…and the endlessness of space. I see God…and He sees me."

EPILOGUE

HUNT AND AVA HAD BEEN IN HOUSTON A WEEK, AND NO MATTER where they went, she still got lost. The city was massive and alive, and she saw a side of Hunt she'd never known. He was a different man here. A man free from the past and at home in his own skin.

He'd shown her every one of his favorite haunts, introduced her to his boss and his friends, and she'd charmed all of them just as much as she'd charmed Hunt, without even trying.

Now every single man Hunt knew kept asking if there were more girls like her back in that Blessings town. And when they did, Ava would just smile and let the chatter roll over her. It was man talk, and she knew how to keep the stray tomcats among them at a distance. But Hunt was proud of her and it showed.

He'd been putting off taking her up until he was certain she was strong enough. Tomorrow, he would start back on his regular schedule with the company, ferrying a fresh crew out to a rig in the gulf and bringing another one home. But this morning was a perfect day to fly.

Hunt made the announcement and Ava's heart skipped a beat.

She was a little nervous, but at the same time so excited. Today, she would see that final side of Hunt that she'd still never seen.

He loaded her up in the Hummer and then they headed south out of the city. They arrived at the company heliport, and after introducing her to some of the flight crew, Hunt got her settled inside the chopper.

He got her headphone adjusted, then went through the flight inspection with the mechanics just like he always did.

Once he was satisfied all was well, he climbed into the chopper and checked then rechecked the seat belts to make sure they weren't too tight against her chest. Once he was satisfied she was comfortable and not afraid, he climbed into the pilot's seat, adjusted the headset, reminded her all she had to do to talk to him was speak into the mic. He gave the crew outside a thumbs-up, then began increasing the speed until it was a solid hum and the rotors were spinning so fast they'd disappeared.

One second they were on the ground, and then they were going up. Ava gasped and then grinned as everything below them kept getting smaller and smaller, and then Hunt tapped her on the arm and pointed to the view before them.

The horizon was water as far as the eye could see, glistening like diamonds on a bed of blue, and the sky above them was so clear and so bright. She watched, her lips parted in awe as the horizon suddenly disappeared and all she could see was sky.

Above them.

Around them.

Below them.

"Oh, Hunt. It's beautiful...so beautiful."

Hunt heard the tremble in her voice and smiled. She got it. She really got it.

Ava was at a loss for words, and the expression on her face told Hunt all he needed to know.

They flew in silence, not speaking.

Finally, as they were heading back, Hunt spoke.

"You're hooked, too, aren't you?" he said.

Ava jumped at the sudden sound of a voice in her ear, and then she looked at him and nodded.

"This is God's realm," he said. "Before, I used to say it was the closest I could get to heaven without dying. But I can't say that anymore."

"Why?" Ava asked.

"Because of you. I don't need to run away from earth anymore, like I ran away from home. You are my home. You are my heaven. God is love, and I see nothing but love when I look at you."

There were tears on Ava's cheeks.

"You know what I thought of when I first saw how clear and bright everything is up here?"

"No, what?" Hunt asked.

"Remember when I told you what I saw when I died? About the light, and how beautiful it was, and that I didn't want to leave until I saw you? That's what this felt like...that you were bringing me back to that beautiful place. Thank you for this. Thank you."

"Always," Hunt said. "Are you ready to go home now?"

There were still tears on her face.

"Where you go, I go. If you're going home, take me with you."

THE END

About the Author

New York Times bestselling author Sharon Sala has 125 books in print, published in six different genres—romance, young adult, Western, general fiction, women's fiction, and nonfiction. First published in 1991, and once a member of Romance Writers of America, she is an eight-time RITA finalist. Her industry awards include the Janet Dailey Award, five-time Career Achievement winner from RT Magazine, five-time winner of the National Readers' Choice Award, five-time winner of the Colorado Romance Writers' Award of Excellence, the Heart of Excellence award, the Booksellers Best Award, the Nora Roberts Lifetime Achievement Award presented by RWA, and the Centennial Award from RWA in recognition of her hundredth published novel. She lives in Oklahoma, the state where she was born. Visit her on Facebook.

ONCE IN A BLUE MOON

New York Times and *USA Today* bestselling author
Sharon Sala brings the comforts of home and
love to you in her Blessings, Georgia series

Cathy Terry is tired of running. Full of fear and hope, she landed in
Blessings, Georgia, not knowing if or when her abusive ex-husband would
catch up to her. In Blessings she glimpses a safe haven and the closest feeling to home she's had in a long time—even more so when she meets Duke
Talbot. The sweet, strong, and handsome rancher provides a shoulder to
lean on—but can Cathy claim a new home and family before her past
claims her?

**"Sharon Sala's Blessings, Georgia series is filled
with unforgettable charm and delight!"**

—Robyn Carr, #1 *New York Times* bestselling author

For more info about Sourcebooks's books and authors, visit:

sourcebooks.com

COME HOME TO DEEP RIVER

Bold, sexy small-town Alaska Homecoming
contemporary romance by Jackie Ashenden

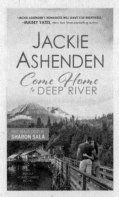

Silas Quinn hasn't been back to Deep River, Alaska, in years, not since he
joined the army. He left behind the best friend he'd ever had. But he knew
Hope Dawson was meant for bigger things than Deep River—and he—
had to offer. What he didn't know was that when he left, he took Hope's
dreams right along with him...

Hope gave up on ever getting out of Deep River. Now Si is back in
town, and his return brings Hope an offer that can change her life. Love,
or adventure, are almost within reach—but what if she can't have both?

"Jackie Ashenden's romances will leave you breathless."

—Maisey Yates, *New York Times* bestselling author

For more info about Sourcebooks's books and authors, visit:

sourcebooks.com

HERE FOR YOU

Emotional, poignant women's fiction from acclaimed
inspirational romance author Pat Simmons

Rachel Knicely's life has been on hold for six months while she takes care
of her great-aunt, who has Alzheimer's. Putting her aunt first was an easy
decision—accepting that Aunt Tweet is nearing the end of her battle is far
more difficult.

Nicholas Adams's ministry is bringing comfort to those who are sick
and homebound. He responds to a request for help for an ailing woman,
but when he meets the Knicelys, he realizes Rachel is the one who needs
support the most. Nicholas is charmed by and attracted to Rachel, but
then devastating news brings both a crisis of faith and roadblocks to their
budding relationship that neither could have anticipated.

**"Pat Simmons pulls at the heartstrings by
focusing on love, faith, and family."**

—Naleighna Kai, *USA Today* bestselling author

For more info about Sourcebooks's books and authors, visit:
sourcebooks.com

NEVER LET ME GO

Kianna Alexander writes tender, emotional
contemporary romance featuring successful men
and the women they're determined to win

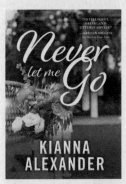

Single dad Maxwell Devers is an in-demand architect, responsible for
some of the most inspired building designs in the mid-Atlantic. But with
his career heating up, he needs a nanny for his baby daughter.

When Yvonne Markham arrives at Maxwell's office, she finds the
handsome businessman struggling to balance a frenzy of obligations. She
doesn't hesitate to help however she can, which is easy since his daughter
is a delight. Falling for her new boss, however, was not part of her plan…

**"A lush, beautifully written story about the indelible mark
of first love. Intelligent, fresh, and utterly lovely."**

—Kristan Higgins, *New York Times* bestselling author,
for *Back to Your Love*

For more info about Sourcebooks's books and authors, visit:

sourcebooks.com

WARM NIGHTS IN MAGNOLIA BAY

Welcome to Magnolia Bay, a heartwarming new series
with a Southern flair from author Babette de Jongh

Abby Curtis lands on Aunt Reva's doorstep at Bayside Barn with nowhere
to go but up. Learning animal communication from her aunt while taking
care of the motley assortment of rescue animals on the farm is an important part of Abby's healing process. She is eager to begin a new life on her
own, but she isn't prepared for the magnetism between her and her wildly
handsome and distracting new neighbor…

For more info about Sourcebooks's
books and authors, visit:

sourcebooks.com

RESCUE ME

In this fresh, poignant series about rescue
animals, every heart has a forever home

A New Leash on Love
When Craig Williams arrived at the local no-kill animal
shelter for help, he didn't expect a fiery young woman
to blaze into his life. But the more time he spends with
Megan, the more he realizes it's not just animals she's
adept at saving...

Sit, Stay, Love
For devoted no-kill shelter worker Kelsey Sutton, rehab-
bing a group of rescue dogs is a welcome challenge.
Working with a sexy ex-military dog handler who needs
some TLC himself? That's a whole different story...

My Forever Home
There's no denying Tess Grasso has a way with animals,
but when she helps Mason Redding give a free-spirited
stray a second chance, this husky might teach them a few
things about faith, love, and forgiveness.

"Sexy and fun..."

—*RT Book Reviews* for *A New Leash on Love*,
Top Pick, 4½ Stars

For more info about Sourcebooks's books and authors, visit:

sourcebooks.com

HEAD OVER PAWS

It'll be love at first bark for Debbie Burns's Rescue Me
series, featuring an animal shelter and the humans
and pets whose lives are transformed there

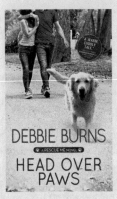

Olivia Graham isn't in a position to have a dog of her own, but her new
role as a volunteer rescue driver for the local animal shelter will keep her
close to her four-legged friends. When she's called to transport dogs and
cats that have been misplaced by flooding, she doesn't hesitate to help, but
her aging car isn't as reliable as she is and sparks fly when she's picked up
by veterinarian Gabe Wentworth...

**"A lovely, easy, and wholesome story that
animal lovers are sure to enjoy."**

—*Night Owl Reviews* for *My Forever Home*

For more info about Sourcebooks's books and authors, visit:

sourcebooks.com

PUPPY KISSES

A heartwarming series by Lucy Gilmore, featuring service
puppies who might just be matchmakers in the making...

Dawn Vasquez never takes life too seriously. But when she rescues a
golden retriever named Gigi, Dawn begins to imagine what it'd be like
to settle down and let someone rely on her for a change. Unfortunately,
Adam Dearborn—a handsome, hopelessly buttoned-up cattle rancher
in need of a guide dog—has also fallen in love with the little ball of fluff
and stubbornly insists that no other animal will do. Adam isn't sure what
drives him to fight to keep Gigi for himself, but he suspects it has something to do with his growing—and unfortunate—attachment to Dawn...

"Uplifting, romantic, and heartwarming."

—*Long and Short Reviews* for *Puppy Love*

For more info about Sourcebooks's
books and authors, visit:

sourcebooks.com

SUMMER BY THE RIVER

Don't miss this heartfelt romantic women's fiction by
bestselling contemporary romance author Debbie Burns

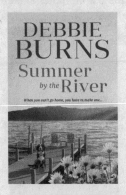

Making a fresh start in a new part of the country is challenging, but fate
and good fortune lead young single mother Josie Waterhill and her six-
year-old daughter to a cozy Midwestern town right on the river. There,
Josie can raise Zoe away from the violence of the life she once knew and
make a new home in the historic tea house where they've been invited to
stay. When a neighbor's interest in Josie inadvertently stirs up trouble, she
thinks she might never outrun it. But her new community is more than
willing to show Josie how to let go of her painful past and create a glorious
future.

"A fun, heartwarming story of love, family, and trust."

—*Harlequin Junkie* for the Rescue Me series

FUR HAVEN DOG PARK SERIES

Mara Wells brings you the love of an adorable puppy
and a forever home in this heartwarming series

Cold Nose, Warm Heart

Caleb Donovan has plans to demolish Riley Carson's
beloved building, but she and her fellow neighborhood
dog park devotees won't go down without a fight.

A Tail for Two

Lance Donovan agreed to dog sit only to help out his
younger brother. Little does he know that an encounter
with his ex-wife and their dog at the local dog park is
going to turn his life upside down…

Paws for Love

Danielle Morrow works tirelessly for greyhound rescue,
though she guards her own heart vigilantly. But now
that Knox Donovan is back, she might be ready for her
own second chance at love…

"Full of humor and heart."
—*Publishers Weekly* for *Cold Nose, Warm Heart*

For more info about Sourcebooks's books and authors, visit:
sourcebooks.com

LUCKY CHANCE COWBOY

Welcome to the Big Chance Dog Rescue, Teri Anne Stanley's heartwarming series where dogs and people get a second chance.

Marcus Talbott is a soldier through and through, and he's not going to let an injury keep him from his Army unit. Sure, his last mission nearly broke his back, but that's nothing his positive attitude and work ethic can't fix, right? In the meantime, he's got a place on the board at the Big Chance Dog Rescue. And flirting with his friend's sassy sister, Emma, is a welcome distraction...

"Love...and puppies...come to the rescue in this heartfelt tale of redemption, healing, and love."

—Jennie Marts, *USA Today* bestselling author, for *Big Chance Cowboy*

For more info about Sourcebooks's books and authors, visit:

sourcebooks.com

HAPPY SINGLES DAY

A funny and fresh romance by author Ann
Marie Walker is something to celebrate!

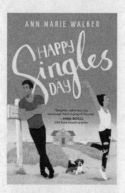

As a Certified Professional Organizer, everything in Paige Parker's world
is as it should be. Perfect apartment, perfect office, perfect life. And now,
the perfect vacation planned to celebrate Singles Day at an adorable B and
B.

As the owner of a now-dormant bed-and-breakfast, Lucas Croft's life
is simple and quiet. It's only him and his five-year-old daughter, which is
just the way he likes it. But when Paige books a room that Lucas' well-
intentioned sister listed without his knowledge, their two worlds collide.
If they can survive the week together, they just might discover exactly
what they've both been missing.

**"A positively delightful romance full of heart, joy,
and enough charm to jump off of the page."**

—Nina Bocci, *USA Today* bestselling author

For more info about Sourcebooks's books and authors, visit:

sourcebooks.com

Also by Sharon Sala

Blessings, Georgia